THE VIRTUOUS WOMAN

BOOKS BY GILBERT MORRIS

THE HOUSE OF WINSLOW SERIES

1. *The Honorable Imposter*
2. *The Captive Bride*
3. *The Indentured Heart*
4. *The Gentle Rebel*
5. *The Saintly Buccaneer*
6. *The Holy Warrior*
7. *The Reluctant Bridegroom*
8. *The Last Confederate*
9. *The Dixie Widow*
10. *The Wounded Yankee*
11. *The Union Belle*
12. *The Final Adversary*
13. *The Crossed Sabres*
14. *The Valiant Gunman*
15. *The Gallant Outlaw*
16. *The Jeweled Spur*
17. *The Yukon Queen*
18. *The Rough Rider*
19. *The Iron Lady*
20. *The Silver Star*
21. *The Shadow Portrait*
22. *The White Hunter*
23. *The Flying Cavalier*
24. *The Glorious Prodigal*
25. *The Amazon Quest*
26. *The Golden Angel*
27. *The Heavenly Fugitive*
28. *The Fiery Ring*
29. *The Pilgrim Song*
30. *The Beloved Enemy*
31. *The Shining Badge*
32. *The Royal Handmaid*
33. *The Silent Harp*
34. *The Virtuous Woman*

CHENEY DUVALL, M.D.[1]

1. *The Stars for a Light*
2. *Shadow of the Mountains*
3. *A City Not Forsaken*
4. *Toward the Sunrising*
5. *Secret Place of Thunder*
6. *In the Twilight, in the Evening*
7. *Island of the Innocent*
8. *Driven With the Wind*

CHENEY AND SHILOH: THE INHERITANCE[1]

1. *Where Two Seas Met*
2. *The Moon by Night*

THE SPIRIT OF APPALACHIA[2]

1. *Over the Misty Mountains*
2. *Beyond the Quiet Hills*
3. *Among the King's Soldiers*
4. *Beneath the Mockingbird's Wings*
5. *Around the River's Bend*

LIONS OF JUDAH

1. *Heart of a Lion*
2. *No Woman So Fair*
3. *The Gate of Heaven*
4. *Till Shiloh Comes*

[1]with Lynn Morris [2]with Aaron McCarver

GILBERT MORRIS

the VIRTUOUS WOMAN

Minneapolis, Minnesota

Cover illustration by William Graf
Cover design by Danielle White

Scripture quotations are from the King James Version of the Bible.

Published by Bethany House Publishers
11400 Hampshire Avenue South
Bloomington, Minnesota 55438

Bethany House Publishers is a division of
Baker Publishing Group, Grand Rapids, Michigan.

Printed in the United States of America

Library of Congress Cataloging-in-Publication Data

Morris, Gilbert.
The virtuous woman / by Gilbert Morris.
p. cm. — (The House of Winslow, 1935)
ISBN 0-7642-2661-4 (pbk.)
1. Winslow family (Fictitious characters)—Fiction. 2. Brothers and sisters—Fiction. 3. Missing children—Fiction. 4. Women prisoners—Fiction. 5. Recluses—Fiction. I. Title II. Series: Morris, Gilbert. House of Winslow.
PS3563.O8742V57 2005
813'.54—dc22 2004020194

To Ann Carroll

This is a dark world we live in, but there are some people who bring light into it. You, my dear sister, are one of those light-bearers, and I thank God for your bright and generous spirit. Your ministry to others (especially to my niece Ginger!) has been a source of joy to me. Your record is on high!

GILBERT MORRIS spent ten years as a pastor before becoming Professor of English at Ouachita Baptist University in Arkansas and earning a Ph.D. at the University of Arkansas. A prolific writer, he has had over 25 scholarly articles and 200 poems published in various periodicals, and over the past years has had more than 180 novels published. His family includes three grown children, and he and his wife live in Gulf Shores, Alabama.

Contents

PART FOUR
September–November 1935

THE HOUSE OF WINSLOW

★ ★ ★ ★

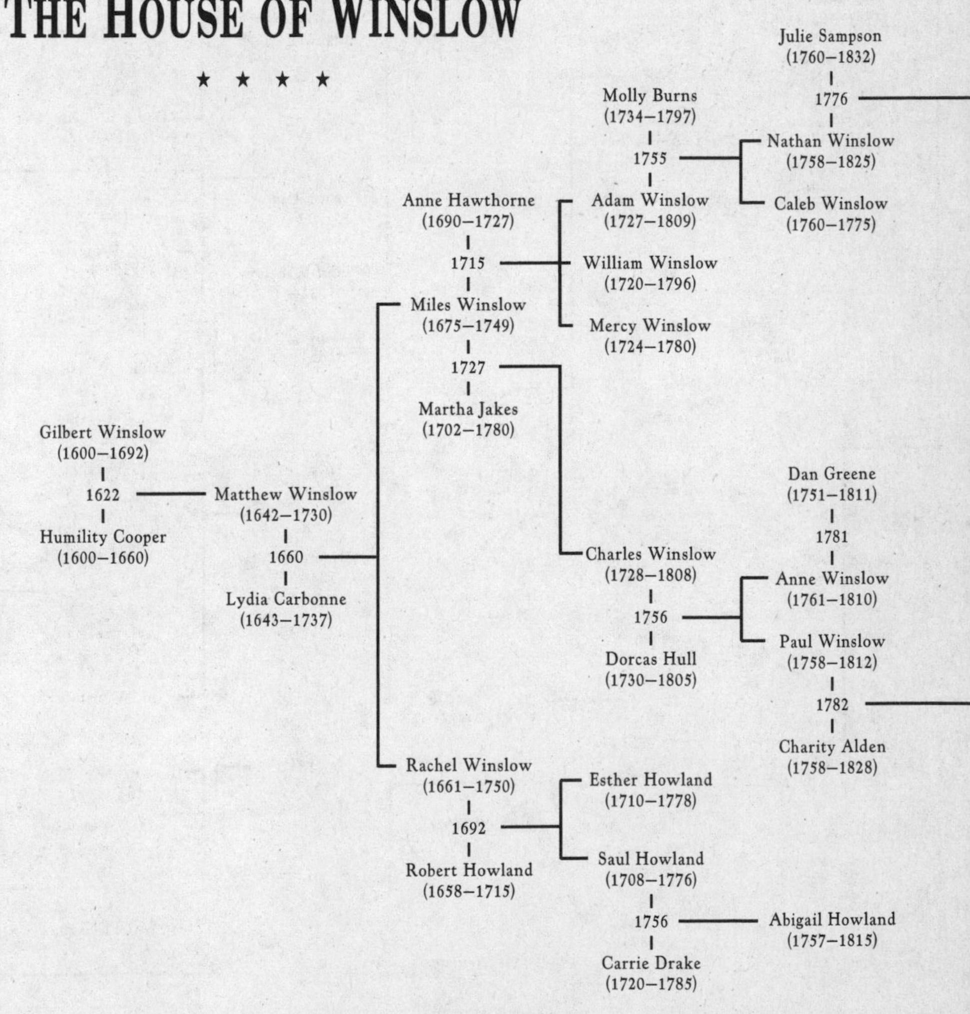

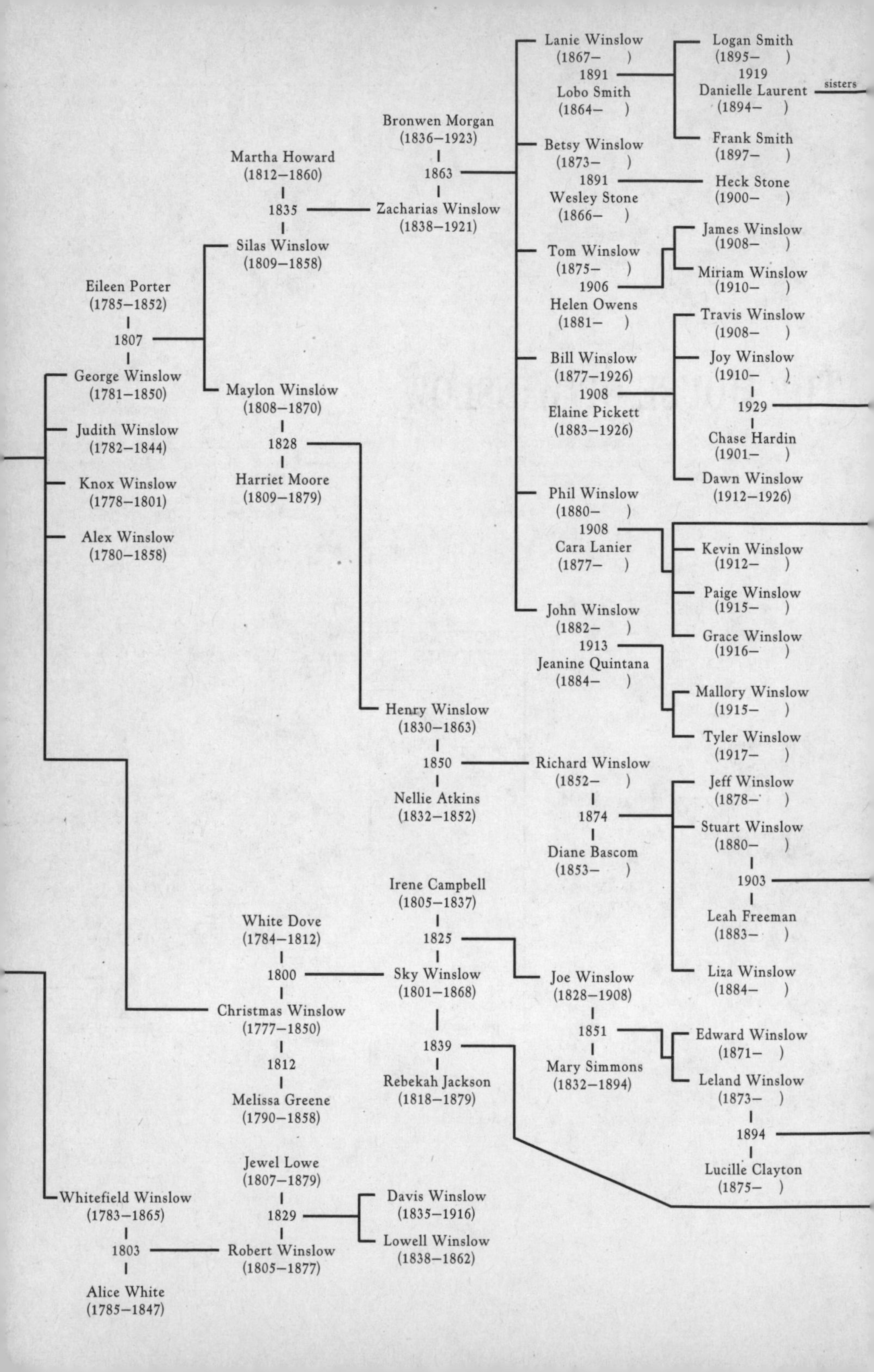

Eileen Porter (1785–1852)
1807
George Winslow (1781–1850)
Judith Winslow (1782–1844)
Knox Winslow (1778–1801)
Alex Winslow (1780–1858)
Whitefield Winslow (1783–1865)
1803
Alice White (1785–1847)
Martha Howard (1812–1860)
1835
Silas Winslow (1809–1858)
Maylon Winslow (1808–1870)
1828
Harriet Moore (1809–1879)
White Dove (1784–1812)
1800
Christmas Winslow (1777–1850)
1812
Melissa Greene (1790–1858)
Jewel Lowe (1807–1879)
1829
Robert Winslow (1805–1877)
Bronwen Morgan (1836–1923)
1863
Zacharias Winslow (1838–1921)
Henry Winslow (1830–1863)
1850
Nellie Atkins (1832–1852)
Irene Campbell (1805–1837)
1825
Sky Winslow (1801–1868)
1839
Rebekah Jackson (1818–1879)
Davis Winslow (1835–1916)
Lowell Winslow (1838–1862)
Lanie Winslow (1867–)
1891
Lobo Smith (1864–)
Betsy Winslow (1873–)
1891
Wesley Stone (1866–)
Tom Winslow (1875–)
1906
Helen Owens (1881–)
Bill Winslow (1877–1926)
1908
Elaine Pickett (1883–1926)
Phil Winslow (1880–)
1908
Cara Lanier (1877–)
John Winslow (1882–)
1913
Jeanine Quintana (1884–)
Richard Winslow (1852–)
1874
Diane Bascom (1853–)
Joe Winslow (1828–1908)
1851
Mary Simmons (1832–1894)
Logan Smith (1895–)
1919
Danielle Laurent (1894–)
sisters
Frank Smith (1897–)
Heck Stone (1900–)
James Winslow (1908–)
Miriam Winslow (1910–)
Travis Winslow (1908–)
Joy Winslow (1910–)
1929
Chase Hardin (1901–)
Dawn Winslow (1912–1926)
Kevin Winslow (1912–)
Paige Winslow (1915–)
Grace Winslow (1916–)
Mallory Winslow (1915–)
Tyler Winslow (1917–)
Jeff Winslow (1878–)
Stuart Winslow (1880–)
1903
Leah Freeman (1883–)
Liza Winslow (1884–)
Edward Winslow (1871–)
Leland Winslow (1873–)
1894
Lucille Clayton (1875–)

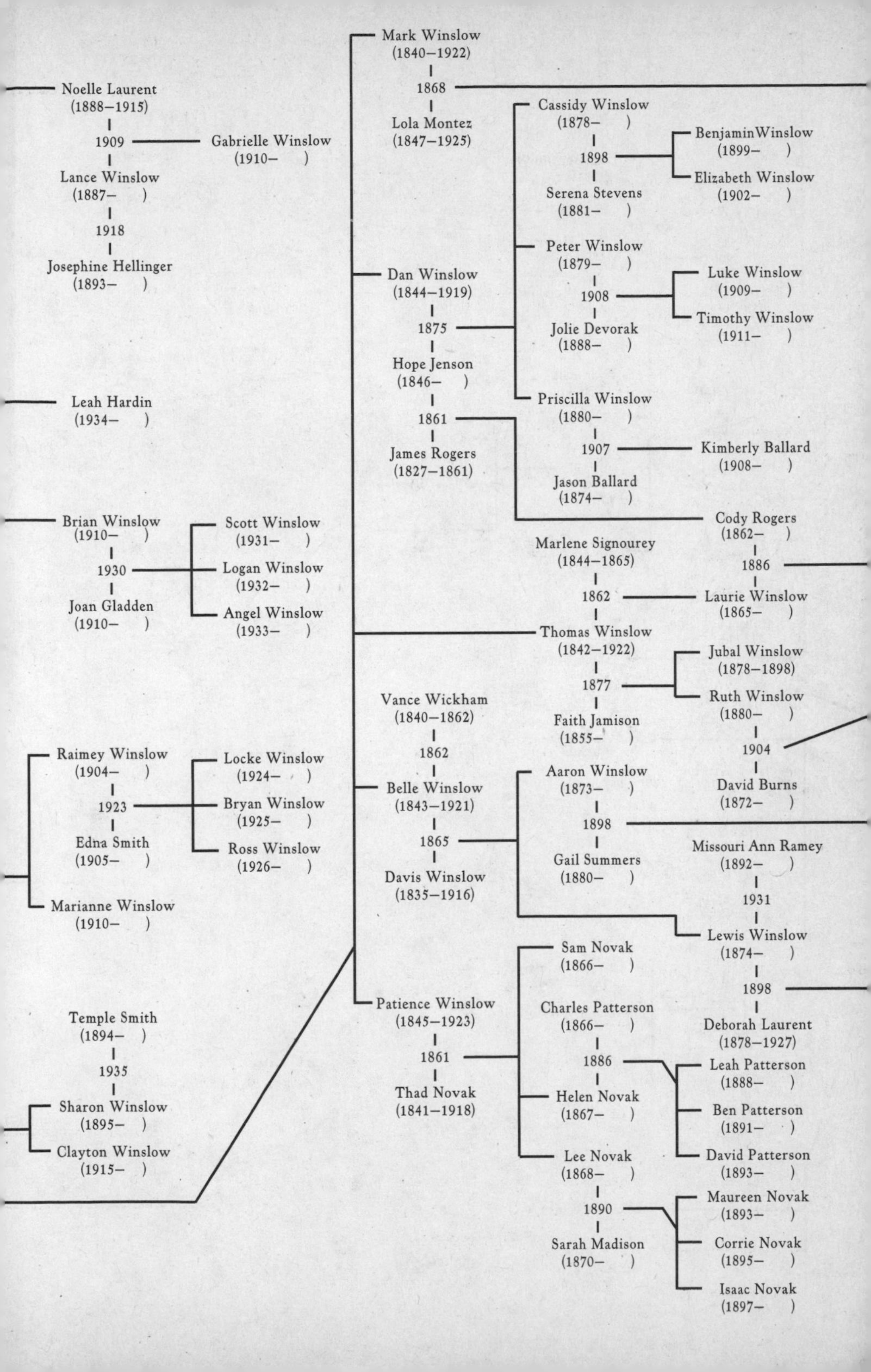

Noelle Laurent
(1888–1915)
1909
Lance Winslow
(1887–)
1918
Josephine Hellinger
(1893–)
Gabrielle Winslow
(1910–)
Leah Hardin
(1934–)
Brian Winslow
(1910–)
1930
Joan Gladden
(1910–)
Scott Winslow
(1931–)
Logan Winslow
(1932–)
Angel Winslow
(1933–)
Raimey Winslow
(1904–)
1923
Edna Smith
(1905–)
Locke Winslow
(1924–)
Bryan Winslow
(1925–)
Ross Winslow
(1926–)
Marianne Winslow
(1910–)
Temple Smith
(1894–)
1935
Sharon Winslow
(1895–)
Clayton Winslow
(1915–)
Mark Winslow
(1840–1922)
1868
Lola Montez
(1847–1925)
Dan Winslow
(1844–1919)
1875
Hope Jenson
(1846–)
1861
James Rogers
(1827–1861)
Vance Wickham
(1840–1862)
1862
Belle Winslow
(1843–1921)
1865
Davis Winslow
(1835–1916)
Patience Winslow
(1845–1923)
1861
Thad Novak
(1841–1918)
Cassidy Winslow
(1878–)
1898
Serena Stevens
(1881–)
Peter Winslow
(1879–)
1908
Jolie Devorak
(1888–)
Priscilla Winslow
(1880–)
1907
Jason Ballard
(1874–)
Marlene Signourey
(1844–1865)
1862
Thomas Winslow
(1842–1922)
1877
Faith Jamison
(1855–)
Aaron Winslow
(1873–)
1898
Gail Summers
(1880–)
Sam Novak
(1866–)
Charles Patterson
(1866–)
1886
Helen Novak
(1867–)
Lee Novak
(1868–)
1890
Sarah Madison
(1870–)
BenjaminWinslow
(1899–)
Elizabeth Winslow
(1902–)
Luke Winslow
(1909–)
Timothy Winslow
(1911–)
Kimberly Ballard
(1908–)
Cody Rogers
(1862–)
1886
Laurie Winslow
(1865–)
Jubal Winslow
(1878–1898)
Ruth Winslow
(1880–)
1904
David Burns
(1872–)
Missouri Ann Ramey
(1892–)
1931
Lewis Winslow
(1874–)
1898
Deborah Laurent
(1878–1927)
Leah Patterson
(1888–)
Ben Patterson
(1891–)
David Patterson
(1893–)
Maureen Novak
(1893–)
Corrie Novak
(1895–)
Isaac Novak
(1897–)

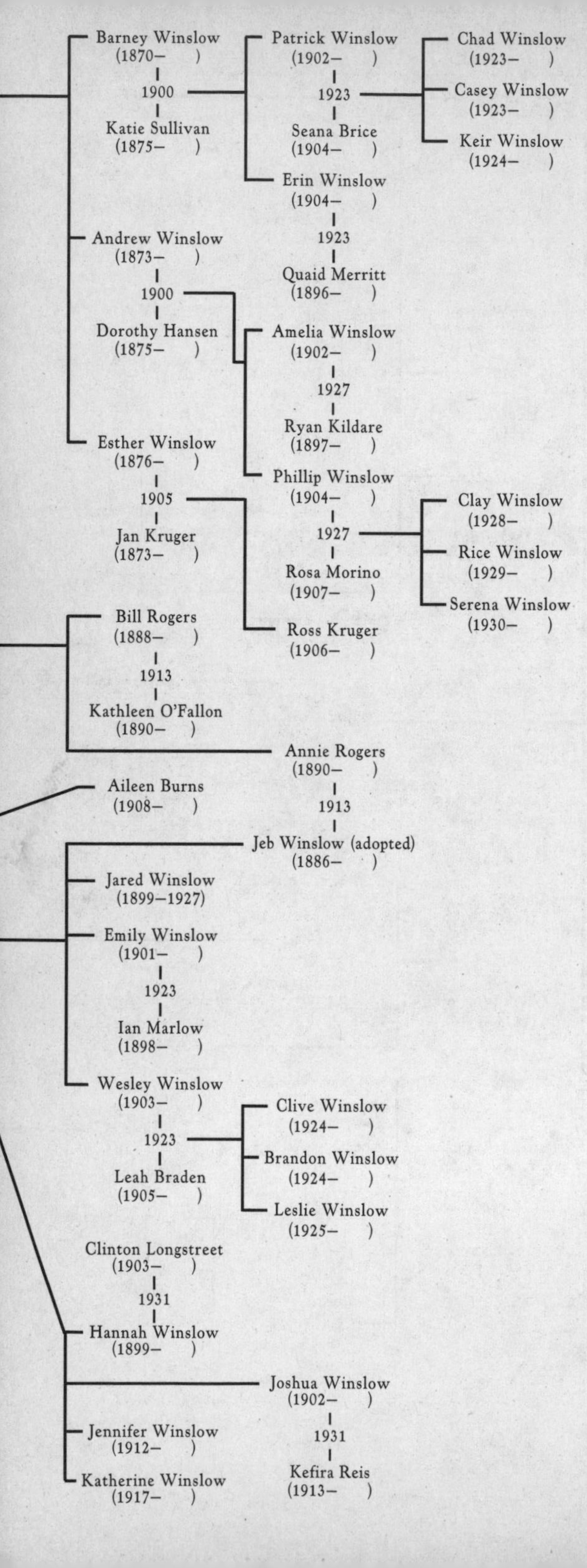

Barney Winslow
(1870–)
1900
Katie Sullivan
(1875–)
Patrick Winslow
(1902–)
1923
Seana Brice
(1904–)
Chad Winslow
(1923–)
Casey Winslow
(1923–)
Keir Winslow
(1924–)
Erin Winslow
(1904–)
1923
Quaid Merritt
(1896–)
Andrew Winslow
(1873–)
1900
Dorothy Hansen
(1875–)
Amelia Winslow
(1902–)
1927
Ryan Kildare
(1897–)
Esther Winslow
(1876–)
1905
Jan Kruger
(1873–)
Phillip Winslow
(1904–)
1927
Rosa Morino
(1907–)
Clay Winslow
(1928–)
Rice Winslow
(1929–)
Serena Winslow
(1930–)
Ross Kruger
(1906–)
Bill Rogers
(1888–)
1913
Kathleen O'Fallon
(1890–)
Annie Rogers
(1890–)
1913
Aileen Burns
(1908–)
Jeb Winslow (adopted)
(1886–)
Jared Winslow
(1899–1927)
Emily Winslow
(1901–)
1923
Ian Marlow
(1898–)
Wesley Winslow
(1903–)
1923
Leah Braden
(1905–)
Clive Winslow
(1924–)
Brandon Winslow
(1924–)
Leslie Winslow
(1925–)
Clinton Longstreet
(1903–)
1931
Hannah Winslow
(1899–)
Joshua Winslow
(1902–)
1931
Kefira Reis
(1913–)
Jennifer Winslow
(1912–)
Katherine Winslow
(1917–)

PART ONE

February–March 1935

★ ★ ★

CHAPTER ONE

A ROSE FOR BERTHA

★ ★ ★

The small greenhouse was brilliant with colors—vivid reds, greens, blues—all contrasting violently with the grim, gray world that surrounded it. Father Anthony Mazzoni, chaplain at the New York State Women's Prison, often said wryly that he was a creator of worlds. Not of *the* world, of course. That, naturally, was the prerogative of God, who made all things. But within the prison confines of concrete, steel, and misery, Mazzoni had managed to create a tiny refuge—a world of his own that burgeoned with fragrant flowers and shimmering color.

Mazzoni smiled as he thought of his battles with Warden Rockland over this greenhouse. *"You're here to save the miserable souls of these women, Father, not grow petunias!"* the warden would say, though not always so politely. The humble priest chose not to remember the sizzling profanity that usually laced the warden's arguments. As he deftly pinched off a faded violet, he relived the moment he had finally obtained the warden's permission. He had set about the work immediately, erecting the small greenhouse in one corner of the prison yard, complete with heater and tubing, at his own expense and on his own time.

The years of dealing with women who had reached the end of everything good in life had left the tall man stooped and gray-haired, with a fine network of wrinkles across his pale face. His energetic dark eyes, however, revealed a vibrant spirit within the aging body. As he moved among the fragile flowers, savoring their fragrance and delighting in the rich dignity of their colors, he paused before his pride and joy—a graceful long-stemmed rose. He plucked off a dead leaf, then added a pinch of fertilizer from a paper bag and stood back to admire the elegant flower.

He heard the door behind him open and he turned to see Warden Rockland, with his usual grim expression. Inmates and guards alike called him the Great Stone Face, and he had a temperament to match. He was no more than five-six, but his huge shoulders and limbs and deep chest gave him the appearance of a human tank. People tended to move out of the way when he entered a room.

"Good morning, Warden," Mazzoni said with a smile.

Rockland had a habit of carefully observing his surroundings upon entering any room, and he ruled this prison with an iron fist—not unlike a tyrannical dictator over a small country. "Morning," he grunted, and then his eyes narrowed. "You know Bertha Zale?"

"Yes, of course."

"She's dying," Rockland said bluntly. "You'd better get down there and fire off a few prayers to heaven. Not that there is a heaven," he said defiantly. Rockland delighted in ridiculing Mazzoni's faith. For four years now he had tried to shake the chaplain's calm, but without success. "The poor woman's got the notion that there's pie up there in that sky. Thinks she's gonna be sittin' around pluckin' on a harp for the rest of eternity. Well, Chaplain, you'd better hurry. She's not gonna last long." He hesitated, and then his mouth drew into a thin line. " 'Course, you can pray all you want, but it won't make any difference. There's nothing out there. When we die, we're gone—just like dumb animals."

Upon hearing the warden's defiance, Father Mazzoni had a rare flash of inspiration. He remembered the one decoration on Rockland's office wall—a black-and-white portrait of a woman with a strong face and a pair of fine eyes. The warden had never mentioned her, but Mazzoni had noted a family resemblance and strongly suspected it was Rockland's mother. "I don't expect your mother would feel that way, would she, Warden?" He saw something flicker in the warden's eyes, as if he'd touched a nerve. But Rockland spun on his heel and left without a word.

After cutting a white rose for Bertha and hanging up his tools, Mazzoni left the greenhouse and made his way through the labyrinthine passageways of the prison, barred at intervals by guarded steel gates. He greeted every guard by name, as he did the inmates he passed. When he reached the door marked Hospital, he stepped inside, where he was greeted by a small man with cadaverous cheeks and moody eyes. "You've come to see Bertha, I suppose."

"Yes, Dr. Zambrinski."

"You'd better hurry, Father. She's almost gone."

Mazzoni moved toward the corner that the physician indicated and found Bertha Zale lying under a thin white sheet. Mazzoni leaned forward, the rose in his hand. "Bertha, can you hear me?" He thought for a moment that she was already gone, but then her eyelashes fluttered and watery eyes stared vacantly from her emaciated face. Her lips were as dry as fall leaves as she whispered, "Father?"

"Yes, Bertha, it's me. Would you like to confess?"

The dying woman nodded slowly and gasped out more sins than the priest thought possible for one person to commit. Finally her voice faded and her eyes closed.

Father Mazzoni thought the woman was finished, but her eyes opened again, and she said in a clearer voice, "One more . . . sin, Father."

Mazzoni listened to her final confession, spoken with unmistakable clarity. Then her voice faded and her eyes shut again. He hastily administered extreme unction, and by the time he had finished, Bertha Zale was gone.

Mazzoni studied the ashen face, worn with troubles and furrowed with lines brought on by hard living. He gently placed the white rose in the gaunt hand. He bowed his head and prayed for her, then turned and walked slowly away.

Dr. Zambrinski met him and asked, "Is she gone, Father?"

"Yes, she is."

"Well, it had to come. She's probably glad to be finished with the pain." He had learned to take death almost matter-of-factly. "We'll arrange for the funeral to be held this afternoon."

"Thank you, Doctor."

The priest heavily retraced his steps back along the corridor, speaking automatically to the guards and inmates who greeted him. When he finally stepped out into the yard, a blast of cold air struck him, and he straightened for a moment. He made his way toward the greenhouse, his thin shoulders slumped as if an unbearable burden had been dumped on them.

I thought I'd heard everything, he thought, *but not this!* Mazzoni was not easily shocked, for he had heard every imaginable sin whispered into his ears. But what Bertha Zale had told him was like nothing he had ever heard before.

"I've got to do *something* about it . . . but what?"

When he reached the greenhouse, he saw Rockland approaching. "She's dead?" the warden demanded abruptly.

"Yes, she's gone."

Rockland shrugged his beefy shoulders. "Well, it's all over for her. Too bad."

Mazzoni did not answer. He watched as the warden wheeled his bulk around and plunged across the yard. The priest entered the greenhouse and stood quietly in front of a rosebush. He thought of the white rose that now rested in the dead woman's still hands and whispered, "It may be over for you, Bertha, but it's not over for me."

CHAPTER TWO

OUT OF THE PAST

★ ★ ★

"But, Dad, you can't *possibly* wear that ratty old suit! Why, you look like a . . . a garbage collector!"

Phil Winslow leaned back in his chair, turning his head to one side and lifting an eyebrow. "I can't believe you're insulting my suit like that!"

Twenty-year-old Paige Winslow had her mother's abundance of soft brown hair, which beautifully shaped her delicate features and small frame. Her fashionable short-sleeved dress was of white silk with a print of large green ferns. It had a V neck, a tie belt around the waist, a shaped bodice, and a mid-calf length, which showed off her white leather high heels. She stood in front of her father but flashed her mother a look of despair. "Mom, you're not going to let him wear that grubby old suit, are you?"

"Your father usually does what he wants to do." Cara Winslow's voice was gentle, as was everything about her manner and appearance. She looked much younger than her fifty-eight years as she smiled at her daughter. "I think the suit looks very nice, and your father looks wonderful in it."

Paige shook her head almost angrily. "But, Mother, it's so

out of fashion! He'll be the only one there who's not dressed properly."

"This suit was good enough for the Prince of Wales," Phil said, straightening up. Whenever he got upset, he drew his eyebrows together, which put two upright creases between them. He was a fine-looking man, three years younger than his wife, with auburn hair that was still fiery under the sun. He had the typical Winslow wedge-shaped face and cornflower blue eyes. His hands were not the hands of an artist—which he was—but rather of a workingman. He had been a cowhand in his youth, working on his father's ranch, and something of the western air still clung to him even after years in Europe and more years of successful painting in America. Now he suddenly got to his feet, towering over his wife and daughter. He was very fond of his daughter but worried about her social aspirations. "Now, Paige," he said patiently, "your mother and I agreed to go to this party, and we will. But you remember what Thoreau said."

"What did he say, dear?" Cara asked.

"'Beware any enterprise that requires the purchase of new clothes.' He was mostly a windy old bore, but at least he hit it right that time."

"Mother, you'll just have to do something with him." Paige fled the drawing room, closing the door behind her with more force than was necessary.

Phil sighed, walked back to his favorite chair, and slumped down. "I suppose I'll have to buy a new suit," he grumbled. "But it goes against the grain."

Cara came over to stand behind her husband and ran her hand over his crisp hair, smiling at him with admiration. "Yes, I think you will, dear. This one is a bit worn, and even the Prince of Wales isn't as society-minded as Paige's future in-laws."

The mention of the Asquiths, the parents of Paige's fiancé, John, brought back the two vertical lines between Phil's eyebrows. "I wouldn't say anything in front of Paige, but to tell you the truth, John's parents give me a pain in the—"

"Now, don't say that!" Cara interrupted. "It would hurt her feelings. But I will admit they are a little into social climbing."

"A little! Why, they make the Astors look like alley rats!" he exclaimed. "I'd hoped that John wouldn't be as much of a snob as his parents, but they've made a pretty strong impact on him."

"I know, dear, but he's young enough to change. He's really a sweet boy."

"He's a mama's boy, that's what he is. When his mama hollers *frog,* he jumps!"

"Don't be so hasty about your judgments," she chided, though in reality she too was concerned about Paige's upcoming marriage into the snobbish Asquith family. She had tried to question Paige about this, but her daughter did not seem in the least perturbed by the thought of marrying into such a socially prominent family. In fact, she appeared to relish the idea. Cara did not think there was much use in arguing about it with Phil, however, nor was there time now to discuss it. "I think I hear the thundering herd," she said, turning her head.

Phil got up from his chair and headed toward the entryway. Before he got there, three children rushed in, clamoring for attention. Four-year-old Scott led the pack, and Phil scooped him into his arms and tossed him up toward the ceiling.

Logan, one year younger, went to Cara, who knelt down to hug him. She also put her arm around Angel, who at a couple months shy of two years was often overrun by her rowdy brothers. As Cara hugged the two youngest, she was struck by how much Scott and Logan had inherited their father's good looks—who, in turn, had gotten his from his own father. Angel, however, with clear blue eyes and blond hair, looked more like her mother, Joan.

"Kids, you can't stampede into your grandparents' drawing room like wild bulls!" Brian Winslow, at the age of twenty-five, was as tall as his father, with the same auburn hair and light blue eyes. He had married Joan Gladden when they were both only twenty and had produced three children in rapid succession. Brian had the look of a successful lawyer, which he was, and of an astute businessman, which he also was.

Cara stood up to take his kiss and smiled. "You don't have to leave so soon, do you?" Brian and his family had been over for a Saturday afternoon visit and now it was time to leave.

"I'm afraid we do, Mom," Brian said, hugging her. "I would think you've had enough of these red Indians anyway."

"I'm not a red Indian!" Scott piped up.

"I am!" Logan said. "I'm a red Indian."

"Boys, you don't have to yell." Joan Winslow was a bright young woman with blond hair and striking good looks. She came over and stood beside her father-in-law. "When are you two going to come see us for a change? We always have to come over here."

"I ought to take you up on your invitation. Come and eat you out of house and home." Phil was very fond of his daughter-in-law, and now he reached out and hugged her. "We'll talk it over. Maybe next Saturday or Sunday."

"You know what we should do," Brian said. "We should all go on a trip together. Go down south and get out of this cold weather. I've never seen such a February." The winter of 1935 had indeed brought unrelentingly frigid weather to New York, and all of the Winslows were looking forward to spring.

The children started jumping up and down, shouting, "When are we going? When are we going?"

"Brian, haven't I told you not to say things like that in front of the children?" Joan said to her husband. "You know they always want it right away."

"They get that from their mother." Brian winked at his mother, then said, "Come along, kids, we've got to go."

"We'll go out and see you safely off," Cara said.

The little procession made its way out of the house, and as they passed through the ornate foyer, Phil had a strange feeling. He looked around the luxurious furnishings and towering ceiling and remembered the plain house of his childhood on his parents' ranch out west. *I never thought I'd be living in a mansion like this,* he thought, *and sometimes I wish I weren't.* Of course, he said none of this aloud. No one but Cara knew he ever had such thoughts.

When they reached the driveway, it took them some time to get the children into the Studebaker. "It's easier to put cats in a sack than kids in a car," Phil quipped as he picked up Logan, stuffed him in, and shut the door firmly. Immediately the window rolled down and three little heads stuck out, all shouting their good-byes and looking for kisses from both grandparents.

"We'll see you soon," Scott said. "Don't forget to bring me a present, Grandpa."

The engine roared, and Brian steered the car out of the circular driveway. Phil reached over and put his arm around Cara. "Those are some grandchildren we've got there." Something caught his eye and his lids narrowed. "Who in the world is that?"

Cara turned to see a taxi driving up. "I'm not expecting anyone," she said.

The two stood waiting until the cab stopped. After a moment's pause, the door opened and a tall elderly man in the garb of a priest stepped out.

"A priest! Why would he be coming here?" Phil wondered aloud.

"I'm sure I don't know. Maybe he has the wrong address."

They both waited until the priest approached and said, "Good afternoon. I'm looking for the Winslow residence."

"I'm Phil Winslow. This is my wife. Can we help you?"

"Yes. My name is Father Mazzoni. I would like to have a few minutes of your time, if it's not inconvenient."

Phil assumed the priest was soliciting money, as he could think of no other reason for such a visit. Since he had made a fortune with his painting, he had become accustomed to monetary requests and showed no sign of impatience. "Well, it's quite cold out here. Why don't you come in? We can talk inside."

"That's very kind of you. I should have called first, but I wanted to be sure to see you in person."

Phil showed Mazzoni inside, where Cara took his black outer cloak and hat and hung them on a coat-tree in the foyer. "Come down this way," Phil said. "We've got a fire going in the drawing room."

"That would be wonderful," the priest said, rubbing his hands to warm them. "One of the coldest Februaries I've ever seen in this part of the world."

Phil motioned toward a chair in front of the fire that was blazing in the fireplace and Phil and Cara sat in chairs opposite him.

Mazzoni sat quietly for a moment, continuing to rub his hands. He seemed ill at ease and cleared his throat before speaking. "This may seem very out of place, but may I ask you if you were in City Hospital on April the twenty-first, 1916?"

Phil and Cara turned startled glances at each other. The date was one they would never forget. "Yes, we were. How did you know that?"

"What I have to say is going to be difficult for you to hear. It might be best if I told you the whole story. Then I'll be glad to answer your questions."

"Certainly. Go right ahead."

The father paused and studied his shoes. Clearly what he had to say was bothering him. He finally looked up and said, "I'm the chaplain at the New York State Women's Prison. Last Thursday I was called to the bedside of a prisoner named Bertha Zale. I don't suppose you've ever heard of her?"

"Why, no. The name isn't at all familiar," Phil said.

"I assumed that would be the case. She was dying when I got there, and I heard her confession. I felt great pity for her. She'd had a very difficult life." Mazzoni twisted in his seat and ran his hand over his hair for a moment, then shook his head. "Before she finished, she told me something that affects you two."

"How could it affect us?" Cara said. "We've never even heard of the woman."

"I know, but the fact is she also was in City Hospital on April the twenty-first—the same time you were there."

"We lost our last baby there," Phil said. "It's been a great source of grief to us."

Mazzoni ran his finger along his nose and tried to think how to put the matter delicately. Shaking his head, he explained, "Mr. and Mrs. Winslow, the dying woman told me that she had a baby the same day you did, although she didn't know you. She told me that her baby died in her arms during the night. Instead of calling for a nurse, she got out of bed and took her dead daughter to the nursery. She managed to slip in when no one was looking and took one of the female babies, switched the name tags, and left her dead baby in its place. Then she went back to her bed."

A deathly silence hung over the room. Phil looked at Cara and saw that her face was as pale as chalk. He shook his head and said, "And you're telling us it was our child she took?"

"I'm afraid that's exactly what I'm saying. I wanted to be very sure about this, so I went to the hospital. They were reluctant to talk to me at first, but when I explained the circumstances, the general administrator gave me access to the records." Mazzoni looked up, and his eyes held the two steadily. "Only one child died on April the twenty-second. That child was listed as Grace Winslow."

"It's true!" Cara cried, standing up. Phil jumped to her side and held her, for she was weaving. "It has to be true, Phil. You remember what I told you—that God had promised me."

"I've never forgotten," Phil said, his own face pale. He explained, "When my wife was pregnant, we committed the child to God. Later in the pregnancy, God promised Cara our child would be used in His service and she would bring great happiness to us."

"And I've wondered all these years how I could have

missed God's word to me so badly," Cara whispered. "Where is she? I want to see her."

"Well, that's the problem, Mrs. Winslow," Mazzoni said as he slowly paced the large, airy room. "You see, the girl had a rough upbringing. That was part of Miss Zale's confession. She was a weak woman in many ways, and the child had a very hard life. Miss Zale told me this herself. Of course, I can't repeat her confession. That's privileged communication, of course, but what *is* important I can tell you. The girl she called Ruby ran away three years ago. Her mother went to prison shortly after that."

"Ran away! How could that be?" Cara whispered.

"According to Bertha she ran away with an actor. Bertha didn't even know the man's name. The girl left a note that said she was never coming back."

"But surely this woman must have had some family. Someone we could ask."

"I don't think she did. I talked to her several times after she first came to prison, and she told me more than once that she had no family at all. She never mentioned the girl she called Ruby—not until she was dying."

A silence fell over the room, disturbed only by the ticking of the clock on the mantel. The bright sunlight that flooded through the tall windows highlighted Cara's face, and Phil could see the mixture of hope and despair in her expression.

"I struggled with myself about bringing this news to you," Mazzoni continued, "especially after I found out that the girl was missing, but I thought it my duty."

"You did exactly the right thing, sir," Cara said warmly.

Mazzoni pulled a card from his pocket. "I've written my name and telephone number on this card. If I can do anything, please don't hesitate to call."

"I'll call you a cab," Phil said.

While he was dialing the number, Cara said, "You must have a hard task facing so many wrecked lives."

"I'm able to reach some of them," Mazzoni said gently. "You'll be in my prayers."

When Mazzoni left, Cara said to her husband, "All these years I've thought about the promise I got from God. It was so clear, Phil. I know He told me that our daughter would serve Him in a great way."

"I remember," he said quietly.

"You know, there have been times when I've felt angry with God for letting Grace die. I was angry and confused because I was so certain He had spoken to me about her life. Now His promise can be made real after all. We can do something."

"We won't know this girl now—or young woman, I should say. She didn't grow up in a Christian home. You heard what the priest said. She's had a hard life. I have a feeling it was even harder than he could say. He was probably trying to spare us."

"You're not saying we shouldn't try to find her, are you, Phil?"

"No, I'm not saying that at all, but we mustn't get our hopes up that we'll be able to."

"Why would God let all this happen, then? If Bertha hadn't told Father Mazzoni, we'd never even know Grace was alive. I believe God's hand is in this situation."

"That's very possible, and that's what I hope. But remember she's a woman now. Eighteen years old, and she's had a hard life."

Cara put her hand on Phil's chest. "We've got to find her, Phil. I believe God still has a plan for her—that no matter what she's done or what she's like, God is going to use her greatly."

"All right, sweetheart. We'll do all we can to find her. I'll get on it first thing Monday morning, but right now we'd better see if Paige is ready to go, even if she doesn't approve of my taste in suits."

CHAPTER THREE

THE TRAIL IS TOO OLD

★ ★ ★

Lieutenant Al Sullivan was almost a caricature of a New York City police officer. If his speech had not betrayed his Irish origin, no doubt his red hair, blue eyes, and ruddy face would have. Sullivan had worked his way up from the beat through hard work and determination to become a lieutenant. Now as he sat in his small office, he felt compassion for the couple across from him. During his years behind this desk, he had lost track of how many people he had seen in those seats. Most of them wanted help he was unable to give, and many of them wanted mercy that was not his to grant.

Glancing down at the paper in front of him, he read the notes he had jotted down as he listened to the couple speak. *Phil Winslow, age fifty-five*. The address told Sullivan these people were pretty well off—unlike the usual sort that sat across from him. His eyes went to the woman: *Cara Winslow, age fifty-eight*. There was a delicate air about the woman, a gentleness one rarely saw these days. She wore no jewelry except for a wedding ring with a small diamond on her left hand, and her clothes were attractive but not ostentatious.

"Why don't you tell me the problem, and we'll see what we can do," he said.

Phil shifted in his chair and leaned forward, his light blue eyes intent. "We've just discovered that our daughter is alive. We thought she died almost nineteen years ago. . . ."

Sullivan listened carefully, his mind sorting out the details. He filed the irrelevant facts into one corner of his brain and kept the ones pertinent to an investigation more accessible. When Phil had finished his story, Sullivan sighed and picked up a pencil, absently drawing circles on his writing pad. He abruptly laid the pencil down and clasped his beefy hands together. "I've never heard anything quite like this, Mr. Winslow. It's very unusual."

"Do you think you can help us, Lieutenant?" Cara asked softly, an intense light in her warm brown eyes, her hands clasped tightly in her lap.

"We'll do all we can, of course, Mrs. Winslow. But it's not going to be easy."

"You do find missing people, don't you, Lieutenant?"

"Yes, we even have a Missing Persons Division that may be able to help you. But I'm afraid it's going to be quite a chore."

"But we know that Grace exists."

"All you have is the confession of a dying woman to a priest. That's not very much to go on."

"You could talk to Father Mazzoni."

"Of course, that would be the first step. But from what you've told me, the woman spoke only briefly of what she had done." Sullivan shook his head slightly. He didn't want these people to get their hopes up. "Have you considered that she may have made the whole thing up?"

"Made it up! Why would she do that?" Phil demanded.

"She may not have done it intentionally. She was dying; she was in and out of a coma. From what you tell me, the priest said she was in very poor condition. She may have been delirious."

"If she made up the story, how would you explain that a

baby did indeed die that very night in that specific hospital? How could she have known that? It seems reasonable she was telling the truth," Cara insisted. "Please, can't you help us some way?"

Sullivan nodded his head, conceding her point. He thought of the unsolved cases his office had stacked up, but nonetheless, he felt he had to try to help. "What you must understand is that most crimes are either solved pretty quickly or they don't get solved at all. There are exceptions, of course, but you'd be surprised how many criminals are caught within a few days. The longer it stretches out, the less chance we have of getting them."

"But I've heard of criminals being caught years after the crime."

"Well, that's true, of course, Mrs. Winslow, but it's rather the exception. I don't want to discourage you unduly. I just want you to understand that this is the way things might work. This crime—if it happened at all—took place almost nineteen years ago. The criminal—the only witness we have—is dead. The only statement we have from her is a few whispered words when she was very far gone. It's been a very long time." He picked up his pencil again and started doodling. "Do you have a picture of the girl?"

"The priest said he went through all of the woman's things, and there were no photographs."

"A picture would have helped. Were there any letters?"

"No, I'm afraid not."

"Well, then, you see our difficulties."

"But can't you do something, Lieutenant Sullivan?" Cara pleaded.

"We'll try, Mrs. Winslow, but I have to tell you that we already have more cases than we can handle." He laid his hand on a stack of papers on the corner of his desk. "These are all cases I'm working on right now—me and the rest of the department. We're overworked and understaffed. What our main job consists of, I'm afraid, is putting criminals in jail who are walking the streets right now."

Phil and Cara listened as Sullivan went on, and both of them saw that he was sympathetic—but also that he had little hope of being able to help them. Finally Cara asked, "Is there anything you can do, Lieutenant? Just be honest with us."

"I'll spend some time on this, I promise. But I'm afraid I can't promise any results."

"Maybe we should hire a private detective—someone who could devote all of his time to it."

"That would be your best bet. If you can afford it, Mr. Winslow, I would certainly advise you to do it."

"Could you recommend a man?" Phil asked.

"Yes, as a matter of fact I can. There are some pretty sleazy private eyes out there you'd want to avoid, but there's one man I've known for a long time who you can trust. His name is Alex Tyson. He worked for one of the largest and best agencies in town up until a year ago. Then he went on his own. I can tell you this," Sullivan said firmly, "Alex is honest. If he can't help you, he won't keep sending you a bill for doing nothing. If you'd like, I'll give him a call."

"Thank you very much, Officer," Phil said. "We'd appreciate it. Could you call him right now?" He turned to Cara and saw her disappointment. "We won't give up, sweetheart," he said as he took her hand. "Not until we've tried everything."

★ ★ ★

"Well, Detective Tyson certainly doesn't intend to impress anybody with his neighborhood, does he?"

Cara glanced up and down the street on Manhattan's Lower East Side. It was not as bad as some of the tenement areas, but it was an older section of town, and the buildings were showing their age. Most of them were no more than two or three stories high, built before the invention of the elevator. The other pedestrians they passed were obviously not from the upper class of New York society.

The two had come directly from the police station to search out Alex Tyson. The journey was disturbing, for the crash of 1929 had left its mark on New York—as it had on every city in America. They passed many shabbily dressed men, their faces drawn with hopelessness, trying to warm themselves by fires burning in trash cans. Three men were selling apples, and Phil bought an apple from each of them. "Poor guys!" he whispered. "All they want is work, and there's none to be had."

"There's our building," Cara said.

The two stepped inside and found a long corridor with a stairway at both ends. "It's on the third floor," Phil said, glancing at the address the lieutenant had jotted down for them. The two climbed the stairs, and by the time they got to the top floor, he was puffing. "Whew! I'm getting out of shape. I'll have to spend more time walking—and you will too, darling."

"You're right," Cara said breathlessly. She held on to his arm as they walked down the dim corridor until they found a door with Tyson's Investigations on the glass. Phil opened the door for Cara and followed her into a waiting room with four chairs and a coffee table with several magazines on top—*Collier's Weekly, Time,* and *National Geographic*. The walls showcased some surprisingly good paintings. Phil moved closer to inspect the artwork and said, "Why, these are originals and not prints!"

The inner office door opened, and a man of medium build with a ruddy face and sharp gray eyes stepped outside. "Mr. and Mrs. Winslow, I presume? I'm Alex Tyson." He put out his hand, and Phil grasped the steely grip.

"It's good of you to see us on such short notice, Mr. Tyson."

"Come on into my office. I let my secretary go. Didn't really need one."

Cara stepped inside, and the two men followed her into the comfortably decorated inner office. There were some chairs around a small coffee table on an oriental rug, a single bed in one corner, a filing cabinet, a window overlooking the street, and a large desk and chair in front of the window. As in the waiting room, the walls were lined with paintings.

Studying the artwork, Phil noted again that the paintings were all originals. One of them was by John Sloan, one of Phil's old friends from the Ashcan School. "I admire your taste in paintings. This is a really good example of Sloan's work."

"You might like that one on the wall behind you as well," Tyson said with a smile.

Phil turned and exclaimed, "Why, that's mine!"

"I bought it before you became so expensive."

Memories flooded back over Phil Winslow. He had painted this scene when he had first come to New York City, penniless and living from hand to mouth. The scene featured a dirty little girl with curly black hair on Hester Street in the Jewish quarter of New York. She was fetching a doll and had an engaging smile. Phil had always thought the painting captured the atmosphere of Hester Street. "That brings back old memories. I'm flattered that you put me there alongside some pretty good artists."

"I once thought I'd be a painter myself," Tyson said. "I still dabble, but I don't have what it takes to make it a livelihood."

"I'd like to see what you've done."

Tyson blinked with surprise. "Well, I'd be happy to show my paintings to you sometime, but first let's talk about your problem. Please have a seat. Would you like some coffee or tea?"

"Tea would be good, but I'd hate to put you to any trouble," Cara said.

"No trouble. I'm a tea drinker myself."

"Fine. I'll have tea also," Phil said, and he walked around examining the paintings while Tyson made tea and poured it into delicate china cups.

"I don't think tea really tastes good unless you have fine china," he said. "It's one of my few luxuries."

Tyson served the two and joined them in a chair by the

small coffee table. Phil continued to study the paintings as he drank his tea.

"You've done very well with your art," Tyson commented. "I understand you nearly starved when you first came to New York."

"How did you know that?" Phil asked.

"I know some artists. I attend most of their shows."

The three spoke about some of their mutual acquaintances in the art world, and finally Tyson turned to the business at hand. "Lieutenant Sullivan told me a little about your problem, but I'd like to hear the story from your point of view. Please don't leave anything out."

Phil told the story very slowly, being careful to give every detail, but in truth there was not all that much to tell. When he had finished, he spread his hands wide and said, "That's about all we have. We want desperately to find our daughter, Mr. Tyson. Can you help us?"

"I don't know," Tyson answered. "I can try."

"Oh, if you could only find her," Cara whispered, and tears came to her eyes. She shook her head and blinked them away. "I'm sorry. I'm a little emotional."

"Very understandable, I'm sure. You have other children?"

She told him the names and ages of their other children.

"You understand, of course," he said gently, "that your daughter won't be the young woman she would have been if she had lived with you since she was an infant."

"We're ready for that, sir," Cara said earnestly. "Just please try your best to find her."

"It won't take me long to see what I can do. I'll either find some leads quickly, or I'll find out just as quickly that I can't do anything at all."

"How will you go about it?" Phil asked curiously. "I have no idea how detectives work."

Tyson leaned back. "Well, the first thing is to go to Father Mazzoni. Then I'll talk to every inmate and any prison guard that will give me a moment of their time. It all depends on how much leeway the prison officials will give me. In any case, that's where I'll begin."

The Winslows asked a couple more questions, and when they rose to leave, Phil took the detective's hand. "You understand that I'm not one of the Astors, but God has blessed us financially. Please don't worry about the expense. As a matter of fact," he said with a smile, "find our daughter, and I'll give you an original painting with my blessing."

"That's quite a bonus, but as much as I admire your work, I'd try just as hard without it. I'll call as soon as I know anything."

* * *

The next few days passed slowly for Phil and Cara, their nerves on edge as they waited for Alex Tyson to call. They had decided not to say anything to the children until they knew something more definite, but in private the two talked considerably about the strange situation that had turned their lives around. They spent much time in prayer, both together and alone, and the two also fasted. While Phil spent much time in his studio, Cara spent an equal amount of time in their bedroom on her knees. God seemed very real to her during that time, and she knew there must be some reason God had allowed this to happen.

Tyson called on March 7 at eight in the morning and said he had some information for them. Less than an hour after the call, Tyson was at the Winlows' front door.

"Come into the drawing room," Phil invited. "We'll have some tea and something to eat if you like."

"Just tea, thanks."

As the three sat down to tea, Cara's eyes were fixed on the detective. "I don't have good news," he said. "I've been at this every waking moment since our conversation in my office, but the truth is that Bertha Zale was a loner. She apparently had made no friends at all in the prison. A real recluse. She had a cell mate for a time named Mary St. Clair. Mary said she was the worst possible cell mate. Wouldn't speak a word. Just lay on her back staring at the ceiling or sitting in a chair. It sounds like she might have had serious mental problems. She had a sexually transmitted disease that may have affected her mind."

"Did you talk to the guards?"

"I talked to everybody," he said. "But nobody knew anything."

"She never mentioned to anyone that she had a daughter?"

"No, I'm afraid not." Tyson put his cup down. "I wish I had better news, but honestly I don't think I can help you."

"I know you did your best," Phil said heavily. "Just send me a bill."

"I don't feel comfortable doing that."

"Nonsense. You did your job, and besides I've got a painting for you."

"But I didn't find your daughter."

"You tried. Come along. It's in my studio."

"Just a minute. There's one more thing." Tyson hesitated, running his hand nervously over his hair.

"What is it?" Cara said. "What's on your mind, Mr. Tyson?"

"I don't know if it's worth anything to you, but it came to me last night when I saw I wasn't really getting anywhere. I worked with Rader Investigation Agency for several years. They're the best of the big agencies. There was an agent that worked for them for a while. He was the best man I ever saw at finding people."

"Why, then, maybe we could go to the Rader Agency."

"No, he doesn't work for them anymore. He quit even before I left, which was about a year ago."

"What was his name?"

"Francis Key."

"What's he doing now?"

"He got a case of religion and decided he wanted to do

something different. For a while he thought he'd be a preacher, but that didn't work out. He never felt comfortable with it. We got pretty close. He had always been a literary sort. Better educated than the rest of us. He didn't tell too many people, but he told me he wanted to write novels with a Christian outlook."

"Why, that's wonderful!" Cara exclaimed. "But I don't think I've read anything by him."

"That's because he never sold anything—at least not that I know of. You know how it is. A starving artist in an attic somewhere. You went through some of that yourself, didn't you, Mr. Winslow?"

"Yes, I did."

"Well, that's what Francis did. He quit work and wrote night and day until he ran out of money. Then he came back to the agency and worked long enough to get enough to support himself for a while again. Smartest man I've ever met. Intuitive about finding lost people. Nobody knew how he did it. I guess it's like Beethoven. He wrote symphonies, but I doubt if he could tell anybody how he did it. It was that way with Francis. He'd come up with something that none of the rest of us ever thought of and just wouldn't let go until he'd solved the mystery."

"Do you know where we could find him?"

"I have an old address for him. I think he might still be there. He's a rather strange fellow, but if I had your problem, I'd go straight to Francis Key."

CHAPTER FOUR

THE WINSLOWS FIND THEIR MAN

★ ★ ★

As Cara and Phil made their way down Hester Street in Lower Manhattan, Phil pointed up at a tenement building. "I had some Jewish friends who lived in this area when I first came to New York. A man named Paul Jacobs and his family. Lost track of them, but they were good people."

"Has the street changed much? That was a long time ago, Phil."

"It hasn't changed a whole lot. Still full of peddlers. And what I remember most is the wash hanging out on all the balconies."

The street had not changed all that much from what Phil remembered. Peddlers with trays suspended around their necks approached them, urging them to buy shoelaces, matches, and ribbons. Others shoved pushcarts around, and even in the bitter cold of early March the babble of vendors hawking their wares hung on the air.

"I thought that the city had gotten rid of most of these old tenements," Cara commented.

"They have torn down a lot of them, but I suppose there'll always be tenements in New York."

The two made their way down the street until finally Phil located the building they were looking for. "I think this is it," he said doubtfully. "Not much to look at, is it?"

The building was gray with age, and as they entered the front door, they were met with the rank smells of cooked cabbage mingled with unwashed bodies and worse. "I remember this smell," Phil said grimly. "I guess that never changes." He looked at Cara and said, "It's on the fifth floor. You think you're up to it?"

"Yes, I can do it."

They climbed up the dark staircase, passing children who screamed as they flew up and down the steps, most of them going out to play in the streets, the only playground they knew. Some of them stared curiously at the couple. An old man, a Hasidic Jew, stood aside to let them pass. "Good afternoon," Phil said.

The man stared at him, his earlocks dangling as he bowed his head. "God bless you," he said.

"And you too, sir," Cara replied.

As they climbed they had to stop once to let Cara catch her breath, and by the time they reached the fifth floor, both were winded. "I'm glad there's not ten stories," Phil said. "Are you all right?"

"Yes, I'm fine."

He led the way down the darkened corridor, which had only a small window at either end, both too grimy to admit much light. He stopped in front of number 507. "This ought to be it." He knocked on the door, and they both heard a chair being scooted back. "Well, at least he's home. I'd hate to have to make this trip twice."

The door opened, and a small young man stood blinking at them. "Yes?"

"My name is Phil Winslow. This is my wife, Cara. Are you Francis Key?"

"That's me."

The speaker was no more than five-eight. He was unremarkable in appearance, with brown hair that fell over his horn-rimmed glasses. His eyes were gray and penetrating—the only interesting aspect of his pale face.

"Would you like to come in?" Key asked. "It's a little crowded, I'm afraid."

"I don't want to intrude," Phil said.

"No problem. Step into my palatial apartment."

As Phil and Cara stepped in, Key said, "One of you can have the chair, and the other can sit on my bed."

"We won't stay long," Phil said, noticing a second chair that was hardly recognizable under stacks of books and papers. "Cara, have a seat."

Cara took the empty chair and glanced around the room. It appeared to be nothing but a storage room for books. Handmade shelves lined most of the wall space, each packed with books of all sorts—leather bound, paperback, and oversized ones that lay flat. In front of the cases on the floor were more books in stacks, some waist high. A table with an ancient typewriter on it was covered with papers and books. A cot pressed against one wall, neatly made up with a brown blanket and a single pillow. Squeezed in between two bookcases was a very small stove and what served for kitchen shelves. The room was relatively clean, but it was so full of books that it was hard to tell.

"Alex Tyson gave us your name, Mr. Key," Phil started.

"How is Alex? I haven't seen him for a while."

"Doing very well, I take it. But he couldn't help us with our problem, and he thought perhaps you might be willing to do what you can."

"You want to find someone?"

"How did you know that?" Cara asked.

"Well, it was what I mostly did at the Rader Agency, but I'm not a detective anymore."

"So Mr. Tyson told us, but would you at least listen to what we have to say?"

"I can listen, but I don't have anything to offer you. I'm sorry."

"That's all right," Phil said hurriedly. He sat down on the

cot while the shorter man remained standing. The man listened with a steady, almost devouring interest as Phil told their story. He seemed to be recording every word on some part of his brain. "And so Mr. Tyson thought you might be able to help us find our daughter," he concluded.

"I'm afraid Alex has an exalted idea of my abilities."

"But he said you could find people that nobody else could."

"Well, I did find a few that were difficult, but as—"

Cara stood up and reached out her hand in a plaintive gesture. "But Mr. Key—"

Her words were cut off when a raucous voice screamed, "Prepare to meet thy God!"

Cara saw a flash of brilliant color and an explosion of movement. She flinched as a bird struck her hair. She did not cry out, but it frightened her.

Phil jumped to his feet, but Francis reached out for the bird and set it on his shoulder. "Prepare to meet thy God!" the brilliantly colored parrot said again, its eyes fixed on Cara.

"I'm sorry," he said. He reached up absently and stroked the bird with his right hand. "She's very jealous." A smile touched his wide mouth. "Jealous of women. Doesn't like them to get close to me."

Phil laughed. "She's like all other females, I suppose."

"She's so beautiful. What's her name?" Cara asked.

"Miriam. I've had her for a couple of years now. I named her Miriam because Miriam was a prophetess. So I decided to let this Miriam speak the Word of God. Would you like to hear her say a few things?"

"Yes," Cara said eagerly.

"Miriam, Luke."

"Except ye repent, ye shall all likewise perish!" Miriam squawked.

Phil laughed again. "That's the authentic King James Version, I believe."

"Does she know any more?"

"Oh yes," he said. "Acts, Miriam."

"Believe on the Lord Jesus Christ, and thou shalt be saved!" Miriam shrieked.

"That's really marvelous. I've never seen anything like it!" Cara said.

"It really startles people sometimes. I just whisper the name of the book and she quotes the Scripture." He stroked the parrot fondly and said, "She'll behave all right as long as you don't try to touch me."

Cara sat down again, fascinated by the bird. "She's very pretty."

"She's a rather romantic bird. She lays eggs all the time, but of course they're not fertilized."

"Why don't you get her a mate?" Phil asked curiously.

Francis smiled shyly, which made him look even younger than the twenty-seven or twenty-eight years Phil had pegged him at. "I don't want to be raising a bunch of baby prophets and prophetesses." He caressed Miriam's head while the bird snuggled close to him and gently pecked at his ear. "I really don't think I can help you."

"Mr. Tyson told us that you feel God has given you a work to do," Cara said.

Interest brightened his gray eyes. "That's right. I do feel that way. Are you folks Christians?"

"Yes, we are," Cara said, "and we feel that God wants us to do something too. You see, even before our last child was born we named her Grace, and God gave me a promise that she would do great things for Him and be a comfort to us. But when we thought she had died, I lost faith, I suppose. But now that we know she's alive, we believe that God can complete the work He wanted to do through her. So you see, if you could only find Grace, I feel you'd be serving God in that way."

Francis stood very still. There was something about him that Cara could not completely identify. Alex Tyson had told them he was the smartest man he had ever known, and she could almost hear his brain cells at work. But there was more to the man than mere intelligence. *As soon as I told him about*

God's promise, he became interested, Cara thought. Aloud she said, "Please, can't you at least try to help us?"

He was silent for a moment. "It's a question of what God wants me to do most. I feel He wants me to write books that will glorify Him."

"Have you had any success?" Phil asked.

"No, not yet. I think I've got the novel God wants me to write in its embryonic stage, but I've run out of money, and I need to go back to Rader for a while to earn enough money to live on. Then I can quit again and write the book."

"If you had uninterrupted time," Phil said, "do you think you could write the novel God put on your heart?"

"I'm sure of it," Francis said eagerly, showing a satisfied smile of perfect white teeth. He was not handsome but was appealing in a boyish way. "I know that God wants me to do this, and somehow I'm going to."

Phil glanced at Cara, who gave him a slight nod. They understood each other very well. "How about this, Mr. Key. You take off from writing your novel and try your best to find Grace." Phil stood up and paced in the small room, never taking his gaze off the detective. "Do everything you can. Tyson was confident that if anyone could find Grace, you could. We'll all pray that you find her, but in either case, after you've done your best—whether you find her or not—I'll finance a six-month period for you in a better place than this. Go wherever you like where it's quiet, and I'll foot the bill."

"Please try, Mr. Key," Cara begged. "It would mean everything to us."

A silence fell on the room, and Cara almost held her breath. She felt certain that God had led them to this man.

Finally he whispered something to Miriam, who instantly screamed, "Put out the light! Put out the light!"

"Oh, Miriam, that's Shakespeare, not the Bible." He thought for a moment, then nodded. "All right. I'll do my best—with God's help."

Phil and Cara both felt relief wash over them. Phil put his arm around her and drew her close. "I believe we found our man, Cara. Thank you, Mr. Key."

"Please call me Francis. Everybody does."

CHAPTER FIVE

ON THE TRAIL

★ ★ ★

As Francis Key entered the prison, the smell assaulted him and brought back bad memories. He had always hated prisons, but this one seemed worse to him because only women were incarcerated. He thought of Miriam and hoped that she would be all right. His landlady would stop by to feed her, but Francis knew the parrot would be lonely without him. *Hang in there, baby,* he thought. He followed the guard down the corridor, feeling the cold steel and the blank gray concrete walls closing in on him. Ever since he had agreed to try to find Grace Winslow, he had felt overwhelmed with the impossibility of the task, and now it seemed more hopeless than ever.

"Right over there you'll find Father Mazzoni," the burly guard said as he pointed.

"Thanks."

Francis walked across the yard, pulling his coat closer against the cutting north wind. He hated cold weather and dreamed of going south. The warm breezes and gleaming hot sand of the southern coast of Florida looked pretty good to him about now.

Reaching the small greenhouse in the corner of the prison yard, he saw a figure inside shrouded by greenery. He tapped on the glass and the door opened at once. A tall priest smiled at him. "Can I help you?"

"Father Mazzoni, I'm Francis Key. I'd like to have a few minutes of your time. I need to speak with you about Bertha Zale."

"Oh yes." Mazzoni nodded. "Come in. It's warm in here."

Francis stepped inside the greenhouse and smiled. "It sure feels good in here." He looked around. "Beautiful violets."

Mazzoni smiled as he leaned over and touched one of the purple blossoms. "Look at how delicate the color is. I don't think an artist could make a paint that would even approach this."

"I expect paintings of flowers are for people who don't have access to the real thing."

Mazzoni stroked the plant tenderly and mused, "Flowers are nicer than people . . . in some ways."

"At least they don't wind up in prison."

"That's right," he said with a chuckle.

"You think there'll be violets in heaven, Father?"

Mazzoni's chuckle turned into a warm smile. "I'm certain of it. You know, I don't care for the description of heaven given in the book of Revelation."

Key was intrigued by this odd statement. "I've read that many times. Gates of gold and pearls. It sounds beautiful."

"Not to me. Gold is hard, and pearls have no warmth either. No, my heaven would be green grass, violets, tall trees rising high into the air." He shook his shoulders and grinned sheepishly. "I suppose I'm a heretic."

"I don't think so. Maybe heaven will be to us what we like best. But in any case," he said with a smile, "we know that Jesus will be there. Which theologian was it that said, 'For me heaven without Jesus would be a hell, and hell with Jesus would be a heaven'?"

"I don't know," Mazzoni said, "but I like what he said. He sounds like a wise man."

Key paid close heed to the change of expression on the tall man's face as they talked, all the while thinking, *This priest is my only hope.* Aloud, he said, "Father, would you mind telling me what you've already gone over with the others?"

"You mean about Bertha Zale's baby?"

"Even before that. Everything you can think of. Every word she said that you can remember."

He nodded. "You don't mind if I go ahead working with the flowers while I talk?"

"Not at all."

Mazzoni relayed how Bertha Zale had been withdrawn, almost catatonic at times. Most of their conversations had been one-sided, with the priest doing most of the talking. She had rarely spoken a word.

"What exactly did she tell you about her daughter leaving home?"

"It wasn't really much. She was weak and dying, you understand." He shook his head sadly, and his voice grew soft. "She was very grieved over the kind of life she had forced the girl into. She had been a simple woman herself and, of course, trying to raise a child in the right way was impossible for her. She said the girl began growing rebellious when she was twelve or thirteen—started running with the wrong crowd, the wrong kind of boys."

"Did Bertha say anything about the man her daughter ran away with?"

"Very little. She only met him once, and her daughter never called him by his real name."

Francis looked up quickly. "What did she call him?"

"Something like Serge. Maybe Sergion. Bertha was fading fast. It was hard to understand her," he said apologetically.

Key took notes throughout their conversation, and Mazzoni was surprised at how well the detective could jog his memory with his questions. "You're very good at this," he said.

He shrugged. "Most people remember more than they think."

Mazzoni lifted the watering can and watered a violet sparingly. He put the can down, then asked directly, "Do you think you'll be able to find this girl?"

Francis's eyes twinkled with humor. "If God wants me to, I will."

Mazzoni laughed. "You sound like you have God all figured out."

"No, hardly that." He smiled. "But I am convinced that God has plans for everyone."

"I'll agree with you there, but most of the time we get out of His plan and into something we design for ourselves."

"Sadly, that's my story too. You met the Winslows, didn't you?"

"Yes, I did. Fine people. Very devoted Christians, from what I could tell."

"Mrs. Winslow thinks that God gave her a promise back before the child was born, and she's convinced that it is God's timing that this information has come to light now. And her husband is convinced that I'm the one God is going to use to find her."

"I will add my prayers to theirs that you'll be successful, Mr. Key."

"I certainly need all the prayer I can get. If you think of anything else, you'll give me a call, won't you?"

"I'll do that, and could you drop me a line if you do find the girl? I'd like very much to know how this turns out."

"I'll do that." Key shook the priest's hand, then turned and left the greenhouse. The cold wind seemed even harsher now, and as he strode quickly toward the steel gates, he wondered if anything Mazzoni had said would be of any help to him.

★ ★ ★

For the next two days Francis Key did little else but sit in his room staring at the walls and thinking. He broke his concentration only to eat or to lie down and rest or to spend time with his loquacious parrot, teaching her two more Scripture verses.

"Revelation," he said on the third morning as the bird watched him eat breakfast.

"Even so, come, Lord Jesus," spouted the parrot.

"That's good. You get a reward for that." Francis cut a small piece from his apple and gave it to the parrot, then finished the rest himself. After putting his dishes in the sink, he grabbed his coat and went out for a walk. He pulled his coat tightly around him, wishing he had a warm hat as the breeze ruffled his hair.

For two hours he walked the streets of New York, going over his conversation with Mazzoni and mulling over the results of Tyson's interviews with others at the prison. He always worked like this, concentrating on the problem to the exclusion of everything else. From time to time he would pray simply and to the point: "God, help me find this woman." He didn't take much stock in long, elaborate prayers, preferring in all things to cut to the chase.

He walked the streets all day, then returned home at nightfall. He did not call the Winslows, for he had nothing to report. On his note pad he wrote down a prayer and dated it: *God, help me to find Grace Winslow. I'm not smart enough to do it by myself, so I'm asking you to put into my mind something that will help.*

Exhausted, he put the pad away and lay down on his cot. "Good night, Miriam," he said. The parrot immediately called back, "Good night, Francis."

Key tossed for a while but finally fell into a deep sleep. The next thing he knew he was sitting up straight in the bed, startling Miriam, who began squawking and quoting Scripture. Key paid her no attention, for he knew something was taking shape in his mind that was not of himself. Perhaps it was the result of all the questions he had asked, but in any case he knew it was time to quiet his mind and listen. He sat there in the silence of the room while various thoughts came to his attention—like pieces of a jigsaw puzzle. He made no attempt to put them together, but let them configure themselves into a logical picture. He smiled and murmured, "Thank you, Lord" and then lay down and went back to sleep.

★ ★ ★

As Francis Key mounted the worn concrete steps that led up to an ancient brownstone building, he had the sensation of time long gone. Years of wind and weather had stripped away the building's surface, leaving a dull, pitted exterior. He entered the dark foyer and thought of how he came to be here. After the epiphany he'd had in the middle of the night, he had waited until a reasonable hour and then called Finley Crane, a man he knew in show business. Crane had been a help to him in a case he had worked on before, and when Key questioned him, Crane said in his booming voice, "You want somebody that knows all about the history of show biz? You're talkin' about Blanche Fountain. If she don't know it, it never happened. I got her address right here."

Key approached the third door on the right and knocked gently. There was no answer, so he knocked louder, and finally, after what seemed like a long time, the door swung open with a creak. Key found himself looking at a woman dressed in a brilliant crimson gown. Her hair was as black as night, but the eyes that regarded him were not young. "Mrs. Fountain?"

"I'm Blanche Fountain. Who are you?"

"My name is Francis Key. I would like to talk with you if I might."

"Are you a reporter?"

"No, but I understand from a mutual friend of ours, Mr. Crane, that you know everything about show business."

"Oh, so Finley sent you. Well, in that case, come in, young man. I can give you a few moments."

He entered the room and was struck by an assortment of

odors—the place smelled of age and deterioration and cat. Several cats of various sizes, shapes, and colors regarded him conspicuously. The room was as jammed as his own, every wall covered with posters from Broadway shows, new and old.

"I was just about to have my tea. You will join me."

Since it was not a request but a command, Francis smiled and said, "I'd be honored, Mrs. Fountain." He sat down in a fragile-looking antique chair that he distrusted, but it held his weight. He watched as the woman fixed the tea and fetched the cream and sugar. She had obviously been a beautiful woman in her youth, but that day was long gone. Now she was made up heavily, the wrinkles unsuccessfully covered by pancake makeup, the eyes accentuated by heavy mascara, and her dry, brittle hair woven into a complicated arrangement. Her hands gave away her age, for they were thin and covered with liver spots.

"I understand you've been in the theater a long time, Mrs. Fountain."

"Oh yes, all of my life. I was born in a dressing room in Madison, Wisconsin. My parents were doing *Julius Caesar* there." She did not mention the date but went on quickly to say, "I am planning my comeback, you know."

"That must be very exciting. What will you be doing?"

"None of this modern garbage, I can assure you. Oh no, my dear man, it will be Shakespeare."

"And which play is your favorite?"

"I think my best work," she said after a long pause, "would be *Ophelia*. I did it a few years ago. I still have the clippings if you'd like to see them."

"I'd like to very much."

Key sat still while Blanche retrieved a scrapbook from a stack of leather-bound books on her table. He studied the reviews and noted that the dates went back twenty years.

Part of his success in finding out things from people was his monumental patience. He could listen to people by the hour as they spoke pontifically or described their boring hobbies, all the while giving the impression that he was fascinated. As a matter of fact, he *was* fascinated by Blanche Fountain. She had been in the theater practically since Lincoln was shot, and he would not have been surprised to hear her mention the name John Wilkes Booth as one of her leading men. Her stories jumped back and forth over the years, mixing up modern events with those plays and actors and actresses who had long ago turned to dust.

When his tea had been gone for some time, Key said, "I'm afraid I may be wasting your time, Mrs. Fountain."

"Why would you say that? What is your name again?"

"Francis Key."

"Named after Francis Scott Key, I suppose."

This was not true, but Francis had learned long ago to simply agree, so he nodded noncommittally. He had actually been named after an uncle on his mother's side and was no relation at all to the composer of "The Star-Spangled Banner."

"I actually am trying to trace a man, and I have no idea where to start. That's why Mr. Crane suggested you might be able to help me."

"Well, what's the man's name? I know a great many people in the theater."

"That's the problem," Key said, allowing distress to show on his face. He made a rather good actor himself, able to convincingly reflect different emotions when necessary. "Actually, all I have is a nickname."

"That's very strange. What's the nickname?"

"Well, even that is not clear. It's something like Serge."

"Serge?"

"Yes. Well, not that, but something like that. Maybe Sergion."

"Oh, you must mean Sergius."

"Is that a character in a play?"

Blanche threw up her hands. "What *do* they teach you children in school these days! Of course Sergius is a character. He's one of the major characters of Shaw's *Arms and the Man*."

"Sergius. Well, that might be a help. Is he the only character named Sergius you know?"

"He's the only Sergius in a play," the actress said firmly. "You should know that."

"I certainly should. That helps me a great deal. Now I'll have to find out if that particular play was being staged in New York three years ago."

"Why, it's no problem to find that out."

Relief washed through him. "It would be a great help to me, Mrs. Fountain. I'd be most grateful."

Blanche began to search through her books, files, magazines, and boxes and finally came back triumphantly. "Here it is. I have the very cast of characters. It took place at the Majestic Theater."

"May I see it?"

"Of course."

He took the program and marveled at the woman's pack rat instincts. "You keep all the programs?"

"Certainly. I need them to keep up on my history of the theater. Besides, many people call or come to see me looking for information. What is the man's name? I've left my glasses in my bedroom."

"Well, the play starred Harry Sinclare and Diane Mobley."

"Oh yes, I saw it. He did very well, but Diane made a miserable job out of her role. I could have done so much better myself!"

"It says here the actor who played Sergius was named Charles Bannister."

"Oh, *him*!"

Key looked up quickly. "You didn't care for Charles Bannister?"

"He's a pitiful excuse for an actor! He moved across the stage like a zombie. And his voice—oh my, Mr. Key, he sounded like a crow!"

"This was only three years ago. Do you suppose he's still acting?"

"Oh no. He went into motion pictures."

Key could not resist the smile that came to his lips. "You

don't regard people who make motion pictures as actors or actresses?"

"Why, certainly not! They do every scene entirely out of context. There's no continuity to it. They have people standing on every side telling them exactly what to say. That's not theater, and it will never last."

"I'm sure you're right, Mrs. Fountain. Well, this makes my job much simpler. Now all I have to do is find Charles Bannister."

"Let me make a call for you, Mr. Key. I know an agent who knows the status of every actor in the business."

He could not help feeling that God himself had sent him to this place. "That would be most helpful," he said.

Francis waited while Blanche got her glasses, perched them on her nose, and dialed a number. She spoke to a man who gave her another name, and finally she called an agent by the name of Abe Goldfein.

"Mr. Goldfein, this is Blanche Fountain." A pause, and then she said, "Certainly you must remember me. I have a gentleman here who needs help finding Charles Bannister. Would you know his whereabouts?"

Key was sitting straight up listening, and when the actress reached for a tarnished brass pencil to write something down, he felt the burden of finding this man lift from his shoulders.

Putting the phone down, she handed him the slip of paper and said, "He's in Hollywood. Awful place!"

Key rose, and when she put her out hand, he bent over it and kissed it as if he were a prince. "Thank you so much, Mrs. Fountain. You've been so helpful. I know this is not usual, but I would have spent money finding out this information." He reached into his pocket, pulled out a money clip, and removed a twenty-dollar bill. "Please give this to your favorite charity in your name."

"Why, certainly I will be happy to do that."

Francis was certain that her favorite charity would be Blanche Fountain, but that didn't bother him. "I'll be eagerly anticipating your comeback, Mrs. Fountain. Look for me in the front row."

"Certainly. You must come backstage after the performance."

★ ★ ★

"Mr. Winslow, I think I found the man that took your daughter away from Bertha Zale."

Phil Winslow's voice crackled with excitement over the telephone. "That's great! Where is he?"

"He's in Hollywood. Los Angeles, actually. I have his address. I can't guarantee he'll be there, Mr. Winslow, but this is the best lead I've come upon."

"I want you to go out there at once, but come by here first. I'll get you a ticket for the train and I'll give you some money. You've done good work."

"You can thank Blanche Fountain."

"No, I can thank you," Phil said with relief in his voice. "I'll have the ticket and the money ready for you."

CHAPTER SIX

THE RING OF DEATH

★ ★ ★

The taxi pulled up in front of a single-story building stretched behind a line of tall royal palms. Francis eyed it suspiciously. "This is Bellingham Hospital? It doesn't look like a hospital to me."

The burly cab driver turned around to face him. His face and arms were bronzed by the California sun, and he had two teeth missing. "It ain't no hospital if that's what you want," he grunted. "If you're sick, you'd better go someplace else."

"What do you mean it's not a hospital?" Key demanded. He searched the building in vain for a sign, but he saw none. "Isn't this Bellingham Hospital?"

"I said it ain't no hospital. It's just a clinic. It ain't even that. It's a place where rich people come to dry out when they get the DT's."

Key chewed his lower lip thoughtfully and pushed his reading glasses up with his forefinger as he checked the address again. "If there's no hospital by that name, I guess this is it, then. How much do I owe you?"

"One seventy-five."

He pulled two dollars out of his billfold and handed it to the driver.

"You know, a lotta them movie actors come to this here clinic," the man said as he took the money. "I brung John Barrymore here twice already. The place is filled up with famous drunks. Hey, thanks for the tip."

"You're welcome."

Key stepped out of the cab and glanced up at the azure sky through the towering palm trees. Light, fleecy clouds drifted lazily along. It was like a spring day in the tropics, with the breeze barely stirring the trees. As he walked up the steps, a gigantic yellow cat appeared from nowhere and stared at him suspiciously before turning and running, intent on some urgent business of his own.

Key stepped inside the glass door and approached the information desk to the right. A curvaceous woman in a white nurse's uniform sat behind the desk, reading a fan magazine. "Can I help you?" she said, smiling brilliantly.

"Do you have a Mr. Charles Bannister as a patient here?"

"Oh yes, indeed!" Her blue eyes quickened, and the smile became even more engaging. "Are you in the movie business?"

"No, I'm afraid not."

The smile disappeared, and the receptionist fluffed her auburn hair. "His room is two twenty-six, but you'll probably find him out sitting beside the pool. Right down this hall and to your left. You can't miss it."

"Thanks. I hope you make it in the movies."

"How did you know I wanted to be a movie star?"

"Doesn't everyone?" Francis grinned at her and winked before striding off down the hall. He turned left and followed the signs, stepping outside into the open air at the back of the hospital. To his right was a pool shimmering like a huge emerald. He passed several chaise longues and chairs occupied mostly by female patients. Francis slowly walked along until he saw a man lying on his back with a towel over his face under a colorful umbrella. Francis cleared his throat, and the man lifted the towel. "Who are you?" he mumbled.

"My name's Francis Key. Are you Mr. Bannister?"

"Yeah, that's right." Bannister sat up and looked Key over carefully. He was tall, finely tanned, and had a rather muscular body, spoiled by a roll of fat around the middle. "I don't know you, do I?"

"No, you don't."

"What a shame for you," Bannister said with a grin. He had an actor's voice, full and strong, and spoke a little too rapidly. "You're not from Liberty, are you?"

"Liberty?"

"Yeah, Liberty Pictures. You know."

"No, I'm afraid not. I'm from New York, and I'm working on a case I thought you might be able to help me with."

"A case? You a doctor or a policeman?"

"Neither one," he said carefully, wondering how best to approach Bannister. It was a touchy situation, and he did not want to offend the man. "I don't know how to tell you this—it's actually a little embarrassing."

Bannister laughed, and his capped teeth flashed against his tanned skin. "I doubt if anything you could say would embarrass me. Just spit it out, partner."

Key nodded, understanding that straightforward tactics would work best with this man. "I'm looking for a young woman named Ruby Zale."

Bannister's eyes opened wide but almost immediately narrowed with suspicion. "You're lookin' for Ruby? What for?"

"It's confidential, I'm afraid."

"That means you're a cop."

"Not at all," he said quickly.

"You have to be a cop if you've come all the way out here lookin' for Ruby."

"Actually, Mr. Bannister, I once served as a private investigator for the Rader Agency. Now I'm employed by a family that's anxious to find the young woman." He hesitated, then added, "I think there might be some money in it for her."

Bannister shook his head, and his mouth twisted in a

grimace. "It couldn't be from her old lady. She didn't have a pot to plant petunias in."

"Is there any reason," Key said carefully, "why you can't help me with this?"

"I don't want to get into any trouble."

"No trouble. I just need to speak to her." He turned his head to one side. "Why should she be trouble for you?"

"Well, to tell the truth, she was only a kid when we took up together, and we crossed the state lines. I think there's some kind of law about that."

"That's right—it's called the Mann Act. I understand she was only fifteen when she ran off with you."

Alarms went off in Bannister's head, and he clamped his lips together. "That was a while ago, and you can't prove anything."

"Look, Mr. Bannister, I'm not trying to prove anything. I'm just trying to find the girl, and I think the situation will be a help to her. I can't force you to tell me anything, but you must have felt something for her at one time. If you did, you can help her by helping me."

Bannister picked up a jug of orange juice and poured some into a tumbler. He drank it, then set the glass down, seeming to come to a decision. "She's a wild broad, Key. A good-lookin' woman. But I'm tellin' you she doesn't care about *anything*!"

"What do you mean by that?"

"I mean she's kind of nutty. Oh, she can be as sweet as sugar one minute, but what a temper. Why, I've seen her cryin' over a dead bird and not ten minutes later hit a guy with a blackjack. You know she carries a blackjack?"

"No, I didn't know that."

"Well, she does, and she knows how to use it too." He reached up and rubbed his temple as if it were sore. "She laid me out cold one time. Believe me, I never forgot it."

Francis followed the flight of a small bird that swooped over the pool. "Do you have any idea where she is?"

"We got in a fight, and she split on me. Just walked out

with nothing more than the clothes she had on. I'll give Ruby this, she never asked me for money. I gave her things, but she never asked for them."

"When did she leave you?"

"Almost a year ago—no, more than that. Probably fourteen months. Yeah, that's right. She found me with another woman, and I thought she was gonna kill us both. But she just gave me a look that would burn a hole in steel and walked out. Never even said good-bye."

"You don't know where she went?"

"Oh, sure," Bannister said. "I looked around for her and found out she took off with a biker."

"You mean a motorcycle rider?"

"That's right. One of the real tough ones, from what I hear. A guy named Hack Keller."

"And you never saw her after she left?"

"Yeah, as a matter of fact, I did once. I heard she was at this carnival doing an act with Keller, so I went to catch it."

"An act? What sort of act?"

"Oh, you've probably seen them. It's this big round steel thing called the Ring of Death. A guy on a motorcycle starts it up on the bottom and runs it up around the walls." He made a face. "Pretty hairy, if you ask me. They could get killed doin' that."

"And you saw Ruby there?"

"I'll say. After Keller got through runnin' around like a squirrel on a treadmill, he stopped his cycle and Ruby rode in on another motorcycle. She had on black leather. I'm tellin' you, she was a knockout. Her helmet was off, and that hair of hers could knock your eyes out."

"What color is her hair?"

"Strawberry blond, and it's the real thing. I know that for a fact. Anyway, she brought in that cycle and both of them started up around the cage. They went around together at first, and then Keller reversed so that the two of them were going in opposite directions." Bannister shook his shoulders.

"I wouldn't get in a thing like that if they gave me the state of New York!"

"Did you talk to her after the show?"

"Yeah, just for a minute. I went around to their trailer, but I didn't get anywhere. She took one look at me and showed me the gate. I tried to argue, but about that time Keller came back and threatened to take my head off. A real troglodyte!"

"Do you remember the name of the act they were with?"

"It was the Royal Shows. Just a two-bit carnival was all." Bannister swallowed hard and leaned forward. "You ain't got a drink on you or a hip flask, have you, pal?" he whispered.

"Afraid not." Francis looked at him quizzically. "I thought you were in here to get away from that."

"Yeah, I am, but I've had about all I can take. I'll get out of here tomorrow. I'm not a drunk like the rest of these people here. I just enjoy a drink now and then."

Key nodded. "Thanks for the help."

"Hey, if you see her, tell her I'm thinkin' about her. And you can tell her she can come back if she wants."

"I'll tell her."

★ ★ ★

The carnival was not terribly difficult to locate. It only took Francis three phone calls to discover that it was set up just outside of Los Angeles. He took a cab the next day, arriving at the fairgrounds at dusk. He was carrying his suitcase, which was as light as he could make it. Shifting it to his free hand, he walked down the middle of the midway with the noisy crowd. Garish lights flooded the place, and loud calliope music filled the air. The merry-go-round pumped the horses up and down as parents held their children steady on pink and green and red horses with flaring lips. Farther on, shills called out to passersby to try their luck at games of chance. Key stopped long enough to throw some baseballs at a fake batter and, to the chagrin of the owner, succeeded in winning a huge kewpie doll.

"You must be a professional pitcher," the man complained.

"Not really. You can keep the kewpie doll."

Key made his way through the carnival until he found the Ring of Death. There was a platform outside, and a huge and poorly executed painting of a man and a woman on motorcycles. The woman had on a skin-tight black biker's outfit, her helmet under one arm and her strawberry blond hair blowing freely. Key studied the picture, wondering if the face was true to life. He approached a heavily made-up woman who was sitting behind a ticket box. "When does the show start?"

"Ten minutes. You want a ticket?"

"Yes." He paid for his ticket and then started up the ramp that wound around to the top of a large steel sphere, where a crowd had already begun to gather. He found a place where he could set his suitcase next to him. As more people came he clung tenaciously to his place as the crowd tried to find good seats.

While he waited he thought of his mission and wondered how he was going to convince Ruby Zale that she was Grace Winslow. *I'll have to try to get her to some quiet place by herself in hopes that she'll listen to what I have to say.*

A few moments later a roar split the air and a motorcycle drove into the cage. The rider got off, shut the steel gate, and locked it firmly. He was a big man, Francis observed, with shoulders like a wrestler. His goggles were up, revealing his close-set beady eyes. He had a pugnacious jaw covered by a beard. He looked at the crowd and grinned mirthlessly, then pulled his goggles down into place. He climbed onto the motorcycle and gunned it and then began circling the cage. The bike started slowly but rapidly gained speed. The man leaned down over the handlebars and let centrifugal force take over. He went around the lower part of the drum, then came up to where he was only a few feet below the audience. Key felt he could have reached out and touched him.

Keller went from the top to the bottom, sometimes quickly,

sometimes slowly, and then after five minutes slowed the speed and brought the cycle to a stop. The gate unlatched, and a woman rode out astride a motorcycle. Her helmet was off, and Key got a good look at her face. He was struck at once by her freshness, which he had not expected. Somehow he thought the hard life Ruby Zale had led would have left marks, but if there were marks, they were inward ones, not outward. She had a lovely girl-next-door face with beautifully shaped eyes. As she looked up and smiled, he saw that they were either green or blue; he could not tell which. Her hair was her most outstanding feature—a true strawberry blond—not out of a bottle, according to Bannister. The black leather outfit she wore clung to her body almost as if it had been painted on, and the top of her jacket was left open invitingly. She put the helmet on, tucked her hair in, and then started around, closely followed by Keller, until the two of them were rolling around the drum at a frightening speed. Fascinated, Francis watched as they changed positions, one leading, then the other, sometimes missing each other by a fraction of an inch.

Then Ruby slowed her machine and descended to the lower part of the cage while Keller continued to circle. She turned around and started up the wall again, going in the opposite direction from Keller. The two got so close they reached out and slapped hands as they passed.

Francis could not help gasping with the crowd as the woman wrenched her machine up and went over the top above Keller. They were performing a wild dance in steel and roaring engines as they missed each other by the merest fractions of an inch.

Finally the roar of the engines diminished and they descended. Both of them looked up and acknowledged their fans as the audience applauded. The man opened the door and the duo peeled their motorcycles out. Francis waited until the crowd stood and moved away, giving one last look down at the Ring of Death. "That's a hard way to serve the Lord," he muttered.

He exited down the ramp and went over to the ticket seller. "When's the next show?" he asked.

"Forty minutes."

"I'd like to meet the artists," he said, giving her his best smile, which almost seemed to bounce off the hard features of the woman.

"I wouldn't advise it."

"Why not? I'd just like to congratulate them."

"They don't need none of that. Especially Hack. He's mean and stuck up. And you wouldn't get nowhere with Ruby."

"Well, I'd like to try."

"Your funeral. They got a trailer out behind here." She returned to her magazine with its lewd cover, and Key noticed that she moved her lips as she read.

Key had learned from hard experience to be cautious, and as he moved between the Ring of Death and the neighboring act, the House of Horrors, he cautiously sought out the trailers where the performers stayed. The area was lit by some naked light bulbs hanging from wires, and he kept to the shadows until he saw a small trailer with the two motorcycles just outside. He hesitated, for he had heard enough about Hack Keller to know that it would not be wise to include him in the interview.

As luck would have it, the door of the trailer opened, and Keller emerged, almost blotting out the inside light as he stooped to get through the doorway. He turned and walked rapidly away, disappearing into the midway area.

Key's heart jumped at the chance to talk to Ruby alone, and he quickly approached the trailer and knocked on the door. After a moment Ruby Zale opened it with a drink in her hand. "Whadd'ya want?" she said flatly.

"Miss Zale?"

A sneer twisted the woman's lips to one side. It was a good sneer, one she had evidently worked on quite a bit. Still it was not enough to distort the symmetry of her beautiful face. "Look, Jack, I don't need no admirers. That's what you want, ain't it?"

"I just want to have a talk with you."

A slight laugh escaped Ruby's throat, and she shook her head and started to close the door. "Beat it, buster, before you get hurt."

Impulsively Francis stepped forward and put his hand on the door. "Please, Miss Zale, I need desperately to speak with you. It's not what you think."

"I know what you want, but here's some good advice. Get out of here before my guy comes back. He'd pulverize a runt like you."

"It won't take but—"

He did not finish his sentence. He heard footsteps, then felt a grip with frightening strength seize his arm. He was jerked aside and turned to look up into the bearded face of Hack Keller. "This guy puttin' the moves on you, Ruby?"

"Ah, he's harmless. Just help him find his way out," Ruby said with a laugh. "He's too scrawny to be much of a masher."

"Get out of here and don't come back!" Keller snarled. He whirled Key around and shoved him hard, driving him to the ground.

Key lifted his head and spit out some dirt. Through a daze, he heard Ruby laugh. "Don't bust him up, Hack. It ain't worth it."

Keller laughed. "Pitiful little runt, ain't he?"

Key got to his feet and dusted himself off thoughtfully. He was not offended by being called a runt; he was accustomed to such remarks from larger men. He picked up his suitcase and walked quickly away from the trailer. He found a dark alley between two exhibits where he could stay out of sight for a while and wait. He put his suitcase down and sat on it.

"I might be a runt," he muttered, "but I'm a patient runt."

CHAPTER SEVEN

HEADING EAST AGAIN

★ ★ ★

"Well, you *are* a persistent little devil, aren't you?"

Ruby stood in the doorway of her trailer, her hand on her hip, staring in disbelief at the man on her doorstep. "You must have a death wish! Don't you know what Hack will do to you if he finds you here again?"

"I need to talk to you, Miss Zale. My name is Francis Key."

"What'd you do—wait until you saw him leave?"

"That's right."

"Look, you must be pretty stupid or else you've got a hearing problem. Now, let me make it plain. I don't go out with other men. I've got a guy, and that's it."

"That's not why I'm here, Miss Zale."

"I've heard that before."

He grinned at her, and Ruby thought it made him look young and innocent, but she had seen innocent faces before. She shook her head and demanded, "All right, what's your pitch, buster?"

"Could I come inside?"

"No."

"Well, then, could you step over here with me out of the doorway?"

"No."

"All right," Key said in a resigned tone. He pulled a card from his pocket and handed it to her. "I used to work for the Rader Investigation Agency in New York City."

"You're a private cop?"

"Something like that. Anyway, I took on a special job, Miss Zale."

Suspicion narrowed Ruby's eyes. "Look, I don't know what you're after me for, but you ain't got nothin' on me."

"Oh, I'm certain I don't. Really, this is another matter entirely."

"All right. Spit it out, then. Hack'll be back any minute. He just went to get some cigarettes."

"I hate to be the bearer of ill tidings. You probably haven't heard, but Bertha Zale died recently."

Ruby did not speak for a moment, then asked, "What'd she die of?"

"I don't know really. She was in prison."

"Yeah, I heard she went to the pen. Look, if you're expectin' me to show some kinda grief, you might as well forget it. I ran away from her 'cause of the way she treated me. Too bad she's dead, but that's the way it goes."

"There's more to it than that, Miss Zale."

"Don't tell me the old lady got rich and left me a bundle." She smiled cynically, passing her hand up over her hair. "You'll never make me believe that."

"It's not exactly that."

"What do you mean 'not exactly'? Come on, I'm tellin' you Hack will be back, and you'll be in real trouble."

"If you'll just listen to me without asking questions, I have something important to tell you. When I finish, I'll answer any questions you have."

"All right. Let's have it."

"Your real name is not Ruby Zale. It's Grace Winslow. Your parents are Phil and Cara Winslow, who live on Long Island in New York State. Bertha Zale was at Manhattan's City Hospital to have a baby at the same time that Mrs. Winslow was there having hers. Bertha's baby died, and she exchanged her dead child for the living Winslow child. . . ."

Ruby listened to the rest of the story without speaking. "And so you see," he finished, "you've really been living in the wrong circumstances all of your life."

Ruby let out a good firm laugh from deep in her throat. "You really expect me to believe that cock-and-bull story?"

"I was afraid you wouldn't," he said regretfully, "but it's true."

"So my mom told some priest all of this when she was dyin'. Don't you know she was on dope and booze? She made up stories all the time, Key. It's just another one of 'em."

"Not this one. It's been very carefully checked. The only death recorded at City Hospital in New York on that date is that of Grace Winslow, but you're Grace Winslow."

"Look, get out of here, will ya. I haven't got time—" Suddenly the roar of a motorcycle split the air, and Ruby warned, "You've gotta get out of here."

"But you can't stay here, Miss Zale. You need to go back—"

"Get out of here now! He's drunk, and he won't think twice about smashing in your skull."

Francis turned with alarm and started away, but Keller brought the motorcycle right in front of him, jumped off, and let the machine fall to the ground. His eyes were bloodshot, and rage reddened his face as he bellowed, "I told you what would happen, you little punk!"

"Leave him alone!" Ruby called out. "He didn't mean any harm. He's just some kind of nut."

But Keller ignored her. He grabbed Key by the lapels and swing his huge fist. Key managed to turn his head so the blow struck him over the left eye. Yellow stars exploded inside his skull, and a loud roaring drowned out everything else. He felt himself propelled backward and hit the ground hard. He lay there unable to move, and through a fog he heard the woman cry, "Don't do it, Hack! You'll kill him!"

Before he could guess what was coming, Key felt Hack's heavy motorcycle boot catch his left arm and smash into his ribs. The pain was unbelievable, and the force of the blow rolled him over.

Ruby grabbed Hack by the arm. "That's enough! You're breaking his ribs!"

"I'm gonna stomp him into the dust!" Keller grunted. "Get out of the way."

Ruby jumped in front of him, blocking his path. "You're drunk, Hack. You'll kill him and wind up in the pen. Is that what you want?"

"Get outta the way, Ruby."

"No, I won't. Come on inside. Let him crawl away."

Keller slapped Ruby in the face, which spun her around, but she did not lose her balance. Keller started back toward Francis and prepared to kick him in the head. With one swift motion, Ruby drew a blackjack from her hip pocket and brought it down on Hack's head. He grunted and staggered as she yelled, "That's enough, Hack! I'll lay you out."

Keller grabbed her by the throat, and Ruby lifted the metal-filled weapon again and slammed it into his head with all of her might. It struck his head with a dull, meaty sound, and his eyes rolled back, showing white. He collapsed limply to the ground, and Ruby stood breathing hard, staring down at him, her face tingling from the force of his slap. She shoved the blackjack into her pocket and stepped around to where Francis was struggling to get to his feet.

"Are you okay?"

"Just . . . a little woozy."

"Can you get up? He's out, but when he wakes up he'll kill you. And me too."

Ruby pulled Francis to his feet and saw that his face was twisted with pain. "He may have busted your ribs, but you've gotta get out of here."

"What about . . . you?" he gasped.

"I think I'd better get out too. He's crazy enough to kill me."

"Then get your stuff and we'll go."

Ruby stared at him. "To New York?"

"That's right," Key said painfully, holding his right side. The blow had split his eyebrow, and he wiped the blood away with his free hand. "I'm telling you the truth. You're Grace Winslow."

For one moment the woman stood absolutely motionless. Key thought she would refuse, but then she laughed metallically. "All right, Francis. That's your name, ain't it?"

"That's right."

"Let me get my stuff and we'll get out of here. Whatever's in New York can't be as bad as him."

Key bent over, trying to catch his breath. He could not breathe very deeply, for each breath was like a knife slicing his ribs. He felt the blood trickling down his face but was hurting too much to worry about it. It was all he could do to stand up, and finally when the woman came out with two suitcases, he said, "Can you hand me mine?"

She grabbed his suitcase and put it in his left hand.

"Come on," she said. "You have a car?"

"No, I came in a cab." He walked stiffly, each step jarring his side, and the woman beside him watched him curiously.

"Can you make it?" she asked.

"I'll make it. Just get us to a cab."

The trip seemed to take forever, but finally the sounds of the carnival grew fainter, and Key heard the woman holler, "Hey, taxi, over here!"

Swaying on his feet, he felt the woman take the suitcase. The door opened, and he almost fell inside. She had to lift his legs in, and he heard the door slam. He was eased back in the seat, and he heard her get inside.

"Take us to the railroad station, driver," he instructed weakly.

"You better get some stitches in that eyebrow first," Ruby said to him. "Driver, take us to the nearest hospital instead."

Key did not respond. It was all he could do to keep himself from crying out as the taxi bounced over the ruts of the vacant lot. As he felt the ride get smoother and the tires begin to hum on pavement, he felt himself losing consciousness. It felt good to slip into the warm blackness and leave the pain behind.

★ ★ ★

"Well, you don't have any broken ribs, but they're pretty well bruised."

Francis tried to take a deep breath and grimaced. "They feel broken, Doctor."

"They're going to hurt for a long time. The bandages will help, but every time you breathe, they're going to give you some pain. My advice is to go to bed and stay there for a couple of weeks."

"What about those stitches?" Ruby asked. She had been allowed to stay in the examining room, where she had watched the proceedings. The young doctor on duty seemed rather inexperienced. Thread dangled from the messy stitches in Key's eyebrow and were covered by a goopy orange medication.

"They can come out in five or six days."

"Thanks a lot, Doc. How much do I owe you?"

"Pay at the desk as you go out."

Key carefully eased himself down off the table and caught himself as his feet hit the floor and jarred him.

"You're not gonna get far like that," Ruby said.

"Let's go to the station."

"You'll pass out."

"Well, put me in a wheelbarrow and drag me. We've got to get on that train. There's nowhere else we can go."

Ruby called a cab and got Francis into it, along with the luggage, and when they reached the train station, she got him inside and seated on a bench in the waiting area.

"What do we do now?" she said.

Key pulled out his billfold and handed her some cash. "Go buy two tickets to New York City. Get one sleeping compartment and one day coach. This ought to cover it."

Ruby looked at the money. "I might run off with this."

"I wish you wouldn't," he said.

Ruby stared down at the man and shook her head. "You are a piece of work, Francis Key. Okay, I'll get the tickets."

★ ★ ★

Ruby looked at the door the porter had opened, then stepped inside. "Hey, this is classy," she said.

"I'll get your bags, miss, and put 'em right in here."

"Keep mine in here if you will," Key whispered to Ruby.

"Where are you goin'?"

"Day coach, two cars down."

Ruby stared at him and nodded.

Key's face was pale, and he was perspiring. "You keep the billfold. The porter here will show you to the dining car." He shuffled painfully away.

"That ain't your husband, miss?" the porter asked. "He don't look too good."

"He had an accident. And no, he's not my husband."

"He looks mighty poorly. Anyway, if you'd like something to eat, let me know. The dining car is the one up ahead."

"All right." Ruby stepped back and shut the door and then explored the tiny sleeping compartment, the first one she had ever seen. She had only ridden in day coaches when traveling with the Royal Shows. When she discovered the sink, she cried with delight and immediately stripped off her biker's outfit and took a sponge bath. After drying off, she opened one of her bags and put on one of her two dresses.

Leaving the compartment, she went directly to the dining car, carrying Francis's money in a small purse.

A white-coated server met her. "You'll be dining alone, miss?"

"Yeah."

"Here's a nice seat right here by the window. Can't see much right now, but when we pass through a town you can see the lights."

Ruby sat down nervously, and the waiter put a menu before her.

"Can I bring you something to drink while you're waiting?"

"Maybe some coffee, please."

"Yes, miss."

Ruby studied the menu and was amazed at the variety. She ordered lobster, which she had never had before, and when it was placed on the table, her eyes opened wide. "How do you get at this thing?"

The server's white teeth flashed in sharp contrast to his shiny black face. "You use this nutcracker, miss, to crack the claws. Then you pull the meat out. You dip it in this melted butter here."

Ruby found the lobster delicious and unlike anything she had ever eaten before. She ordered fresh strawberries and cream for dessert and had another cup of coffee. She sat there feeling full, and as the train sped through the night, she leaned her head back against the seat and thought about Francis Key. He had appeared from nowhere, and she had thought at first that he was a con artist. Some suspicion still lurked in her mind, but at least he had gotten her away from Hack Keller. She had planned to leave him soon anyway, for he was abusive and not a man any woman would stay with for long. He had been virile and tough enough to attract her attention, but now she felt almost dirty as she thought of the time she had spent with him.

She smoked a cigarette, then ground it out and got to her feet. The waiter was there immediately, and she said, "How do I pay for this?"

"You can pay me if you'd like, miss."

Pulling out the roll of folded bills, she paid the tab and added a little extra for a tip. "It was real good," she said.

"Thank you, miss. We have a good breakfast too. Anything you like."

Ruby left and went back to her compartment and sat down. Wondering where she was supposed to sleep, she tried to figure out how the berth worked. By experimentation, she discovered there was an upper berth that could be pulled down.

A knock on the door startled her and she jumped up to open it.

"May I make up your bed, miss?" the porter asked.

"Yeah, sure. Thanks."

She stood back while the porter expertly made the seat into a lower berth and then said, "Good night, miss. I hope you sleep well."

"Thanks."

When the door closed, Ruby ran her hand across the clean white sheet. It smelled so fresh, and the pillow was fluffy and inviting. She started to undress but quickly changed her mind and left the compartment. She passed through one coach and entered the next, which was a day coach. She spotted Francis at once in the half-full car. He was halfway down, leaning his head against the window, holding his side. She moved down the aisle and stood over him. He was breathing in short breaths, and perspiration wet his shirt. "Francis," she said, "are you all right?"

He opened his eyes and whispered yes.

"You don't look all right. Those ribs are giving you a hard time."

"I'll be all right," Key managed to grunt.

"This is silly. There are two beds in that compartment. Come on, you might as well use one of them."

"Maybe I'd better not."

"Don't be stupid," Ruby said impatiently. "You're gonna pass out here. Come on, and don't argue."

She stepped back, and Key got to his feet painfully. He

could not straighten up fully and moved like an arthritic old man as he made his way down to the sleeping compartment. Ruby followed him down the corridor, and when they reached the door, she opened it for him.

"I've discovered that there's another bed up here," she told him. She swung the upper berth down, which already had sheets and a pillow and a blanket.

"Okay, get your clothes off and get in that bottom bunk."

Key was too woozy with pain medication to argue. He pulled off his coat, which was damp with sweat, and started unbuttoning his shirt. He looked at her and said, "That's good."

"No it's not. You'll be miserable. Go ahead and take your shoes and pants off."

He sat down on the bunk and she removed his shoes. "That's enough," he managed to say as he carefully lay down on the sheet and finally relaxed. "That feels good," he whispered. He felt her pull the blanket up over him, and he was out.

Ruby straightened up and looked down at the unconscious man. *That really is rich,* she thought with a smile. *Most guys are tryin' to get me into bed, and here I'm puttin' one into bed.* She undressed quickly and put on a white cotton gown, then climbed up into the bunk. She pulled the sheet and blanket up over her and lay still, listening to the *clickety-clack* of the wheels until she fell into a deep sleep.

CHAPTER EIGHT

"DON'T YOU LIKE WOMEN?"

★ ★ ★

Ruby sat across the table in the dining car, sipping coffee out of a fine china cup. They were nearing the end of their long trip across country, and Francis was feeling better. During the early part of the trip he had mostly slept, only staying awake long enough for Ruby to give him his pain pills, help him to the bathroom, or give him a little food.

"You're lookin' better. You got some color." Ruby tipped her cigarette ashes into an ashtray, then settled back to study his face. He was finishing his meal, which was primarily vegetables. He had only nibbled at the glazed chicken but seemed to relish the asparagus. "You eat like a rabbit," she said.

He managed a smile. "I guess I do. The food's good, isn't it?"

"Best I've ever had. You ever traveled on one of these things before?"

"Once or twice."

The two sat there quietly and ate their dessert, Key taking small bites of his lemon meringue pie. He moved carefully when he reached for his water but did not show the agonizing discomfort he had experienced at first.

"Tell me more about these Winslows," Ruby demanded. "I still think this is the nuttiest thing I ever heard of."

"Strange things happen all the time," he said. "You'd be surprised at how many babies get stolen. Just disappear."

"Who takes them?"

"People who can't have babies and want them, nuts, psychos. I once worked on a case where I tried to help a young couple who'd had their first child taken. The baby was only two months old and someone just picked her up out of her buggy in the general store. When the woman turned around, she was gone." The memory seemed to trouble Francis, and he shook his head. "That mother was in pretty bad shape."

"You never found the baby?"

"Never did. Nothing to go on. Just like she disappeared off the face of the earth."

Ruby sobered at the thought and quietly listened to the now-familiar rhythm of the train wheels. It was late now, and most of the passengers had already eaten. Only an older couple down the way and a young woman with a baby occupied the car. "What about these Winslows?" she asked again.

"All I know is that Phil Winslow is a professional painter—an artist. He grew up on a ranch out west, left and went to Europe to study, then came back and had a hard time making a living in New York. But now he's famous. You can see his pictures in museums."

"How much do painters make?"

Key grinned. "More than I do. Some of them don't make anything. Others, like Mr. Winslow, get hundreds or more for every picture."

Ruby thought about this for a while. "You say he's got three kids?"

"Yes—they're grown now. All in their early twenties. One of them is married and has three children."

"Won't they be happy to see little Grace," she said sarcastically.

Key lifted his eyes. "What do you mean by that?"

"I mean, I'm one of the family now. When Popsy kicks the

bucket, I'll get a fourth of all of it."

Key shifted uncomfortably. "I don't know what to say to that."

"They won't be happy to find out they have another sibling. I can guarantee you that." Ruby puffed on her cigarette. "You know anything about my brothers and sisters?"

"Only that there are two brothers and one sister."

"So what are you going to do?" she said. "Just deliver me like a sack of groceries?"

He grinned. "Just about. That's all I'm hired to do."

Ruby studied him. She had been curious about Francis from the moment she had first seen him, and now their time together on the trip had heightened her curiosity. At first he had been so helpless from his injuries that she had felt the faint stirring of a maternal instinct. But now that he was feeling better, she kept expecting him to attempt some intimacy. Each night she stepped outside the compartment while he got undressed and into bed, and when she came in, he rolled over and faced the wall while she changed into her nightgown. His good manners had become a challenge to her, for she had never known a man who did not eventually try to take advantage of her. Now she considered the pale face of Francis Key and could not fathom him.

"You're not a detective anymore? Is that right?"

"Just when I have to be."

"What does that mean?"

"That means I want to be a writer. It takes all of my energy. I write until I'm broke, and then I go back to work to make some money so I can write again."

"What kind of books do you want to write?"

"I've been working on a novel for some time now."

"What kind of novel—a love story?"

"Most novels are love stories, but there's more to my story than that."

"Tell me about it."

"I can't do that," he said quickly. When he saw her resentment, he added, "I've got a theory that you shouldn't tell people what you're writing. If you tell it, you wear it out and then it can't come out when you're trying to get it on paper. I'll talk about anything else, though."

"Do you expect to be rich someday?"

"I doubt it. Most writers aren't."

"Why are you doing it, then?" A puzzling expression crossed his face as he seemed to struggle with the answer. This surprised her, for he was usually an easy man to read.

"I guess it's just something I think I should do."

Her eyes narrowed. "You're not tellin' me the truth."

Key smiled. "That's right. I'm not."

"Why would you lie about a thing like a book?"

"It sounds silly when I say it. Or it would to you, I think."

"Try me," Ruby said, puffing on her cigarette and leaning back.

"Well, I hate to sound like a preacher, and I'm not. But God's been good to me and I'd like to write a novel to show how God works great things in people's lives."

Ruby shook her head in disbelief. "I don't believe in any of that religion stuff."

"I didn't think you did, but you asked me."

A silence rose between them. The last thing Ruby wanted to talk about was God. She watched the waiter clear dishes from the other empty tables.

"You married?" she asked.

"No."

"I knew you weren't," she said with a grin. "I can always tell when men are married."

"Because they wear rings?"

"No, a lot of them take them off. But they always look guilty. Why aren't you married?"

"Haven't found anyone I want to share my life with, I guess."

"What about girlfriends?"

"What about them?"

"Are you dense? I'm askin' you about your love life!"

Francis's face reddened and she laughed loudly. "I don't

believe it! I didn't think there was a man left in America that could blush. You oughta do something about that."

"Not that much to tell in that area," he said, looking uncomfortable or maybe even angry.

"Why not? How old are you?"

"Twenty-eight."

"Twenty-eight and no girlfriend! What's the matter? Don't you like women?"

"Which women?"

"You've got a mind like a butterfly," she said. "What do you mean 'which women'?"

"I mean, I like some women, and I don't like others."

She laughed and leaned across the table. "What about me?"

He looked daunted by her aggressiveness. "It wouldn't matter if I did. I'm not your type."

Now she was the one who was angry. "You think Hack was my type?" She waited for him to answer, and when he did not, she said, "I'm goin' to bed."

"I'm tired too. We'll be in New York tomorrow."

Ruby left the dining car, leaving Francis to pay the check. She wasn't sure why the conversation had angered her. Perhaps because he seemed so innocent and she was not. She was a woman of sudden impulses, and as she reached their compartment, she had an idea. "We'll just see how innocent he is and what a big Christian he can be with a real woman." She went into the compartment and waited. When he came in, she said nothing but went into the tiny bathroom and brushed her teeth. When she came out, he was lying in the bed looking up at the underside of the bunk above. She opened her suitcase and pulled out a sheer black gown, remembering what she'd thought when she had first seen it, *You can read a newspaper through this thing!*

She started to take off her skirt and immediately Key rolled over to face the wall, groaning slightly with the effort. She stripped down and put on the sheer nightgown. Instead of climbing up into the bunk, she sat down on the bed beside him and touched his shoulder. "Key," she whispered.

He rolled over. "What is it?" When he saw the sheer gown, he stiffened and turned his head away. "What is it, Ruby? Something wrong?"

A sense of disappointment swept through her. Any other man she had ever met would have interpreted what she had done as an open invitation. She had been hoping he would too. Not that she would have let him follow through, but she thought she could expose his hypocrisy. Ruby leaned forward and pressed her figure against his arm. "Don't you ever get lonely, Key?"

He did not answer, and she reached out and touched his face. "Turn over," she said. "Look at me."

But instead of turning toward her, he shifted his body away from her and said in a strained voice, "Good night, Miss Winslow."

Rage boiled up in Ruby. Such rejection was a new experience for her and an unpleasant one. The mirror told her she was attractive, and enough men had made that evident. Now this little runt was turning her down. She stared at the back of his head and wanted to hit him, but she got to her feet, clambered up into bed, and jerked the cover over her. As the train ran on through the night, she clenched her fist tightly and thought of ways to torment Francis Key. He couldn't treat her like this!

Her hard life had taught her to be on her guard, but she had not always been cautious, and more than one man had taken advantage of her. She thought she had built up enough defenses to withstand anything, but now, besides the outrage at being rejected, she was surprised to feel a sense of shame. Something about the small man who lay quietly in the bunk below had disturbed her. She could not identify it, but she didn't like the feel of it.

He's like all the rest of them, and I'll prove it someday. She closed her eyes and lay stiffly until the rhythm of the train wheels put her to sleep. She slept fitfully, however, awakening several times and thinking about what had happened. She was determined to prove that Mr. Francis Key wasn't as holy as he thought he was.

PART TWO

April 1935

★ ★ ★

CHAPTER NINE

AN UNWELCOME ANNOUNCEMENT

★ ★ ★

Brian Winslow pulled his Studebaker up in front of his parents' house, stopping with a vicious jolt, the wheels locking. He jumped out of the car, slammed the door hard, and took the steps up to the long porch three at a time. He jerked the door open and was met by his sister. "What's this all about, Paige?" he demanded, snapping his fingers nervously and shifting his feet. "Dad wouldn't tell me anything. Just that he wanted the whole family to come together for an important announcement."

"I don't know what it's about," she said with exasperation. "Dad didn't tell me any more than he told you—and I can't get a thing out of Mother."

"Where are they?"

"In the drawing room."

"Come on, then," he said impatiently. "Let's find out what this is all about. I canceled an important meeting at work because Dad said it was urgent."

The two made their way down the spacious hallway, turned down a corridor, then went in through a set of double doors. Brian practically burst into the room, where his father sat beside one of the mullioned windows. "What's going on, Dad?"

Phil glanced at Cara, who was sitting in one of the antique chairs. "Something has come up that the whole family needs to know about."

"Well, what is it?" Brian demanded.

Cara got to her feet. "We'll have to get Kevin here first."

"Oh, Mother," Paige said, "if it's business, you know Kev. He won't care. He never does." Paige was fond of her brother but had little respect for his abilities.

"That's right, Mom," Brian said. "He doesn't know what's going on—and he doesn't much care either."

Cara's ordinarily gentle voice became surprisingly firm. "Your brother *must* be at this meeting. I'll go get him." She left the room, closing the double doors behind her. She walked down the long hall, passed through the spacious kitchen, and went out the back door. She followed a brick pathway around to the east side of the house, where she found her younger son digging industriously in a flower bed in the early April sunshine. He did not see her approach, and for a moment Cara paused, examining him. The left side of his face was toward her, and, as always when she saw the terrible scars that marked her son, Cara felt a pang of remorse. She could not help thinking back to what a handsome young man he had been before the accident. When he was fourteen years old, a worker on the estate had lit a cigarette and thoughtlessly tossed the match, accidentally igniting the can of gasoline Kevin was carrying.

Kevin's clothing had helped protect his body, but his face had received the full impact of the explosion. Cara thought of the long weeks of waiting at the hospital to see if he would live, and she knew she would never forget the sorrow and regret in Dr. Olson's eyes when he said, *"He'll live, but he's going to be terribly scarred, Cara. We'll do the best we can, but there's a great deal of damage."*

Kevin turned and the right side of his face came into view, still handsome and unscarred. He was much like his father, tall and strong, with the handsome features of the Winslow men. From the right side he was as attractive as any matinee idol, but his left side was a disaster. The flesh had been burned away, and despite several operations, the eye was drawn down into a permanent squint and the left side of his mouth was twisted.

Cara had grieved for years over her son, not only for his physical disfigurement but for what it had done to him emotionally. She would never forget what a happy, outgoing, joyous spirit Kevin had had before the accident. Always laughing, involved in everything, loving to be with people. He had worked hard and earned his rank of Eagle Scout at the earliest age of anyone in the history of scouting, was active in his Sunday school, and was popular with everyone he met.

But that had changed with the terrible blinding explosion. She had hoped that after he recuperated and was strong enough, he would pick up his life—but he never had. He absolutely refused to go back to school and would not even attend church. For years now he had stayed on the estate, working expertly with the flowers and plants. His other interest was engines, and he kept all the vehicles running like fine watches. But the rest of the time he kept to his room and refused to see anyone other than his family.

"Oh, hello, Mother, I didn't see you." He instinctively kept the scarred side of his face turned away, even from her.

"We're waiting for you, Kevin. Did you forget the meeting?"

"I wanted to finish preparing this bed."

"You can finish that later. Come along now."

"I'm too dirty," Kevin protested. He was wearing a pair of faded khaki trousers and a blue shirt with the sleeves rolled up. His arms were lean and muscular, and he had strong hands from years of working in the soil and with engines.

"It doesn't matter."

He gave her a cautious look. "Will there be anybody else there?"

"No," she assured him at once. "It's just the family. Come along now."

He drove the shovel into the ground and reluctantly joined her. She took his arm, thinking how much he looked like his father. The same cornflower blue eyes, wedge-shaped face, and thick auburn hair. *So fine looking and yet so ruined!*

"What's this all about, Mom?"

"Let's just wait until we get there, and your father will tell you all about it."

★ ★ ★

"I'll tell you, Dad, you can't afford to miss out on these stocks. I've looked into it from every angle, and it's a sure thing."

Phil stood looking out the window, only half listening to Brian. "I don't understand the stock market," he said. "Wasn't it amateurs dabbling in stock that brought this depression on?"

"This is different, Dad," Brian said, his eyes sparkling with excitement. He was shorter than his father by two inches but well built and knit together like the athlete he had been. "It's a sure thing! There's no way to lose."

"I wonder how many people said that who lost their shirts in the crash. There are men selling apples now who gambled everything on some stock."

"Dad, you've got to listen to me—"

"Brian, be quiet," Paige interrupted. "You know Dad's not going to get involved in any of your stocks!" She turned petulantly toward her father. "Daddy, you've got to promise me we'll have the party we talked about."

"Another party?" Phil groaned and ran his hand through his hair. "The last one took just about all my savings."

"But it's important, Dad. We have social obligations."

Phil sighed. He loved his beautiful daughter deeply, but some of her desires seemed a little extravagant to him. "It seems like such a waste to spend thousands of dollars just to have a bunch of people come eat and drink and talk and then go home."

"Oh, Daddy, it's more than that, and you know it! John's parents gave a party, and we owe them one in return."

John Asquith, Paige's fiancé, was the son and heir of Helen and Roger Asquith. They were prominent in society, and like the founder of the Winslow family, their ancestors arrived on the *Mayflower*. It delighted Phil to bring up that similarity in conversation. The Asquiths, of course, were fabulously wealthy—and fabulously stuck up, in Phil's opinion. "We can have the Asquiths over anytime, but I can't stand those monstrous parties."

Their argument was silenced when the door opened, and Cara came in holding Kevin's arm.

"You look like you've been wallowing in the dirt, Kev," Brian said with displeasure. He loved his younger brother but felt that Kevin should make more of an effort to get back into the world. He had often told him, *"You've had a tough break, but you can come back. You've just got to face up to it."* Now he shook his head. "Why don't you hire somebody to do the gardening?"

"Leave him alone, Brian," Cara said. "He's made this place the most beautifully landscaped spot on Long Island, I believe." She patted Kevin's arm. "I never go outside without thinking how beautiful it is."

Impatiently Paige spoke up. "All right, Dad, we're all here. What's the big mystery?"

"Everybody sit down—I think you're going to need it."

"That sounds ominous," Brian said as he threw himself into a chair. "Have you gone broke or are you moving to Europe? Which is it?"

Phil looked over at Cara, and she came to his side. He put his arm around her and took a deep breath. "I've got some news that's going to change things for the family." He saw alarm come into Brian's eyes and noted that Paige stiffened. Kevin leaned back against the walnut paneling, his arms across his broad chest. He kept the left side of his face averted, as always, but he was watching with mild expectation. He assumed this change would not affect him, for his world consisted of the estate, the landscaping and vehicles, and his thousands of books in the large library.

Phil continued with the speech he had carefully planned. "A few weeks ago we had a visitor, a Roman Catholic priest named Anthony Mazzoni. He came just after you left with the children that cold day in February, Brian."

"A Catholic priest! Was he taking up a collection?" Brian asked.

"No, he brought us some surprising news. I'll say it as simply as I can, and you wait until I'm finished before you say anything. Mazzoni told us he had been with a dying woman in the New York State Women's Prison. . . ."

Cara watched the faces of her children as Phil told the story Mazzoni had shared with them. She was apprehensive, for she knew this news would not be as welcome to them as it had been to her. Both Brian and Paige loved their family, but they were too proud of their family status. They even resented it when friends tried to break into that intimate circle. As Phil broke the news that their child had been stolen and was still alive, she watched Brian come to his feet, his fist clenched.

"Why, that can't be—it's impossible!" he exclaimed.

"Of course it's impossible," Paige put in. "The woman must have been crazy. You say she was dying and was no doubt a drinker."

"All that's true, but still the fact remains that one child died, and it was on the night we were in the hospital just hours after Grace was born."

"But at the hospital did you see the dead child? You must have noticed something different."

"It never occurred to us that we should examine our baby," Cara said. "I was so overcome with grief—and so was your father—that all we could do was weep. New babies all look a great deal alike, and this child was dead and wrinkled, and such a thought never crossed our minds."

"I think it's a fraud, Dad," Brian said. "Somebody's just trying to get to your money. You've got to have the police check this out."

"We have checked it out, Brian, and it's not as though this young woman, who I'm sure is our daughter, has come looking for us. We had to hire a private detective to find her, and it wasn't all that easy."

"But where is she now?" Kevin spoke up. "Is she coming here?"

"Yes, she'll be here very shortly. I just got a call from the detective I hired, and they pulled into New York on the train from Los Angeles an hour ago. They're coming here now in a cab."

"You should have given us more warning, Dad," Brian said angrily. "We really need to talk this out."

"There's nothing to talk about, son," Cara said. "When we hired the detective we weren't sure if we would ever find her, so we didn't say anything. If we hadn't found her, then we would never have told you, I suppose. But now we know she's alive, and she's coming back into our family."

"But what kind of person is she?" Paige said. "From what you've told us, she's had a terrible life. She might be perfectly awful."

Kevin broke in with unusual boldness. "Come on, Paige. If she really is our sister, we don't have any choice."

"You can say that," Paige said, "because you don't ever do anything but hide when people come. But if she is awful and becomes a part of our family . . ."

A silence fell over the room, and color touched Paige's cheeks. She was actually a very kind young woman, just too concerned with her social position. "I mean . . ." She faltered again.

"We know what you meant, sis," Brian said. "I really think we should keep all this quiet until we've checked her out. There must be some way to prove whether she really is our baby sister. Some legal way, I mean."

He's afraid she'll take part of his inheritance that he wants for his children, Cara thought, and it grieved her that she had a child who would put money before relationships.

"She may be different," Cara said aloud. "That would be understandable." Cara seldom raised her voice, but now there was steel in her tone, and her entire family looked at her with astonishment. "The woman who took her was not a good woman, and from what Father Mazzoni and the detective have told us, the child had a very hard life. But that's all the more reason why we should love her, and that's exactly what we'll do."

Phil pulled her close. "Yes, you're right, darling." He looked at his children and said, "We'll love her, and we'll take her into this family. If she has faults—well, she'll fit right in with the rest of us."

CHAPTER TEN

A New Family Member

★ ★ ★

Ever since Francis Key had rejected Ruby's advances on the train last night, there had been nothing but a solid silence between them. Ruby spoke only when Francis spoke to her and then only in monosyllables. The antagonism in her eyes was unmistakable. Since the embarrassing encounter he had tried hard to think of what he could say that would ease the tension between them, but nothing sounded right.

Francis studied her covertly as the cab wound through the countryside toward the Winslow estate on Long Island, making a mental list of the things about Ruby Zale that needed to be changed. He often made such lists to make things easier to organize mentally, and with Ruby the list was not at all difficult.

Number one, she wore far too much makeup. Her lips were flaming red, her eyelids thick with eye shadow, and her eyelashes globbed with mascara. Her beautiful complexion was spoiled by the rouge she inexpertly applied. Her fingernails were painted a flashing scarlet, and her hair, which had a beautiful texture and color, was a mess.

Number two, she evidently only had two dresses, and the

one she had on was suitable only for a low-rent saloon. Francis was no fashion expert, but he could point out that it was (a) too tight, exposing her abundant curves; (b) the wrong color, a bright emerald green; and (c) overly adorned, with fringes around the edge of the sleeves and the bottom of the skirt. It simply looked frightful—but this was Ruby's idea of fine clothing.

Number three, she wore too much jewelry. Large imitation diamonds—and not very good imitations at that—dangled from her ears. The fake gold was chipping off, exposing the dull base metal. She wore a large, showy necklace with imitation rubies, and her hands sported several gaudy rings, all featuring imitation gems.

Number four, she was chewing gum and popping it in a most annoying fashion, the way low-paid shopgirls did. Key wanted to tell her to spit it out, but he wasn't sure that he dared.

Number five, her shoes had four-inch spike heels, which made her four inches taller than Key. He did not mind that, being accustomed to his modest height, but the shoes were in poor repair and shiny black, except where the imitation leather was peeling. She also was rather unpracticed in wearing them and tilted precariously as she attempted to walk.

Number six, she was holding a cheap black velvet purse adorned with a garish sequined dragon design, and she was twisting the long, wide strap between her fingers.

The list could have gone on, but he already had plenty to convince himself that the situation was hopeless. *I wish I could give her some kind of warning, but if I say anything she's going to blow up.* He sat there silently noting that Ruby was getting tenser by the moment. Her hands were doubled up into fists, and she sat with her back as straight as a poker, her bosom lifting and falling quickly as she took short breaths.

Finally Francis knew he had to say something. "You don't have to be nervous, Ruby."

She turned and looked him full in the eyes. "I'm not nervous," she said flatly.

He did not challenge the statement but instead said what had been on his mind for hours. "Ruby . . . about last night. I wanted to explain to you why I acted as I did."

"I know why you acted as you did. You're a holy man."

He flushed and shook his head. "No, that's not it. I never claimed such a thing for myself."

"Then you're no man at all!" She kept her eyes fixed on him, daring him to speak.

He knew that whatever he said, she would pull it to pieces. So he merely replied, "I'm sorry."

She gave her head an angry shake and turned to look back out the window.

They were now passing several large estates, and Key leaned forward. "Go through those gates right there, Driver."

"Right you are, buddy."

Ruby stared out the window at the emerald grass that spread out before her and the large trees scattered about the estate and lining the drive. *It looks like a park,* she almost said aloud but held her tongue, determined to stay silent.

Then the car turned out of a stand of enormous oaks, and Key said quietly, "There's the house."

Ruby stared at the mansion before her. The three-story brick home was dominated by four white columns in the front that framed a large porch leading to elegant double doors with stained glass windows flanking each side. On the left side of the house, near the massive chimney, dark green ivy twisted its way up the brick, almost reaching the black slate roof. The porch itself was decorated with large green plants and bright potted flowers, and the windows all had clean white shutters.

"Kind of overwhelming, isn't it?" he said.

Ruby did not even turn her head. A feeling of fear had been growing in her, and now as she looked at the magnificent house and the beautiful grounds, with flowers already blooming even this early in the year, she felt as if she could not get enough air.

The cab driver drew up in front of the porch and got out.

Key followed suit and walked around to open the door as the cab driver pulled the suitcases out of the trunk. Key got a quick glimpse of Ruby's face and saw that beneath her heavy makeup she was pale, and he wanted to comfort her, but the wall between them was too high.

Key paid the driver, who gave him a cheerful "Thanks, buddy" and drove off. Before Key could even bend to pick up his suitcase, the front door opened. He caught a glimpse of Ruby's face as Phil and Cara Winslow rushed down the steps. She was absolutely still, her face frozen, her eyes wide and unblinking.

Key saw that there were tears in Cara's eyes as she came forward. She put out her arms and embraced Ruby, who remained as still as a statue. "My dear, I'm so glad you're here!" Cara said, her voice filled with emotion. She turned to Phil and said, "This is your father, Phil."

He stepped forward and put his hand out, and when Ruby awkwardly took it, he smiled. "It's good to see you, Grace."

The group stood in awkward silence for a moment, and then Cara said rather nervously, "Why are we standing here? Come inside. The rest of the family is waiting."

As she led Ruby toward the steps, Phil turned to Key. He took one look at his bruised and stitched face and asked, "Who beat you up?"

"Oh, just a fellow." He bent down to pick up his suitcase and grimaced.

"I've been hurt like that," Phil said. "It must have been pretty bad."

"I've had worse. I shouldn't have let that cab driver go. I wasn't thinking."

"No, come on in. I need to pay you, and we need to talk. I want to hear all about your trip. Here, let me take that suitcase."

"I can handle it if you can get the others."

But Phil ignored him and picked up all three suitcases. "How has she been, Francis?" he asked.

"It's been a real test—and I'm afraid it's going to get tougher."

"She looks scared to death."

"I think she is, but she'll probably cover it up. She can be pretty tough."

Francis accompanied Phil inside, and they caught up with the two women, who were waiting in the foyer.

"The children are in the drawing room," Cara was saying. "Are you very tired after your long trip?"

"No, I ain't a bit tired."

Key caught the slight antagonism in Ruby's voice. She was holding her purse tightly, and her skin was drawn across her cheekbones. It was almost as if she'd had a serious car wreck and was in a state of shock. *Poor kid. She's able to handle a monster like Hack Keller, but she's never experienced anything like this before.* He himself felt out of place in the opulent setting. Still, he wanted to see the reaction of the rest of the family. More than that, he wanted somehow to help Ruby, but could think of no way to do so.

As they stepped inside the drawing room, Key got an impression of spaciousness and very expensive paintings and furniture, but his focus was on the faces of the young adults, who he assumed were the Winslow children. He saw shock run across the features of the young woman who was beautifully and expensively dressed as she took in the newcomer. It was as if the young woman were holding up a huge sign that read, *Oh no, this can't be! She's a tramp pretending to be a Winslow!*

Key's eyes went to the smaller of the two young men. The man hid his expression carefully, but something flickered in his eyes, and Key felt that this man would be Ruby's real enemy. He was conscious of Cara calling their names, and when she introduced Brian, Key saw his lips pull into a tight line. Brian nodded his head and merely said hello.

The other Winslow son stood back against the wall, his face turned away in a rather awkward position. He was wearing a working man's outfit: a pair of khakis, heavy boots, and a faded blue shirt. He smiled when he was introduced as Kevin and said, "Just call me Kev. Everybody does." His voice was warm, and Key thought, *At least this one's open to what's happening*. The young man finally faced them, and Key saw the terrible scars on the left side of his face. A great compassion arose in him, as always happened when he encountered anyone who was crippled or maimed in any way.

Key moved slightly so he could get a better view of Ruby's face, and as he expected, she kept her expression blank. She merely nodded and said hello after Cara introduced each one.

A silence fell across the room after the introductions. Brian broke it by saying, "Well, I guess we came as quite a surprise to you, didn't we? I understand you didn't know anything about all this."

Ruby put her eyes on Brian and saw the same hardness in his gaze that Key had sensed. "I guess I'm more of a surprise to you, ain't I?"

Paige Winslow winced as Ruby began chewing her gum and surveying the room. "Hey, these are some digs. I ain't seen nothin' this classy in a while."

Key was accustomed to Ruby's rough grammar and rather shrill voice. Her voice wasn't always shrill, for she usually spoke in a perfectly well modulated tone—it was rather deep, as a matter of fact. Somehow he knew she had learned to be shrill in order to make herself heard, but the combination of her voice and her dress, the cheap jewelry, and her attitude were clearly having a negative impact on Brian and Paige.

"You'll want to see the rest of the house," Cara said, "but I know you'd like to have time to freshen up. Come along, and I'll show you your room."

"Wait a minute, Mom," Brian said quickly. "I thought we might talk a bit."

Cara gave Brian a warning look. "Not now, Brian. We'll have plenty of time to talk later, but I'm sure Grace is tired."

At the use of the name Grace, Key picked up a slight change in the young woman's eyes. She laughed harshly and said, "Grace! That'll take a little gettin' used to. I ain't never been called nothin' but Ruby."

"If you like Ruby better," Phil said, "that's what it'll be."

The young woman was clearly surprised, and Key saw a fleeting softening in her features before her lips grew tight again. "Naw, if I'm gonna be a part of this bunch, I can get used to that name. If I don't pay no attention when you call me by it, you just tell me to watch what I'm doin'."

"Come on, dear."

Francis watched as the girl gave Brian a hard look and then shifted her level gaze to Paige. She smiled and laughed. "I guess we'll probably never get used to each other. Right?"

Kevin approached Ruby, and she couldn't hide the shock in her eyes when she saw his terrible scars up close. Kevin was accustomed to such reactions, however, and he smiled and said, "Welcome home, sis."

"Uh, th-thanks," she stammered. "It's . . . nice to be here."

As soon as the two women had disappeared, Brian said, "Dad, we've got to talk about this."

"Not now, Brian. I need to talk with Francis. Come along into my study."

The two men left, and Brian said, "I don't believe she's who she says she is for a minute, Paige. She doesn't look like any of us. There's no family resemblance at all."

"You're right. She doesn't look like Mother or like me. But there's no way to prove it, is there, one way or another?"

"There's got to be a way. Maybe I'll talk to that private detective. I want to know how he found her." The two fell silent, and finally Paige whispered, "She is just *awful*! I can't imagine introducing her to John or his parents—or any of our friends."

"She doesn't fit," Brian agreed, "but I think there's more to it than you've considered. If she's who she claims to be, or even if Mom and Dad assume she is without proof, have you thought what it will mean?"

"What are you talking about?"

"I mean she'll become an equal heir. Sooner or later this

estate will have to be divided up. I always thought it would go three ways. Now it'll be four. In effect, she's taking money away from my kids."

"Maybe she won't stay," Paige said hopefully. "She's so . . . so *different*! She may feel so uncomfortable she'll leave. Maybe Dad will pay her off and she'll go away and be satisfied with that."

"Not likely, sis. She's a hard cookie. Women like that will squeeze a man dry, and I bet that's what she's planning to do to us." He reached out and took her arm. "This is a real mess, Paige. We've got to do something about it!"

CHAPTER ELEVEN

GRACE'S NIGHT OUT

★ ★ ★

The midmorning sun sent pale shafts of light through the tall windows, illuminating the canvas that stood before Phil. He mixed some pale blues on his palette and carefully applied the color to the painting with his brush. He had spent much of his later life in this studio and found it the most comfortable room in the entire mansion. He had been reluctant at first to buy such a large place, but once he saw the studio, and then saw that the rest of the house pleased Cara and the children so much, he had no doubt that this was to be their home. He took a break from his painting and gazed around at his studio. The ceilings in the twenty by thirty room were over fourteen feet high, giving it an air of spaciousness. He'd had bookcases built in to one wall, and the other three walls were lined with the paintings of various artists he admired. The room was not neat, for old canvases were piled up on each other in two corners. A small table and two chairs stood near the easel.

He rolled his shoulders back and scrutinized his painting. With a fine brush, he applied a tiny bit of color with a steady hand and was pleased with the results. "I still don't know how long my hands will be this steady," he murmured, "but I hope for a long time."

He had hardly moved from this spot since before dawn. He found that the early morning hours were the best time to work undisturbed. He meticulously cleaned his brush, put it in a large Ming vase along with several other brushes of assorted sizes, then walked over to the mullioned window. He arched his back, for he had worked hard. *If anybody had ever told me, when I was punching cattle back on the range, that painting would be such hard work,* he thought, *I would have told him he was crazy.* He thought briefly of his youth, and a smile touched his broad lips as he considered how far he had come from those days. He remembered the struggle that had gone on in his mind and emotions when he had first felt the urge to become a painter. Nobody in the family had ever done anything like this, and when he finally told his father and mother his desires, he had fully expected them to laugh him out of it. They had taken him seriously, however, as had the rest of the family.

As he looked out the window, a flash of movement caught his eye, and he leaned forward to watch Kevin digging industriously in a flower bed. A pang seized him as he thought about his younger son. He loved the boy with all of his heart, but tragedy had marked Kevin's life, and it seemed nothing could be done to set his feet aright.

Even at this distance he could see the scars on the left side of Kevin's face, and he vividly remembered the explosion, the doctors, the many surgeries. Phil watched for a while as Kevin made the dirt fly. *He's become a wonderful landscape artist. I believe he knows every blade of grass and every tree and every flower on this place. I guess he planted most of them. I just wish he weren't so afraid to let people see him.*

Turning his head the other way, he saw another figure emerge from the house and walk along one of the brick walkways that wound through the grounds. He fastened his attention on his newly found daughter as she bent over to smell a flower. She was wearing the same dress she had worn when she arrived yesterday, and an impulse suddenly took Phil. He left the room, going down two flights of stairs to the first floor and exiting. He quickened his pace, and when he was within twenty feet of her, he called out, "Good morning, Grace."

She stopped and faced him, and he could see a look of resistance on her face, but he showed no reaction to it and just smiled. "I missed you at breakfast. It was a good one. Cara made her world-famous pancakes."

"I slept late, but she heated up some that were left. She's a good cook."

"Your mother could always cook. Her own mother taught her." He felt ill at ease trying to talk to this daughter he didn't even know. *What's going on in her heart?* he wondered. *What does she think about me? She must be terribly afraid and confused.*

"Do you like your room, Grace?" he finally asked.

She frowned. "Sure I do. Who wouldn't? It's nicer than anything I ever had."

"I'm glad you like it. Let me walk with you. I always like to look at the early flowers."

"Okay."

The two walked along, and Phil pointed out some of the flowers, commenting, "Kev put all these in. He's got a wonderful gift for growing things. Me, I've got a brown thumb. Everything I touch curls up and dies."

"What happened to his face?"

Phil explained how Kevin was injured. "Before the accident he was the most outgoing young fellow I ever saw. Just filled with vim and vitality and got along fine with people, but now he never goes out."

"He's scared people will make fun of him, huh?"

"I suppose so."

"Yeah, they would too."

"Some of them would, but some wouldn't."

"They'd all look at him, though, and that's what he's afraid of, ain't it?"

"I think it is."

"Can't the doctors do nothin' for him? You know, make him look more normal."

"He's had several operations, but they don't have much to work with. We're hoping that over the next several years some doctor will develop some new techniques that will help him, but I think his hurt is more on the inside than on the outside."

"I know what that's like."

The remark caught at Phil. He turned toward her and saw that beneath the heavy makeup, her skin was smooth and beautifully textured. She had clear-cut classic features and lovely eyes. "You look a lot like your grandmother," he said. "Cara's mother. She was a very beautiful woman."

"Is that right?"

"Grace, you didn't look like the woman who raised you, did you?"

"No, not at all."

"Did she ever talk to you about your father? You must have wondered about him."

"Nah, she had so many men, she lost track of 'em."

"Must have been hard for you."

"It's just the way it was." Grace looked at him strangely and said, "I don't know what to call you. It sounds funny to call you Dad, and I'm too old to call you Daddy."

"Call me Phil if you like."

"That would be easier for me. I don't feel like—"

She broke off and looked off into the distance.

"You don't feel like I'm your father," he said. "Well, that's understandable. We just met. I think fathers and children build a relationship over time, but I hope we'll be good friends, Grace."

She smiled. "I don't know. I ain't had too many of those."

"Well, I'm going to try."

They walked on through the garden, and Phil encouraged her to tell him about her childhood, but she put him off. He knew her past was rough, and her manners were totally unpolished. Finally she told him, "I'd like to have a drink. Maybe a beer."

"I'm sorry, Grace, we don't keep any alcohol around."

"I didn't think you would."

"Prohibition just ended a couple years ago, and during all that time we didn't break the law."

"I did. It was as easy to buy booze as it was to buy soda pop."

Phil longed to ask her how much she drank, but he knew this wasn't the time for that question, so he changed the subject. "Listen, I know Cara's going to want to take you shopping to buy you some clothes and whatever else you need." He pulled a billfold from his pocket and extracted several bills. "Take this and spend it all up."

She stared at the cash. "That's a lot of money, Phil."

"Well, I'm eighteen years behind on spoiling you. This is the first payment."

She still did not take the money, so he took her left hand and put the cash in it. Closing her fingers over it, he laughed and said, "You'll have to have lessons from your sister. She's not hesitant about taking money from her old man."

"All right." She laughed a little and looked at it. "I'm really used to working. I been working, I guess, since I was twelve years old."

"What did you do when you were twelve?"

"Washed dishes in a restaurant."

"What about school?"

"Oh, I quit that when I was fifteen. I'm used to working."

"Do you still want to work? I don't mean washing dishes, but is there anything you'd really like to do?"

"I never thought about it much. I just went from day to day, I guess. Just earning enough to have some clothes on my back and something to eat."

"Let's talk about it," Phil said. "Come on. Let's go see if Cara has any ideas."

★ ★ ★

"You've simply *got* to do something about her clothes, Mother," Paige said urgently. She had come to find her mother, who was sitting in the drawing room reading a book. "She can't continue to wear those awful clothes! Why, she looks like a . . . like a streetwalker!"

"I don't think she looks that bad," Cara protested.

"Yes you do. You just won't admit it. We've got to do something with her. Why, we couldn't take her out to visit any of our friends."

Cara sighed. "Well, I know your father gave her some money to buy new things."

Paige stared at her mother. She was a strong-willed young woman, spoiled from being the only girl in the family and used to much attention because of her good looks. Now she shook her head, and her brown hair swung from side to side. She pulled herself up to her maximum height of five-four and pleaded with her large, expressive blue eyes. "Mother, you know she can't go out and buy her own clothes. She wouldn't know where to go in the first place."

"I suppose that's true. I thought about taking her myself, but you two are almost the same age. Why don't you take her, Paige? It would be a chance for you two to get acquainted."

Paige nodded firmly. "That's a good idea."

"Here, let me get some money for you as well. It'll be more fun if you can both do some shopping." Cara rose and went to her room and quickly came back. "Here you go, dear. You can be a great help to her."

"She needs a lot of help," Paige said grimly. She took the money and sighed. "You know, Mother, this looks hopeless to me. You have to start when girls are young to put manners and breeding in them."

"Now, that's wrong! Breeding is what God gives you in your genes. Manners can be taught, but Grace comes from good blood. She's got your father's family and mine running in her veins."

"Well, that may be so, but the way she acts is terrible. You heard the way she talks."

"She talks the way she was brought up, and we're going to change all that."

Paige was as doubtful as she had been since she had first heard of the existence of her sister. She had a good heart, but too many years of having her own way and then finding the social world of New York exciting had spoiled her. Her fiancé's family was very cautious of anyone who came from outside their select little circle. Paige had worked hard to make herself acceptable in their sight, but she knew that she was now facing a precarious situation. Here she had a major social obstacle in this crude, loud, ignorant young woman who was part of her family. The Asquiths, she knew, would not like the girl at all.

"I'll go get her, Mother."

Cara tried to go back to her book, but she couldn't help thinking how she had failed to instill a democratic and gracious spirit in Paige. Especially since she had become engaged to John Asquith, she had become quite snobbish.

A few minutes later Paige reentered with a puzzled look. "She's not in her room."

"She's probably outside."

The two women got up and went outside but found no sign of Grace. Finally they went to the garage, where they found Kevin with his head stuck under the hood of the Oldsmobile.

"Have you seen Grace this morning, Kev?" Cara asked.

Kevin lifted his head. A mark of grease decorated his forehead, and by force of habit he kept his scarred features situated so they could not see them. "Why, yes, Mom. I saw her get a taxicab."

"A taxi!" Cara was surprised. "Did she say where she was going?"

"No, I just saw her get in."

"When was that?"

"Oh, about an hour ago. Maybe an hour and a half."

"Mother, what can we do? There's no telling what she'll buy," Paige moaned.

"It'll be all right. Don't worry," Cara said, but she had a sinking sensation and wished that Grace had not disappeared so abruptly.

★ ★ ★

"You mean she's been gone all day?" Brian had come for dinner, bringing his family with him. The children were gathered at the dining table, listening to Phil as he kept them entertained, while Brian and his mother talked in the kitchen.

"She left in a taxi about noon," Cara said.

"Did she have any money?"

"Yes, her father gave her some to buy new clothes with."

Brian shook his head. He was neatly dressed in a light gray double-breasted suit with creased and cuffed trousers. A white handkerchief peeked out of his breast pocket, and a large diamond stick pin glittered from his red tie. "Why didn't you go with her?"

"Paige was going to go with her, but Grace left before she could find her."

"Well, I hope nothing's happened to her."

Cara looked alarmed. "You think something might have?"

"A woman by herself in a city like New York? You know what it's like in some places downtown."

"Surely she wouldn't go there."

"Mother, you don't understand her. That's *exactly* the sort of place she would go."

"I don't believe that. She just went out to buy clothes. She'll be back soon."

Brian knew his mother was a good woman in every way, but she was a little idealistic. She could not grasp the fact that this girl, who had burst into their lives like an explosion, was almost an alien being. She did not fit in with the world the

Winslows inhabited, and the sooner his mother and father came to realize it, the better.

"Let's go in and join the family," Brian said. The two went into the smaller of the mansion's two dining rooms, a beautifully furnished room dominated by a long shiny mahogany table. The chairs were also made of mahogany, as was a sideboard that stood under a long mirror that reflected the diners. Every spare space was filled with antiques.

Brian pulled out a chair for his mother as he told the others, "I guess we're not going to wait on Grace."

Phil was seated beside Scott, and he reached out and ruffled the boy's hair. "We might as well start. Scotty, can you ask the blessing?"

Scott, only four, looked very much like his grandfather, with auburn hair and light cornflower blue eyes. "Sure I can, Grandpa." The sturdy young fellow bowed his head. "Thank you, God, for the food. Amen."

Phil could not help laughing. "Well, that's getting right down to it."

"I don't like long blessings, do you, Grandpa?"

"Not very much."

Paige sat next to her sister-in-law, and Joan said, "Tell me about your plans for the wedding, Paige."

"Oh, we're not planning to get married for at least six months."

"I thought June was the month for weddings."

"Well, John's parents are going off on a cruise to Europe, and we'll have to wait until they come back."

"What'll John do while they're gone?" Joan asked as she ladled some gravy over the mashed potatoes that Logan was begging for. The three-year-old looked so much like his older brother that they were sometimes taken for twins.

"They've been trying to get John to go with them, but I've been arguing against that," Paige said.

"Why don't you two get married and make that your honeymoon?" Phil suggested with a smile. "That way you'll get to know your in-laws. Taking them with you on the honeymoon seems like a novel idea."

"Don't be silly, Daddy!" Paige said crossly. She knew that her father had little admiration for the older Asquiths, and it disturbed her. "It takes time to get ready for a big wedding."

"It didn't take us long to get ready for ours, did it, Cara?"

"No, it didn't," she said. "But then you stole me."

"I've always thought that was so romantic." Paige smiled at the thought. Cara had had a domineering father who frowned on his daughter's choice of a husband, and Phil and Cara had practically eloped. At the last minute, however, Cara's father had appeared at the church and given the bride away.

The mealtime conversation continued in a pleasant vein, but all of the adults were silently wondering about Grace.

Finally Brian lifted his head. "Listen, there's a car coming up."

They all stopped talking except for Angel, the little girl who was almost two, who was telling a story until her mother put her hand over her mouth. "Hush, Angel. Listen."

The front door opened and then closed, and Phil rose and said, "I'll go tell her we're in the dining room."

He started toward the door, but just as he did, Grace appeared, followed by a man in a dark blue suit.

"Hello, Grace," Phil said. "We've been worried about you."

"Why, hello, Popsy," she said and laughed meaninglessly. Her eyes were slightly glazed, and her steps were unsteady as she entered the dining room. "Sorry to be late, but I met up with Vic here, and we decided to go out and do the town. Vic, this is my brand-new family."

The man called Vic was tall and thin, and his hair was slicked back on his head. "Hi," he said. "I'm Vic Costello. Nice place ya got here."

Grace looked at the family gathered around the table and was sober enough to see the displeasure on most of the faces. "What's wrong with you?" she said loudly. "Ain't you never seen a good-lookin' guy before?"

Phil saw the situation getting out of control, and he said quickly, "Come in and sit down."

But Grace was looking at Brian and saw his scowl. "What'sa matter, brother? You too stuck up to meet anybody new?"

Brian flushed and said, "Grace, you've been drinking."

"Sure I been drinkin'. What about it?"

"Maybe you'd like to go up to your room, dear," Cara said. Her face was pale, and her hands were so unsteady she had to clasp them together.

Paige was glaring at the pair. "What do you mean getting drunk and bringing a total stranger into our home! Don't you have any decency?"

"Well, la-di-da!" Grace spat back. She glared at Paige and then laughed coarsely. "It wouldn't do you no harm to get a real man. Ain't that right, Kev?"

When Kevin said nothing, anger swept through Grace. "For pete's sake, this is some dull bunch! Come on, Vic, let's get outta here and find us a livelier crowd."

"It's too late, Grace," Phil said. He moved quickly to stand close to her. "It would be better if you didn't go."

Grace scowled at him. "A little late for you to be wondering about your wanderin' daughter, ain't it, Pops?"

"I think you'd better go, Mr. Costello."

"I'll go with him," Grace said. She started for the door but was so drunk she had difficulty staying on her feet.

Only Phil's quick reaction stopped her from falling. He grabbed her arm and held her upright. "Good night, young man."

Costello's face grew hard. "It's your house," he said.

"Gimme a call tomorrow, Vic," Grace mumbled.

Costello turned and walked away, his back stiff.

"He's an important guy," Grace muttered.

Phil put his arm around her as she slumped against him. "You'd better go to bed, Grace."

She blinked her eyes, and her head rolled slightly. "I guess I am a little high. Maybe I better hit the sack." She looked around the table and saw the horrified glances. "Well," she said with a giggle, "I bet none of your other kids ever came in drunk, did they?"

Cara rose quickly and took Grace's other arm. "Come along, dear."

As Phil and Cara left, escorting Grace between them, Scott asked curiously, "What's wrong with that lady?"

"She's not feeling well, dear," Joan said.

Brian and Paige exchanged glances. Both were stunned by the enormity of this family disaster.

Seeing the expression on their faces, Kevin said quietly, "We've got to remember where she came from."

"Well, she's not where she came from now," Brian snapped. "I think it's too late for her."

Kevin did not answer. His eyes were troubled, and he simply shook his head.

CHAPTER TWELVE

THE PARTY

★ ★ ★

Grace woke up with a start and looked around wildly. For several seconds she was confused, not knowing where she was, but then her memory came pouring back. She looked down and saw that she was still wearing one of the two dresses she had bought for herself, and a sense of shame came over her. Throwing the blanket back, she saw that her shoes had been removed. She vaguely remembered buying the dress and then going into a bar. She had been drinking, and a man named Vic had talked to her—but from then on it was hazy. Like a kaleidoscope, she remembered a series of bars and dancing and then resisting Vic's advances.

She stood up abruptly, then closed her eyes tightly, for a headache struck her like a red-hot ice pick being pressed through her temples. She held on to her head for a moment as she swayed. She took a deep breath, then slowly moved her hands and opened her eyes. She walked carefully to the window and looked out, noting that it was sometime in the morning, for the sun was not far up in the sky. The grass was bright green, and the large oak trees that framed the driveway were bright with their early spring growth. As she stood there, she remembered fighting Vic off in the taxi on the way back to the house. She had a horrible taste in her mouth, as she always did when she drank too much, and felt disgusted with herself. She always hated the morning after her drinking binges because she suffered frighteningly painful hangovers, yet despite the consequences, she continued to drink too much.

Finally she turned from the window and went to the bathroom adjoining her room. She drew a hot bath, undressed, and soaked in the tub until her head felt better. She rinsed and got out, drying off with a fluffy white towel, then put on the new underwear she had bought, pleased with the silkiness of the garments. She slipped into her other new dress, even though she knew—despite the high price—that it was not the sort of dress a young Winslow woman would wear. It was too tight and the color was too bold—a brilliant peacock blue. But to her it was beautiful, and if Paige didn't like it, that was just too bad. She put on her stockings and shoes, then sat down on the vanity and brushed her hair. She was sorry now she hadn't washed it when she was in the bath, for she realized it smelled of smoke. But she didn't feel well enough to go to the bother now. She studied her image in the mirror and began to put on her makeup. She had noticed that Cara used almost no makeup, and Paige used it sparingly. She thought about experimenting with less, but a defiance rose in her, and she quickly lavished on her favorite red lipstick and applied even more eyeliner than usual.

Finally she pulled on the jacket she had bought. It was made of a smooth lightweight wool and felt good in the morning coolness of the house. She went down to the kitchen, where she found a short, heavyset woman working at the sink. She assumed this must be the cook, whom she had not yet met.

The woman turned and said, "Good morning. You must be Miss Grace. I'm Betty, the Winslows' cook."

"Good morning, Betty."

"You want some breakfast?"

"No, just coffee."

"You ought to eat some breakfast. It ain't good to go without eatin' in the morning."

"Well, maybe a piece of toast with some jam."

"You sit down and I'll fix it for you."

Glad enough to obey the cook's order, Grace sat down and laced her coffee heavily with sugar and cream. When the toast came, she buttered it and put a thick layer of blackberry jam on it.

"I done make that blackberry jam myself. You like it?"

"It's real good. How do you make blackberry jam?"

Betty looked at her wryly, her eyebrow lifted. "You don't know how to make jam? Why, there ain't nothin' to it. You first pick the ripest, plumpest berries you can find, then wash 'em and crush 'em in a big saucepan. You add water and sugar, heat it to boilin', and stir until the sugar's dissolved. You boil it till it's thick, then you put it in jars and cover 'em with wax. How come you don't cook, I wonder?"

"I never learned to do much except open cans."

"Maybe I can learn you how to cook a little if you wants to know."

"Yeah, maybe." She nibbled at the toast. "How long you been workin' here?"

"Twelve years. Me and Luke, we come here right after we got married. He's a regular handyman, he is. Fixes things, does some of the rough cleanin' and the like."

Grace ate her toast while Betty told her about some of the things Luke had fixed. She felt somewhat better by the time her toast and coffee were gone. "Thanks, Betty."

"You're welcome, Miss Grace. Your mama's gone with Miss Paige, but your daddy is workin' in his studio."

"Oh? I've never been there."

"It's up on the third floor. It's fixed up real nice and you get a wonderful view of the grounds from the big windows. You go up the stairs, turn to your left, and there's some more stairs."

"Thanks, Betty."

Leaving the kitchen, Grace made her way up both sets of stairs and paused outside the heavy oak door. She was ashamed to face Phil, but she preferred to face up to things rather than put them off. She opened the door and saw Phil standing in front of an easel by one of the tall windows.

Phil turned at the sound. "Why, come in, Grace."

"I don't wanna bother you. You probably don't like people watchin' you work."

"Not a bit of it. Come on over. I've got a pot of hot tea here under this tea cozy."

"I don't drink much tea."

Phil was wearing a pair of light brown trousers and a white shirt stained with paint. He laughed as he noticed Grace's eyes settle on his shirt. "I don't wear a smock. Makes me feel too much like an artist. I just wipe my fingers on this old shirt. Cara's been trying to get me to throw it away for years." He put his paintbrush down and waved at the small table. "Here, sit down and we'll have some tea. Did you have breakfast?"

"Yeah. I just came from the kitchen."

Phil made a business of pouring the tea, and then he sat down across from her, leaning on the table with his elbows. "I try to get most of my work done in the morning. The light seems to be best then."

Grace looked down at the cup for a moment, then lifted her eyes. "Sorry I made such a mess last night."

"Don't worry about it."

"I won't do that again—bring a man home, I mean."

Phil nodded. "That might be best—for you, I mean. What do you plan to do today?"

"Don't know. Nothin' much."

"You ought to get Paige to show you around. Maybe you two could go shopping."

"Guess I need somebody to help me with that." She looked down at her dress. "I know this dress ain't what looks good, at least to you."

"I'm no expert on women's clothes."

"Neither am I, I guess." She looked over at the painting on the easel and said, "I don't know nothin' about painting."

"I'd be glad to show you a little. I've spent most of my life smearing paint on canvas."

"Did you start when you were a kid?"

"Oh no, I grew up on a ranch herding cattle. Didn't let anybody know I was painting for a long time. I was ashamed of it."

"Why was that, Phil? What's wrong with painting?"

"Well, cowboys mostly look on artists as sissies."

"Are they?"

"Some of them, I guess."

Grace got up and began to look at the pictures lining the walls. "Did you do these?"

"No, those are all by other artists."

"Why don't you put your own up?"

"I don't know. I guess it'd be like putting your own photograph on the wall. Seems a bit egotistical." Phil grinned and scratched his nose, leaving a small blue mark there. "You want to see some of my stuff?"

"Sure." She looked over at him. "You've got paint on your nose."

Phil laughed and got to his feet, pulling out a handkerchief and wiping it off. "I get it in my hair and everywhere else. Come along. I keep some of my old things over here, along with some of the paintings I don't want to sell."

"How much do you get for a painting?"

"Oh, it depends. Some of them pay pretty well. Others don't."

He opened a large cabinet and began to pull out canvases. He lined them up on a shelf built specifically for temporary displays. "These are some of my early things."

Grace moved closer until her nose was almost pressing against a painting of a poor young woman sitting on the doorstep of a dilapidated old house with a baby in her arms.

"You don't look at them that way, Grace. You stand back. When you stand that close, it's just a smear of paint."

"Why it is, ain't it?" she said with amazement. She had never looked at a real painting. All she had ever seen were reproductions that looked about the same up close as far away. She stood back and tilted her head to one side.

"Why do you paint poor people?" she said with some distaste. "Why not paint flowers or something?"

"Poor people are a real part of life, aren't they?"

"Sure they are, but who wants to look at a crummy old house? You see enough ugly things in the real world. I'd rather see a picture of a pretty baby or a lake or maybe a cat."

"I used to paint those types of things when I first came to New York City, but I was stunned when I saw the hard life that people led in the tenements. So I changed my direction. I think artists should show life as it is, you know."

"I guess that's one way to look at it."

They moved on to the next painting, and Grace listened carefully as her father pointed out the colors he had used to create contrasting brighter areas and shadows. "I guess I'm prob'ly the most stupid person in the world when it comes to art," she said.

"You're never too old to learn. I've got some books downstairs."

"I wouldn't understand 'em."

"I could explain some of it to you if you'd like. It might be fun."

"All right," she said, "but not now. You're busy."

"Stay and watch if you'd like."

She hesitated. "Are you sure you don't mind?"

"Not a bit. I think I could paint in the middle of a carnival and not even look up."

He grinned then, which made him look much younger. She was impressed at how handsome he was. He picked up the brush and resumed work on the painting. Grace stood there fascinated by what she saw. She liked Phil Winslow very much. He did not seem like a father to her, and for some reason this made her sad.

Phil worked in silence for the next half hour. Grace

watched him for a while and then went back to study the paintings he had set on the shelf.

"That's that," he finally said. "I'll have to let that dry." He put the paintbrush in the Ming vase. "Did your mother tell you about the party she's having for you tonight?"

"No, I haven't talked to her today."

"It won't be a big affair—she's just having a few people over to meet you. Paige's fiancé and his parents will be here, along with some other folks."

"I don't wanna go."

"Why, it's nothing serious. It'll be fun."

"I dunno. Do you think your friends are ready for me?"

Phil felt a keen pity for this young woman. "I know this has been tough on you, but we're your family. It'll take a while to get used to each other. We'll all have to learn."

"You don't have to learn anything, but I do, and I don't think I can."

Phil put his hand on her shoulder. When she drew back and half closed her eyes, he removed his hand at once. She clearly wasn't ready for any expression of physical affection.

* * *

The knock caught Francis Key off guard. He had been pounding away at the typewriter, and the sound of the sudden rapping on his door made him straighten up. He shoved his chair back and went to the door, wondering who it was. He had few visitors and didn't really want any. With the money he'd earned from the Winslows, he was able to get back to work on his novel again, and he'd been making good progress today. But the knock was insistent.

Opening the door, he saw Grace Winslow standing there. She was wearing a dress he hadn't seen before, but one as tasteless as the two he had seen. "Hello, Grace," he said, not moving.

"Ain'tcha gonna ask me in?"

Key heard the slur of her words and knew she had been drinking, even though it was only early afternoon. He reluctantly stepped back. "Of course. Come on in." He caught the smell of alcohol as she passed by. She was steady enough, it seemed, so at least she was not falling-down drunk. He closed the door and turned to where she was standing in the middle of the room, looking around.

"These are your digs, huh?"

"Yes . . . pretty small, isn't it? How'd you find me?"

"I burgled Phil's desk. He had your name in his address book."

"That wasn't very nice."

"I'm not a nice person, Francis. I thought a smart guy like you'd already figured that out. Everybody else has."

"Oh, come on. Don't talk like that."

"It's true enough. Everybody in the family's tryin' not to look shocked at baby sister Grace."

"Here, sit down. You want something to drink?"

Grace giggled. "I already had something to drink. Maybe I'll have another one. What've you got?"

"Juice. Coffee."

"None of the hard stuff? Nah, you wouldn't have none of that. Not the holy man."

Key shifted his feet. "I wish you wouldn't call me that."

"Maybe I won't if you do me a favor."

Key felt an alarm go off in his head. "What kind of favor, Grace?"

"My new family's havin' a little party for me tonight. I don't wanna go by myself. You come with me."

"Why, I haven't been invited."

"Sure you have," Grace said with a grin. "It's my party and *I'm* invitin' you." She came to stand directly in front of him and asked suddenly, "How tall are you?"

"Five-eight."

"So am I. So we got somethin' in common. But with these high heels on I'm taller than you. You got any cowboy boots?"

Key grinned. "No, afraid not."

"Maybe I can go barefooted. Why couldn't you have been taller?"

"Man cannot add one cubit to his stature."

"Cubit? What the heck is that?"

"Oh, it's just an old measurement—the distance from your wrist to the end of your longest finger, around eighteen inches. It means you can't make yourself taller by wanting to be taller."

"Why do you talk like that? You've been educated too much. That's your problem."

Key laughed. "You may be right. One of my professors told me I'd been educated beyond my capacity. He didn't like me much. Hard to believe, isn't it?"

"Not too hard. So you went to college, huh?"

"Yes."

"I didn't even finish high school." She started reading the titles of some of the books on the bookshelves. Finally she turned back around to face him. "Well, are you goin' to the party or not?"

"I don't think I'd better, Grace."

She tried to look mad, but there was fear in her eyes too. "Well, if you won't go, I won't go neither." She laughed. "I'll just go out to a bar. Whadd'ya think of that?"

"I don't much care for that idea. I'll tell you what. Maybe I will go with you."

"You'd better. I might get drunk if you don't."

"Is it formal or what?"

"Ah, come on. You look all right." Grace giggled, then came over and put her hands behind his neck. "For a little guy, you got a way with women. I wonder—"

She was suddenly struck on the side of the head, and a raucous scream filled the room. "*My* Francis! *My* Francis!" Grace cried out and put her hands over her head.

Reeling away, she caught her balance and stared at Francis, who had captured a brilliantly colored bird. "What is *that*?" she yelled.

"This is Miriam," Francis said, holding the bird tightly.

"She gets a bit jealous. If anyone touches me, she kind of loses it."

Grace regained her poise and came closer to see the bird. "So you *do* have a female!" She laughed. "And you're *her* Francis, huh?" Grace and the bird locked eyes. "Don't worry, Miriam, I won't steal your man."

Miriam uttered a vile oath, and Key thumped her on the head. "I've told you not to say that!" he exclaimed, his cheeks flaming. "She has some bad language left over from a sailor she used to belong to."

Grace was delighted with this. "Cusses like a sailor, eh? What else can she say?"

"Well . . . mostly verses from the Bible."

"Make her say one."

Francis tried to make Miriam speak, but the parrot sulked and kept silent. "She's stubborn sometimes, but—"

"Behold, thou art fair, my love—"

"Miriam, be quiet!" Key said quickly, but the bird shouted, "Thou hast doves' eyes!"

"What's she sayin'?" Grace demanded.

"Oh, it's part of the Bible—"

"Thy two breasts are like two young roes—"

Desperately Key clamped his fingers over the parrot's beak, but Grace's eyes were open wide. "That's in the *Bible*?" she said, amazed.

"Yes, it is, from the Song of Solomon."

"I never knew stuff like that was in the Bible!"

"It's what's called an *epithalamium,* a bridal song. It's kind of symbolic." Key's cheeks were flaming as he said, "Maybe we'd better go." He put Miriam back into a large cage, and as soon as her beak was released, she screeched, "*My* Francis! *My* Francis!"

Grace was tickled. "She's sure jealous, ain't she, Francis?"

"I guess I'm all she's got."

"You got a car?"

"No. How'd you get here?"

"Came in a cab. He's still waitin' outside." Grace suddenly

locked her hands behind his neck and pulled his face forward until her eyelashes were practically brushing his glasses. She laughed as Miriam went wild in the cage. "Come on, runt," she said. "Let's go to a party."

Key disentangled himself from her embrace and grabbed his hat and trench coat, glancing at her uncertainly.

"Don't worry, holy man," she said with a grin. "I won't attack you like I did on the train. Your virtue is safe enough."

★ ★ ★

The large dining room at the Winslow mansion was almost big enough for a ball. The walls were covered with paintings, and the oak floor glowed with polish. The long table had been placed along the wall and covered with a snowy white tablecloth, and two young women in maid's uniforms were serving food and drinks to the guests. There were no more than fifteen people there, and Paige circulated throughout the room, speaking to the guests. She was wearing a simple dark blue silk dress with a buttonhole neckline and short sleeves. The bodice was embroidered with white roses and green leaves, and she wore a pair of matching blue silk shoes and a string of pearls around her neck. She found her fiancé standing alone and said, "John, she's not here. She probably won't come. I told Mother we were doing this too soon."

John Asquith was a thin young man with blond hair and guileless blue eyes. He was not dressed formally but wore a herringbone gray suit. At the age of twenty-nine he had never even come close to marriage before. For a time Paige had wondered at the reason, for as the only son of Roger and Helen Asquith, he was considered quite a catch. He was not as handsome as some men, but he dressed well and was charming and mannerly.

"You're worried about her, aren't you, Paige?"

"She doesn't know *anything,* John. She can't dress, her

speech is awful, she chews gum—even pops it."

"Well, that's not a mortal sin," Asquith said with a shrug.

"And she drinks like a fish."

Asquith gave her a surprised look. "She drinks? You mean she actually gets drunk?"

"She came home last night so drunk she couldn't even stand up. Mom and Dad had to put her into bed. She certainly isn't ready to meet our friends yet."

"I certainly hope she doesn't do that today. Might give my folks a shock. You know how they are about drinking."

Paige knew indeed, for John's parents had been sorely disappointed when Prohibition was repealed. They were passionate nondrinkers, rigid in their views.

"Why don't you go over and talk to Freddie and Lena. They look—" She broke off suddenly and took a deep breath. "There she is—and she's brought that private detective with her."

"Private detective! What do you mean?"

"His name is Francis Key. He's the one who found her out in California. Look at that dress. Isn't it just *awful*?"

"I take it you didn't pick it out."

"No. She did. She has no taste at all."

"We might just have to help her, Paige."

"First I'd like to talk to her alone, John. Go mingle for a few minutes."

Paige approached the pair alone. "We were worried about you, Grace."

"I had to go find my escort, Francis."

"Yes, I know Mr. Key."

"Oh, just call him Francis. He ain't very tall, but he's a good guy."

Paige caught the scent of alcohol and wondered desperately if she could get Grace upstairs before anyone realized she was here. She could make some excuse to the guests that Grace wasn't feeling well. She had no time, however, for John's parents had spotted her. "So this is the newest addition to the Winslow family," Roger Asquith said.

Paige's heart sank, but she put on a pleasant smile. "Yes, this is my sister, Grace. Grace, this is Mr. Asquith and this is his wife."

"Hi, ya." Grace grinned broadly. She put out her hand, and for a moment Roger Asquith stared at it blankly; then he reached out and Grace pumped his hand energetically.

"How ya doin', Missus?" Mrs. Asquith had her hand pumped as well, and then Grace said, "I'd like for you to meet the guy that found me. This is Francis. Francis, this is the Asquiths."

Key had noted the distaste in the faces of the couple and did not offer to shake hands. "Glad to know you," he said quietly.

"C'mon, Paige. Lemme meet the rest of your friends."

"Certainly," Paige said quickly, glad to get her sister away from John's parents.

Key watched Paige lead her away, and as soon as the pair were gone, John came over and put out his hand to Francis. "I'm John Asquith, Paige's fiancé. I don't believe we've met."

"I'm Francis Key."

"Paige tells me you're the one who found her sister."

"Yes, that's right."

"Are you some sort of policeman?" John asked.

"I once worked for a private investigation agency."

Key's quick eyes caught the distaste in John Asquith's eyes, and he thought, *I suppose private detectives aren't very welcome in his circle.* The two managed to make some more small talk, and soon John excused himself to talk to some other friends he had spotted.

Francis had not wanted to come to the party, and he tried to stay out of the way as Paige introduced Grace to the guests. It was a painful thing to watch, for most of them made no effort to hide their astonishment at her appearance. He knew Grace missed none of this and in defense had begun to talk more loudly. He heard her say, "Where's the booze? I need a drink."

He did not hear Paige's reply, but he did not think liquor

would be served at one of the Winslows' parties. Sure enough he was right, for he heard Grace's voice rise loudly. "Whadd'ya mean there ain't nothin' to drink? What kind of a party is this? Not a tea party, I hope."

Key glanced at the Asquiths, who were standing frozen in place. Roger leaned over and whispered something to his wife, and she nodded firmly. Key felt embarrassed at the whole situation as he observed the shocked faces of these prim and proper guests.

Meanwhile, across the room, Cara and Phil were talking with an old friend of theirs, Dr. Laura Maddox, their family physician. "So that's Grace," Laura murmured. "She looks a little like you, Cara."

"She looks very much like my mother, and I can see something of Phil in her too."

"How is she doing? This is quite a switch for her."

"Terrible, Laura," Phil said, shaking his head. "She's had no home life at all. She drinks and smokes and chews gum and seems to delight in shocking people—like she's doing now."

"I think that's probably pretty natural. She's been thrust into the limelight and doesn't know any other way to behave. It's a pretty normal reaction, don't you think?"

Cara glanced over at Roger and Helen whispering together and said, "I'm afraid the Asquiths are shocked."

"They're shocked at anything they don't understand," Phil said shortly.

"I don't know them very well," Laura said, "but they do seem pretty stuffy. I was a little surprised when Paige got engaged to John. He's a nice enough young man, but he doesn't even sneeze without asking his parents' permission."

The party went on uncomfortably for some time, and finally the inevitable explosion came. "What kind of a dead party is this?" came Grace's voice above the others. "Come on, Francis. Let's get outta here."

Key looked over at Phil, who gave him a nod, as if to say, *Take care of her*.

"All right, Grace," Francis said.

"Come on. You're a sorry specimen of a runt, but you'll have to do."

As the two left the room, Roger Asquith said, "Helen, John . . . it's time we went home."

Five minutes later the trio were in their car, their chauffeur making his way down the long driveway.

"There's a weak strain in that family, John," Roger said to his son. "It shows up in that girl."

John tried vainly to argue, even though he had never succeeded in winning any sort of argument with either of his parents. "She was basically brought up on the streets, Dad. What can you expect?"

"We expect you to marry a girl with a family of some decency and respectability, son," Helen said.

"That's right," Roger snapped, shaking his head with distaste. "It has always bothered me that Phil Winslow is nothing but an artist."

"But he's very successful with his art."

"That's quite different from having a good family," Helen insisted. "We've tried to warn you about this before, John. There's something to a family's bloodlines."

"But they're a very good family. The Winslows are—"

"They don't belong to our set. Can't you see that, John?"

He settled back wearily. He was not a strong man when it came to expressing his views, especially where his parents were concerned. Now he simply gave up the argument, as he always did. He stared blindly out the window as he listened to his parents pick apart every member of the Winslow family.

CHAPTER THIRTEEN

"Jesus Loves Misfits"

★ ★ ★

Grace opened her eyes slowly, aware of the pain in her head. The texture of her tongue was like a blanket that had been in a garbage can for weeks. She tried to will herself back into unconsciousness, but sleep had fled, and she knew she must get up. She stared at the ceiling, aware that the sun was pouring its rich yellow beams through the window to her right. She could see thousands of dust motes dancing in the light, and from far away came the sound of a barking dog.

She sat up slowly, moving her head carefully and trying to push the memories of the previous night out of her mind. "They must really love me," she muttered. "Being drunk at their party in front of Paige's future in-laws! I'm surprised they didn't kick me out."

Grace had long had the ability to relive memories vividly. From her earliest childhood, she could still smell the odor of the boiling cabbage on the stove, see the bright colors of a caterpillar as it inched down a tree limb, hear Bertha's shrill voice screaming at her that she was late for school. Most of her early memories were unpleasant, and she had learned to block them out of her mind by willfully thinking of other things.

This morning, however, as she went about the tedious business of getting ready to face another day with a hangover, she could not forget the previous day's disasters. She could see the faces of her siblings trying hard to hide their distaste and her mother's face, sad and grieved. She could also see the faces of Roger and Helen Asquith, who had made no attempt to hide their feelings for her. "Stuck-up idiots," she muttered on the way to the bathroom, where she washed her face and brushed her teeth. She shuffled back to the bedroom to pick out clothes for the day and was painfully conscious again that the clothes she had bought did not fit the new life she'd been thrown into. She thought of Francis and, as usual, did not know what to make of him. He was not like any man she had ever met, and he fascinated her. Yet she had no romantic notions of him. In the first place she had always liked big, dark men, and he certainly did not fit that category. She was impressed with how smart he was, and as she slipped into her dress, she thought, *He could probably do a better job picking clothes out than I can. He'd know about things like that.*

She sat down and brushed her hair out, then put on her makeup. As she looked in the mirror, she was dissatisfied with what she saw. She did like the color of her hair, however, because it was unusual. There were always plenty of fake blondes, along with a few real ones, and there were some women with bright red hair, but she had seen very few strawberry blondes. It was her best feature, she thought, but she wished she could fix it in a better style. She rose and tossed the brush down. *If they'd had to live with Bertha,* she thought angrily, *they'd be as dumb as I am too!*

Leaving the bedroom, she went down to find Cara in the kitchen.

"Good morning, Grace," her mother said.

"Morning, Cara. Where's Betty?"

"It's her day off. I've been waiting for you. Phil's already up in his studio, and Kev is out working on the car."

"He's good with engines, ain't he?"

"Yes, he is," Cara said with a smile. "That and flowers." A shadow fell across her face. "I wish he was better with people."

"He's a real sweet guy. Too bad about the scars on his face."

"Yes, it is."

Grace sat down at the kitchen table and gave Cara an odd look. "Doesn't it make you mad at God?"

"You mean because Kevin had an accident?"

"Yeah. Why did God let that happen?"

Cara took some eggs out of the refrigerator and laid them on the countertop. "It doesn't make me mad at God. I don't think anything could do that."

"But what about all the other terrible things in the world? Little babies burning up in fires, old people getting hit by cars. Rich people havin' it easy while nice poor people suffer. It makes me mad."

"You must understand, Grace, that this is not the world that God made. He made a perfect world and put two people in it who were both perfect themselves. The Scripture says that they walked with God." She smiled and said, "I've often thought I'd like to have seen that—Adam and Eve out walking with God."

Grace tilted her head to the side thoughtfully. "I can't even imagine it. Did they wear clothes?"

"I wouldn't imagine so. There was no need for it at first. And it's hard to imagine how they walked with God because God is a spirit, and you can't see a spirit. So somehow, I suppose, they just were conscious of the spirit of God."

"Well, the world sure ain't like that anymore," Grace said defiantly.

"No, it's not. It's a ruined world we live in. There's a dark power, the devil, that seeks to destroy mankind. But one day Jesus will come back, and the world will be remade. Then everything will be as it once was."

"Most of us'll be dead by then."

"But there's going to be a resurrection. Do you know that, Grace?"

"I don't know nothin' about religion. I never went to church. Bertha didn't like it."

Cara studied her daughter, and Grace's neediness tugged at her heart and spirit. She saw a young woman who was outwardly beautiful, though her appearance was tarnished by poor taste. But she also sensed that inside, Grace was a frustrated, angry young woman who had been battered by life. But beyond that, Cara believed, was a goodness and a sweetness just waiting to be released. She had been praying steadily since she had heard of Grace's existence and knew that she would never stop until she saw the woman before her become beautiful on the inside as well as out.

"How about eggs Benedict this morning for breakfast?"

"Eggs Benedict? What's that?"

"It's a special way of fixing eggs. Come over here, and I'll teach you to make it. I believe you'll like it." Cara showed Grace how to make the hollandaise sauce by melting butter in the top of a double boiler, then blending in egg yolks, lemon juice, and mustard with a whisk. She let this simmer while she poached four eggs, then began putting the dish together. She placed crisp English muffins on each plate, added thin slices of smoky Canadian bacon and the poached eggs on top, then poured a liberal amount of the hollandaise sauce over the eggs and bacon. She filled out each plate with one of the cinnamon rolls Betty had made the day before.

Cara set the plates on the table, and she and Grace sat down. Cara bowed her head, and Grace quickly did the same, although she didn't close her eyes. "Lord, we thank you for this food and for the blessings of the day. In Jesus' name, amen." Cara looked up and smiled. "Now let's see how you like eggs Benedict."

Grace took a bite of the dish, and her eyes widened with surprise. "Hey, it's good!" she said, taking another bite, followed quickly with a taste of cinnamon roll. "Nothing wrong with my appetite. I'll be fat as a pig if I keep this up."

"I don't think so. Nobody on my side of the family or Phil's is really heavy. It's a blessing. We seem to be able to eat anything and not gain much weight."

The two women finished their breakfast and sat drinking coffee while Cara told Grace about her family. "We're going to have a family reunion in about a month. I want you to meet them all."

"They won't be happy to meet me," Grace said.

"Of course they will."

"No they won't." Pushing the plate away from her, she said, "I don't belong here, Cara. I just don't fit in."

"Yes you do. Before you were born, God gave me a wonderful promise concerning you. I didn't understand it when I thought you had died, but now we're going to see it happen."

"It's too late for me." Grace thought for a moment and said, "Kev and me, we're misfits. We won't ever be nothin' but what we are."

Cara leaned forward and put her hand over Grace's. She noticed the strength of it and the beautifully textured skin, but she was thinking of other things. "Jesus loves misfits. He always seemed to be looking for people like that. Did you ever hear of the woman at the well in Samaria?"

"No."

It amazed Cara that this girl had heard nothing of the Bible. She began to tell the story according to the Gospel of John, stressing that Jesus had gone out of His way to find the Samarian woman, and when He found her, He showed such love for her that she trusted Him completely.

"She sounds about like me, that woman, with all those men." Grace's eyes narrowed, for this was, in fact, a confession. "I haven't been a good girl. It's too late to do anything about that."

"There's always a fresh start. Just like the woman at the well. The Bible doesn't tell us what became of her, but I'm sure she became a virtuous woman after that."

"She might be, but I'm not."

Cara yearned to put her arms around her daughter, but it

was too soon for that. The wall Grace had built was too high, and the problems were too sharp and keen in Grace's mind for that to happen just yet. "Why don't we take a walk around the grounds?" Cara suggested. "Maybe go out and watch Kev work on the car."

Grace was disturbed by the conversation. She felt grubby and unclean around a woman like Cara Winslow, and she quickly offered, "I'll wash the dishes first."

★ ★ ★

Brian Winslow loved his work and rarely took time off from it. But for the last few days Brian had been thinking deeply about the problem that had exploded like a bomb in the Winslow family. He could not put Grace out of his mind, and finally at noon he left his office and drove out to the estate. As he pulled up the drive he saw Grace walking across the lawn. He parked the car and went out to meet her. "Hello, Grace," he said cautiously.

Grace turned quickly. "Hi, Brian," she said warily.

"How's it been going with you?" Brian tried to smile in a friendly manner, but inside he wondered, *Why doesn't Mother get her more suitable clothes?* Aloud he said, "Did you see that bed of tulips Kev put in? They're starting to come up."

"Yes, he showed them to me."

"He's made a showplace out of this estate. He could make a lot of money in a landscaping business, but he won't listen to me. I've tried to talk him into it several times. He's just wasting his life."

"Maybe he knows he couldn't handle facing the public."

Brian shook his head. He looked handsome there in the afternoon light, the sun touching his slightly curly, rich auburn hair, his eyes clear, and his chin strong and determined. He was trim and fit, and there was an enthusiasm about him, the air of one who had never been hurt.

"Come along," Brian said. "I'll walk with you to the fish pond."

As they walked along together, Grace said, "How come you're not workin' today?"

"Oh, I took off early. I thought I'd come out and have a talk with you."

Instantly Grace grew defensive. Up to this point Brian had shown nothing but disapproval for her, and she could not imagine that he would feel any differently now. They reached the fish pond, and Brian cast a look at the fish shimmering in the clear water. A small waterfall, run by a pump, created a pleasant trickling sound. Brian turned to face Grace squarely. "I just wanted to see if I could help you find your way, Grace. I know you've had a hard time, but it seems to me you're making it tough on yourself."

"You mean because I got drunk twice and shamed your family?"

The harsh words made Brian's eyebrows rise, and he saw her body stiffen. "There's no need to get antagonistic," he said quickly. "I just want to help you."

"It's clear you don't like me, Brian. You're sorry I showed up. You and Paige have made that pretty plain."

A flush suffused Brian's face, for she had touched on the exact truth. "You shouldn't talk like that. We've got to make the best of what you are."

"What am I, Brian?"

"Well, you're what life has made you, I suppose. But it's never too late for someone to change."

"When are *you* gonna change?"

"What do you mean?"

"You don't think you need to change?"

"I'm not the one who dresses like a—" He was angry, but he caught the word before it came out.

"Like a tramp? Is that what you were gonna say? Let me tell you something, Mr. Brian Winslow. All your life you've had everything handed to you on a silver platter. You're nothing but a spoiled brat and a stuck-up snob!"

Ordinarily Brian was a self-controlled young man, but her comment stung and he allowed his temper to get the better of him. "You're a fine one to be calling me names! Why, you're nothing but a cheap, low woman!"

Grace cursed him and stomped away. She was so angry she did not know where she was going. She just headed across the grounds until she was out of sight of Brian before slowing down and trying to calm herself. "Why do I let him get to me?" she whispered under her breath. "He's nothing but a stuck-up snob! He's not at all like Phil and Cara. He and Paige are both snobs, and I'll never have anything to do with them!"

⋆ ⋆ ⋆

Kevin carefully removed a bolt and dropped it into a bucket of gasoline, then was about to remove another when he heard someone calling his name. He turned around to see Grace enter the garage. "Hi, Grace. Come to help me work on the car?"

Her encounter with Brian was still fresh on her mind, but Grace was calmer now. "I'm just bored."

"Why, there's no point in that. Why don't you go shopping with Paige? She told me she intends to take you."

Grace studied the tall young man before her. He was different from Paige and Brian, and it wasn't just because of his scars. Both Phil and Cara had told her how outgoing and winsome a child Kevin had been until the accident. Now he hid himself away, tinkering with cars and working on the grounds, afraid to face life. Without intending to be mean, she said, "Kev, how can you bury yourself in this place?"

Kevin looked at her without showing the scarred side of his face. "What brought that on, sis?"

It touched Grace to hear him call her *sis*. She would not have cared for such a title from Brian or Paige, but she welcomed it from Kevin. She knew he had a genuine concern for her, just as she knew Brian and Paige did not. "It just bothers me that you hide yourself away. Why don't you get out and find a life?"

"I can't do that, Grace."

"Look, you've had some bad luck. Your face is scarred, but the scars are a bigger deal to you than they are to other people."

"You don't know what you're talking about. You haven't had to look into people's eyes and see the pity. I've tried a few times to go out, but I just can't take the stares."

Suddenly Grace was fired with a desire to do something for this marred brother of hers. "Come on. Let's go to town," she said.

Kevin stared at her. "Go to town for what?"

"Just to look around. To have a good time. You can go shopping with me."

"I don't know anything about clothes. I'd feel silly in a dress shop."

Grace stepped closer and put her hand on Kevin's arm. "Please come. I can't stand staying here all alone. The folks are nice enough, but I know Paige and Brian don't want me here."

"They'll come around."

"Look, until they do, why don't you and I spend more time together? I can't help you with cars, but maybe we can go to the zoo or something."

Kevin laughed. "So you're after a good time. You've come to the wrong person for that."

"I don't believe you. We can find something fun to do together. Will you come?"

Kevin suddenly wanted to go. At that moment the thought of working on the cars or planting flowers lost its appeal. He had no hope that he would ever have much of a life, but he had hopes for Grace and wanted to do all he could to make her feel better about her new life. "All right," he said, "but I'm not much fun."

"You will be. Now, get out of those greasy old clothes."

* * *

The expedition proved successful for both Kevin and Grace. He took her to town, and the two of them went to the zoo. Grace had seen animals at the carnivals she had been in but had never visited a zoo before. Together they laughed at the antics of the monkeys and were impressed by the majestic strength and beauty of the tigers. They ate hot dogs and ice cream and talked a great deal.

Grace noticed that though Kevin might laugh at times, he was always conscious of the looks he got from people. Some of them stared at him with a total lack of manners; others took one look and quickly averted their eyes, which must have been just as painful for Kevin. She learned during those brief hours how hard it was for him, and she tried hard to encourage him.

Once a little girl pointed at him and said, "What's wrong with that man's face, Mommy?" The mother quickly shushed the child, but Grace saw that the remark had pierced him like a sword.

"Don't mind her," Grace said. "She's just a kid."

"I know. I'm used to it," Kevin muttered.

After they had watched every animal in the zoo, Grace said, "I'm hungry. Let's go buy the most expensive meal we can find."

"I'd really rather not go into a fancy place."

"How about an unfancy one then."

Not far from the zoo they found a place called Pete's Bar and Grill. They ordered steaks and Grace ordered a cocktail for herself. She insisted that he have a drink, but he said, "Nothing for me."

"You can at least have some wine," Grace persisted. "That won't hurt you."

"I don't know about that," he said doubtfully. But he was overruled, and before he knew it, there was a bottle of wine on the table and a glass in his hand. "I've never tasted wine before." He took an uneasy sip.

"Do you like it?"

"I shouldn't be drinking it."

"Oh, come on, it's only wine. It's not hard liquor. I'd be the one to get drunk if anybody does." She laughed at the expression on his face. "Don't worry," she said. "I'm not going to."

Grace was true to her word. She did not get drunk—but Kevin did!

He drank two glasses of wine before their meal arrived and then had more afterward. He was listening to Grace tell about her life and was so interested, he didn't realize how much wine he was drinking. It was quite a lot more than his uninitiated system could stand.

Grace became aware that Kevin's speech was getting slurred, and she knew that Cara and Phil would not like it—and certainly Brian and Paige would have a fit. "I think that's enough wine for tonight," she said. "We'd better get you home."

"Home? I'm all right," Kevin said, pronouncing each syllable distinctly. "I'm just a little bit . . ." He blinked several times and could not finish.

"You wait here while I go to the ladies' room. Then we'll leave."

"All right, sis."

Grace went to the ladies' room, thinking, *I gotta sober him up quick. They'll throw me out for sure if I take him home in this condition.*

When she returned, she found a woman standing beside Kevin whose face was heavily painted and whose dress was quite revealing. She had her hand on Kevin's shoulder and was saying, "Come along with me, honey. We'll have us a good time."

Grace intervened loudly. "That's my honey you're talkin' to. Come on, Kev."

"This is Doris."

"Glad to meetcha, Doris. Now good-bye."

The prostitute sneered and found someone else to approach.

"Good-bye, Doris," Kevin said. "She's a nice girl, isn't she?" he said to Grace. "That's Doris."

"I know," she said, pulling Kevin to his feet. "Come on. It's time to go home."

"Wait a minute. I'm a little dizzy. Where'd Doris go?"

"She's gone. Come on."

She paid the bill and led Kevin out of the restaurant. When she got to the car, he started for the driver's side, but she said, "Oh no. I'll drive home."

"I can drive," he insisted.

"No you can't. You get in and sit down." She put him in the passenger seat, shut the door, then went around and started the car. As she drove, Kevin kept muttering, "That Doris, she was a nice girl. She liked me."

"Yes, Kev, I know she did." *Poor baby! He has no idea in the world what sort of woman she was*. Before long he fell asleep and slumped down, his head against the window.

"I shouldn't have done this," she moaned. "It was wrong. Poor guy! Never had a drink in his life."

When she got home, she stopped the car and went around to the passenger side.

She heard her name called and saw Paige rushing toward the car. "Where have you been?"

"Kev and I went out."

"Went out where?" Paige demanded, her eyes flashing. She looked inside and said, "What's wrong with Kev? Is he hurt?"

By this time Cara and Phil had reached them. "What's wrong with Kev?" Phil echoed.

There was no hiding it from them. "He's had a little too much to drink," Grace admitted.

Paige opened the door and Kevin slumped out, almost falling on the ground before she caught him and propped him on the seat. "You've gotten him drunk!" she accused.

"Grace, you shouldn't have done that!" Cara said sharply.

"I know it, but—"

Phil pulled Kevin out of the car.

Kevin came alert and said, "Hey, Dad!"

"Hello, son."

"Where's Doris?" Kevin asked.

"Who's Doris?" Paige snapped.

"Doris is a nice girl. She liked me."

At that moment Grace would have given practically anything to start the evening over again. She had known all along that it was wrong, but somehow she had justified it by saying he never had any fun. But now, looking at the disapproval in the faces of her parents and the furious rage in Paige, she had no defense.

"Congratulations, Grace, you've managed to drag Kevin down to your level!"

"At least I took him out of this prison, dear sister! What did you ever do for him?"

"That's enough, both of you," Phil said crisply. "Come along, Kev. Time to go to bed."

"All right, Dad."

Kevin required Phil's help to keep him steady, but he turned around and put his hand on Grace's shoulder. "It was a fine day," he mumbled. "We'll do it again."

Grace looked at the scarred face with pity and knew that no matter how much Paige hated her and her parents were disappointed in her, she truly cared for Kevin. "Good night, Kev," she said. "I'll see you tomorrow."

As Phil and Cara took Kevin inside, Grace said to Paige, "I was wrong. I shouldn't have done it."

Paige was pale with anger. "How could you do such a thing? You took advantage of him!"

"I didn't mean to hurt him. It seems like I always do the wrong things."

Paige shrugged her shoulders wearily. "Yes, you do." She followed the others, leaving Grace alone beside the car.

Grace sighed with remorse, but at the same time she made a resolution. *I went about it the wrong way, but I'll find a way to help Kev. I know I will.*

CHAPTER FOURTEEN

"WHAT DO YOU REALLY WANT?"

★ ★ ★

The next morning it rained heavily, and after breakfast Grace went back to her room with a movie magazine and the latest tabloid newspaper she had bought the day before. She sat cross-legged on the bed to peruse them, not having anything else to do.

She glanced over the headline story about the German dictator Hitler, but she cared little for politics in her own country, much less in Europe. Another story was entitled "Defeating Demon Rum," and she read it quickly and then tossed the paper aside. "People are gonna drink—and that's all there is to it!" she murmured.

Bored with the paper, she read the movie magazine but didn't find it much more interesting. She thought of Hack Keller and wondered if he had found a new partner to ride the cycle around the Ring of Death. For a fleeting moment she missed her life with the Royal Shows—at least it had kept her busy. Of course, she had hated it most of the time, but the past sometimes looks better in light of the present.

Finally she got up and, seeing that the rain had stopped,

went downstairs. She stopped in the kitchen looking for a snack.

"I made some fresh cinnamon rolls," Betty said. "You want one?"

"Yes, I think I will." She took two of them, wrapped them in napkins, and started out the back door to find Kevin and apologize. Not finding him in the garage, she went out to look for him on the grounds.

She located him at the pond, staring down at the goldfish. He looked up when he heard her, and her heart broke when she saw the look on his face. She held out one of the cinnamon rolls. "A peace offering, brother."

Kevin smiled crookedly. "That's the first hangover I've ever had. It felt like a blacksmith was pounding my head to pieces."

"I'm sorry, Kev. I shouldn't have let you drink all that wine."

"For some reason I didn't think wine made you drunk. I thought you could drink a whole bottle of it."

"Well, you know better now." She gazed down at a large fish that appeared to be watching them. "Look at that," she said. "He's making O's with his mouth. I bet he can't do Z's."

Kevin laughed and took a bite of the cinnamon roll. "This is good," he said. "First thing I've had to eat today."

"Did you throw up?"

"Like crazy! Why do people drink? Do you always feel that crummy the next day?"

"Every single time."

"Then I guess I won't ever do it again."

Grace watched him nibble on his cinnamon roll. "You didn't do nothin' wrong, Kev. I was the one who did wrong."

"Don't worry about it. I didn't die, but this morning I thought I was going to."

"I feel bad about Cara and Phil."

"Do me a favor, will you, sis?"

"Sure I will. What is it?"

He grinned at her. "You mean you're promising without knowing what it is?"

"You wouldn't ask me to do nothin' wrong. You're not like me."

"Don't be silly. I do plenty of wrong things."

"What do you want me to do?"

"I wish you'd call them Mom and Dad."

Grace dropped her head and looked at the lush grass beneath her feet. When she looked up, she was smiling. "That's easy enough to do. Might shock them a bit."

"They'll like it."

"Anything else I can do for you?"

"No. Not that I know of."

"I'm sorry I got you drunk, but it was probably the most exciting evening of your life, wasn't it?"

"I guess so." Kevin grinned ruefully. "Who was Doris? I kept thinking about her last night."

"She was a tart who tried to pick you up!"

"She was?" He looked shocked. "She seemed like such a nice girl."

"Well, she wasn't."

Grace felt better now that she'd apologized. She'd been afraid that Kevin would be angry with her, but there was a sweetness in him she could not resist. They walked around the grounds while he showed her some of the improvements he was making, and they stopped beside a fragrant bush with white flowers. "That smells good. What is it?"

"It's just honeysuckle. You mean you've never smelled it?"

"I may have, but I don't remember." She looked at him and suddenly asked, "Kev, what do you really want out of life?"

He looked at her in surprise. "What do you mean?"

"I mean, you don't want to spend the next fifty years cooped up here. It's like a jail. Oh, it ain't a bad jail, but it's kind of a prison for you."

"It's not so bad," he said defensively.

"But you must want something more than this." Grace

saw his expression change, and she reached out and put her hand on his arm. "What is it?"

"Nothing," he said quickly.

She knew he was not telling the truth, and she wondered what sort of ambition or dream he might have that he could not speak of. Kevin turned the tables and said, "What do *you* want, sis?"

She was surprised that he would ask, but she was a quick thinker. There were things she wanted, but like Kevin, she could not speak of them. "What do I want? Just a brand-new Italian motorcycle—top of the line! Ain't that what every girl wants?"

"Are you kidding me?"

"No, I *love* bikes. That's what I was doing when Francis found me. Ridin' motorcycles for a living."

"I didn't know that."

"I love to ride 'em. They're not like cars at all. You can open them up and go tearin' down the road. That's what I want, all right. A new Italian bike—but they cost like everything. I'll never get one."

Kevin smiled and the smooth side of his face showed warmth, while the other side remained frozen. "Maybe you'll get it under the tree for Christmas."

"Maybe. You know what else I'd like? I'd like to learn somethin' about flowers. Will you teach me?"

"Sure," he said. "Come on. I'll get you a shovel, but you'll have to change clothes. . . ."

⋆ ⋆ ⋆

After digging in the earth with Kevin for almost two hours, Grace looked at her hands and laughed ruefully. "I'm gonna have blisters." She smiled at Kevin. "But it was fun."

"More fun than getting drunk. I bet I couldn't have gotten Doris to dig in the ground like this."

"I don't think you could. I'm gonna go clean up."

Grace went back to her room to bathe and change her clothes, then went out back to the patio. She was surprised to find Cara painting a picture of a potted flower. Approaching quietly and looking at the canvas, Grace remembered Kevin's request and decided to try it out. "That's real good, Mom," she said. A warm light came into her mother's eyes, and Grace knew she was pleased with the name. "I didn't know you could paint like that."

"Oh, I'm just a dabbler compared to your father."

"Go on paintin'. I wanna watch."

"All right," Cara said. "You know, your father rescued me from becoming an invalid. Did I ever tell you that?"

"No, what was wrong with you?"

"I had a childhood sickness, and it took me a long time to get over it. My father was a good man, but he was overly protective. He was hard on his other children without knowing it, but he tended to spoil me because I was ill."

"Whadd'ya mean he was hard on them?"

"He loved them and wanted good things for them, but he was a strict disciplinarian. I was his favorite, and he was afraid something would happen to me. Without meaning to, he made an invalid out of me. I see that now. He kept me in the house and had a doctor there almost every day." She looked into the distance and smiled. "I remember the first day your father came to our house. My brother had been hurt at school, and Phil brought him home. I hadn't had any suitors yet, and he fascinated me. I found out very soon that he was quite interested in me, but my father didn't want me to have anything to do with him."

"Tell me all about it. I want to hear everything."

The two sat at the patio table and Grace listened while her mother told of their eventual courtship and how against great odds Phil won her heart and begged her to leave her father's house and marry him.

"Did your father ever learn to accept him?"

"Yes, to our surprise he showed up at our wedding and gave me away. And after that he was fine. Actually he was very proud of Phil. They became good friends before Dad died."

"You must have been lonely cooped up in a house like that."

"I was dying inside and didn't even know it. I didn't know how to get away, Grace, and then Phil came and rescued me."

"Dad's pretty special to you, isn't he?"

"Oh yes." She had a faraway look in her eyes for a moment. "You've got to learn about the Winslow family. They're wonderful people. They can trace their family all the way back to the *Mayflower,* when Gilbert Winslow came to the New World. His blood is in you, Grace. God isn't going to waste it."

A faint hope stirred in Grace as she saw the love in her mother's eyes. "I hope so, Mom," she said. "I'm a pretty tough cookie, though. I'm not sure God has too much use for me."

"You are very special to God. You never know what He will do with your life." Cara stood up and hugged Grace and then kissed her cheek. "I'm glad you're home, daughter," she said gently.

★ ★ ★

After her escapade with Kevin, Grace deliberately tried to please the family. She let Paige take her shopping, and her sister bought her some more suitable clothes. Grace did not like them as much as Paige did, but she did not let on. She had apologized to Brian for her outburst, and he in turn tried to be more pleasant with her.

She spent most of her time with her parents, sometimes watching her father paint and getting to know him better and sometimes letting her mother teach her how to cook. She also loved being with Kevin. They worked on cars together and went out on test drives; at other times, she worked in the garden with him.

One morning after breakfast, Kevin said, "Come on, sis."

"Come where?"

"Outside. I've got a surprise for you."

"You just want me to dig more holes, that's all."

"Not this time. Come along."

Mystified, Grace followed him, and he led her to the garage. Taking her arm, he said, "Now close your eyes."

"It's not my birthday yet, you know."

"Well, it will be soon. Come on and close them."

Obediently Grace closed her eyes and smiled, wondering what in the world he had planned. He guided her in, and when he pulled her to a stop, he said, "All right, you can open them."

When she opened her eyes, Grace gasped, "It's an Italian bike!"

Kevin was watching her expression. He saw her eyes light up and her lips part with pleasure. "Happy birthday, sis."

Grace ran her hand over the sleek machine. It was a top-of-the-line Italian bike. "I can't believe it," she said, turning to Kevin. "You can't spend this much money on me."

"Why not? You're my sister, aren't you? And this is what you want more than anything else in the world."

"Oh, Kev, you're so sweet!" She put her arms around his neck and kissed him on the cheek. She hugged him tightly, and for some absurd reason she wanted to cry. Fighting back the tears and stepping away, she shook her head. "You shouldn't have done it."

"You got anything you can wear to go for a ride on this thing?"

"Have I! You just wait. I'll be right back."

Dashing away to her room, she quickly changed into the black leather biker's outfit she had worn in the Ring of Death. She zipped the front of it modestly up to her neckline, then pulled on her boots, grabbed her goggles and helmet, and ran downstairs. She passed Cara in the hall, who stared at her in shock.

"Don't worry, Mom. Kevin got me a new motorcycle. This is my ridin' outfit. Come on and see it."

She ran out to the garage at full speed, and when she reached Kevin, he said, "What kind of a getup is that?"

"It's what lady motorcycle riders wear," she said. "Let's start it up. Have you ridden it yet?"

"No. I wanted you to be the first, but I've started the engine. It runs like a top."

Cara came running up, followed by Phil. He had evidently been watching out his window and came down immediately. Paige appeared too, her eyes wide with the shock of seeing Grace in her tight-fitting outfit. "This is what my brother gave me for my birthday," Grace said gaily. "I'm going to take you all for a ride. Go get some ridin' clothes on, Mom."

"Not for a moment would I think of getting on that thing!"

"Neither would I!" Paige exclaimed.

"I may take a ride," Phil said with a grin. "I used to ride a cycle once in a while, but you go ahead and give it a run first."

"Go for it, sis," Kevin encouraged as she pulled her goggles and helmet on.

Grace got onto the seat and kicked the starter, and the engine broke into a riotous roar. "Watch this," she yelled. She drove the cycle out of the garage and opened it up full speed. She flung gravel behind her and felt the wind in her face, once again experiencing the thrill she always felt when she rode a cycle. She had never been on one as fine as this. Her heart swelled at Kevin's kindness, and she thought, *He's the sweetest brother in all the world.*

★ ★ ★

Francis heard the roar of an engine outside his window and got up to look out. He laughed when he saw the shiny new cycle pull up. "Well, it's Ruby back again." He waited for the bang of the outside door, then heard her take the steps two at a time. He opened his apartment door and she burst in from the hallway.

"Come on, Francis. I want you to see my new Italian bike."

"I saw it. It makes more noise than a twin locomotive."

"You've gotta come with me."

"I'm busy right now." He stepped aside, and for the first time Grace saw a pretty young woman who had risen to her feet. "This is Karen Bell," Francis said. "She's doing some research for me. Karen, this is Ruby . . . I mean Grace Winslow."

"Hi," Grace said, her curiosity stirred. "You been workin' for this guy long?"

"No, I just started." Karen was staring at her outfit and said, "I saw your motorcycle. Do you ride it everywhere?"

"I just got it." She turned to Key. "Kev got it for me. Wasn't that sweet of him?"

"I'm not sure. I think those things are dangerous."

"Come on. You've gotta go for a ride."

"Not me," Francis said. "I'd like to keep all my arms and legs."

Grace was happier than she had ever been in her life. She grabbed his arm and squeezed it.

Miriam squawked, "*My* Francis!"

"Be quiet, Miriam!" Grace laughed. "I won't take no for an answer. You won't even need a helmet. Just sit on the back and hang on."

Key gave in and shrugged. "I knew you'd get me killed before this was over." He put down the paper he was holding. "Karen, you can go ahead and keep working. I won't be gone too long."

"All right, Francis."

Grace led the way outside and flung her leg over the motorcycle. She kicked the starter, and when the engine revved, she said, "Come on and get on. I'm gonna show you what a real ride is like."

Nervously Key got on and put his arms around her waist. "No tricks, now. Just take it easy."

"Sure."

Key felt himself pitched backward as she gunned the machine. He gasped and held on tightly. He was very aware of the fullness of her figure and knew that she was delighted at having succeeded at getting him on the bike. He clung to her as she turned a corner, leaning over precariously. "Not so fast!" he shouted.

"You ain't seen nothin' yet, Francis!"

It was the ride of Key's life, and thirty minutes later she pulled up in front of his apartment building. "How'd you like it?" she asked.

Releasing his grip, he stepped off and grinned at her. "It's as fun a way of committing suicide as any I ever saw. Come on in. You can tell me all about this fancy new bike."

When they got inside, Karen was gone.

"Where's she off to?" Grace asked curiously.

"Probably to the library." Key dropped a cover over Miriam's cage, ignoring her protests.

"She's a pretty girl."

"I suppose so."

Pulling off her helmet, Grace said, "You *suppose* so. Didn't you notice?"

Key shrugged. "I guess I did. She's good at research—that's why I hired her. Would you like something to eat?"

"Sure. I'm starved."

"How about tuna fish sandwiches? I made up some tuna salad last night."

"Yeah."

The two worked together to move the stacks of papers and books from the table to the floor to squeeze in enough room for two plates. Soon they were sitting at the table, finishing up their sandwiches and washing them down with soda pop.

"How's the book goin'?" Grace asked.

"All right, I guess. Do you read many novels?"

"Just romances. Does yours have any romance in it?"

"Sure it does."

"I thought writers had to know about things in order to write about them."

Key gave her an indignant look. "I know about romance."

"How? You read about it in books?"

"Sure."

Grace could not sit still. She got up and paced the floor, then came over to stand behind him. "I tried to teach you something about romance, but you didn't want any lessons."

"I told you I'm sorry—"

"Oh, forget it, Francis. You're just the way you are. Tell me about the book." She curled up on the cot, her feet beneath her, and listened as he told her a little about it. He was reluctant to give her too many details, though. Finally she said, "Give me some of it to read."

"Not until it's finished, but you can read this." He picked up a book and handed it to her.

She looked at the title. "*Old Pioneers*. What's it about?"

"Read it, and then we'll talk."

"All right." She got up and said, "I'll let you get back to work now." As she started out the door, she turned and asked, "What about Karen? Are you two havin' a thing?"

"No, of course not. It's just business."

"Didn't you ever have a woman, a real girlfriend, I mean, Francis?"

"That's none of your business."

This only egged her on. "Ever plan to have one?"

"Yes." Francis Key did not like this conversation, and he began to push her out the door. "Thanks for the motorcycle ride."

"When?"

"When what?"

"When are you going to get a real woman, a girlfriend?"

"When I find one I want to spend my whole life with. Somebody I can grow old with."

Grace found this amusing. "So the two of you will lose all your teeth and get gray hair and go creakin' around together?"

"That's it."

"I think that's sweet." She leaned forward and kissed him on the cheek. "I'll come back and give you another ride tomorrow, but I still think you're a freak."

"I guess so."

Key watched as she left the room, then went to the window. As she got on the motorcycle and roared off, he touched the spot where she had kissed him. "I guess I am a freak," he muttered ruefully.

CHAPTER FIFTEEN

THE LAST STRAW

★ ★ ★

Kevin burrowed down into the easy chair with his feet propped up on a hassock and intently studied the book before him. Two walls of his bedroom were covered in floor-to-ceiling bookshelves with books of all sizes and colors and shapes. This was only a small part of his collection—those he used regularly. The rest he kept in the family library downstairs. Lifting his eyes, he glanced around the room and looked at the family portrait his father had painted before Kevin's accident. His father had posed them all outside under a spreading oak tree near the fish pond. The picture captured the spirit of the youthful family well. Kevin rested his eyes on his own image, and he thought how well his father had caught his personality at that period of his life. He had keen, sharp memories of how he had thrown himself into life with a joyous expectancy. He studied the smooth face, unscarred, the eager eyes and the ready smile. Tears came to his eyes and he quickly looked away as he thought of what he had lost. He did not need a reminder of that.

Feeling frustrated, he got up, tossed the book on a table already laden with magazines, papers, and notebooks, and went to look out the window. The sun had just risen and was throwing its fiery beams over the landscape. His eyes ran around the hedges, the flower beds, the pond, and the carefully nurtured young trees, and for a moment he felt some satisfaction with his work. Then without warning, a thought challenged him: *I've done all I can do to this place.*

The thought was disturbing. Ever since he had recovered from the accident, he had taken refuge from the world here on the estate—working on engines or reading or developing the landscaping. He knew every foot of this place—no, not every foot. He knew every inch. He had planted and dug until he wasn't sure what more he could do to add to it. Sadly, he realized he had come to the end of his usefulness here. He had become a lonely young man, and except for his family, he was close to no one. Now the sight of the fully developed landscaping left him feeling empty. "I guess I'm like Alexander the Great, with no new worlds to conquer," he muttered.

Restlessly he turned from the window and moved along the bookcase, slowly perusing his books. He had a fondness for literature and had collected an excellent collection of poetry, plays, and novels. But he also had an entire bookshelf full of technical works—mostly on the history and development of machinery. Another bookshelf was filled with the history of aviation, and on one of the walls not covered with books there was an enlarged photo of the first flight at Kitty Hawk of the Wright brothers' biplane, Wilbur running alongside and Orville at the controls.

Looking over to the section of his library devoted to aviation, he ran his eyes along the titles. He had read them all so many times, he had no urge to read any of them again. He moved back to his chair and picked up the Bible that lay on the table. He was a faithful reader of the Scriptures and was now challenging himself to read it all the way through from Genesis to Revelation. He had done this three times already, and the words of the Authorized Version had become very much a part of him. He opened the book to the fourth chapter of Esther. He had never particularly cared for this book—not as he did for the Psalms or the Gospels or some of the others—but he read it dutifully. He had mentioned once to his father that he didn't see much purpose in the story. His father had said, *God has a purpose for everything, son. That book might not speak to you right now, but it has spoken to God's people throughout history. Someday it might speak to you.*

He had already read how the Jews were about to be massacred due to the hatred of Haman, and how Mordecai, the wise old Jew, had prayed to God to deliver them. He remembered that Mordecai had told her she must go to the king and beg for the lives of her people, and Esther had reminded him that if she were to do that without being summoned by the king, according to the law, she might be executed. Then came the words of the old Jew to the young queen in the fourth chapter. *"Who knoweth whether thou art come to the kingdom for such a time as this?"*

He had never paid more than passing attention to these words, but now they caught at him, and he could not understand why. He knew the rest of the story. He knew Queen Esther did go to the king and he listened to her and consequently the Jews were saved from death. But Kevin could not understand why this particular line was so strong in his mind right now. He bowed his head and closed his eyes. "Lord, I don't understand why this Scripture suddenly seems so important to me. But I ask that you enlighten me and give me wisdom, in the name of Jesus."

For a long time Kevin sat there waiting patiently. He had learned that God does not rush into a man's life or his thoughts, but that meditating on the words of Scripture allows them to become significant and meaningful. Finally he closed the Bible, but he knew he would keep thinking of that simple sentence until it made sense to him.

He had just laid the Bible down when a knock came at his door. He got up to answer it, wondering who would want him this early in the morning. He was usually the first one up. When he opened the door and saw Paige, he said, "What are you doing up this early?"

"I've got to talk to you, Kev."

"Sure. Come on in." He stepped back, and when she entered, he closed the door. "Something wrong?"

She was wearing a light blue robe and fluffy slippers. Her hair was disturbed, and Kevin understood that for her to come to him in this disarray meant something was bothering her. "Is somebody sick?" he asked quickly.

"No, not that. I came to talk to you about Grace."

"Why, sure. Come on and sit down."

"No, I'm too nervous." Paige began to pace back and forth, a troubled air about her. "I've got to talk to someone. Dad won't listen to me, and Mom won't either."

Kevin understood her problem. He had already given it a lot of thought. "I know you're worried about Grace, but I think it's all going to work out."

"Going to work out! How can you say that?" Paige flung her hand in a wild gesture, her eyes pleading with him. "She's ruining the family, Kev. Can't you see that? You know what a spectacle she made of herself at the party. John's parents were horrified, and I don't blame them."

"She's had a hard life, but she'll come out of it. She just hasn't had a good upbringing for her to learn proper behavior. All she needs is love and lots of prayer."

"That's easy enough for you to say, Kev. You don't have to face the world. You've made yourself a little kingdom here, and you're satisfied with it."

Kevin did not answer, but her words stung. He suddenly remembered the Scripture he had been reading: *"Who knoweth whether thou art come to the kingdom for such a time as this?"* The kingdom that he had made did not seem to be much. He had long felt that life was passing him by and he was helpless to do anything about it. He shook off thoughts of his own problems and tried to concentrate on Paige. "Have you talked to John about her?"

"Yes, I have, and he tells me that his parents have spoken to him very strongly."

"I can understand if they're shocked. They're the ones that

live in a secluded world, Paige. Oh, I know I do too, but all they know is the world of the rich. They can't begin to understand what it's like to struggle with poverty and the way that Grace has had to live."

"She doesn't have the same values we do, Kev. Can't you see that? She was brought up in a different world. People can't just step out of one world and into another one. I'll admit, if I tried to go to her world, I'd be a failure. Well, she's a failure trying to come into ours. We just don't believe in the same things. You know that. For starters, I'm sure she's not even a Christian. On top of that she smokes and drinks and runs around with men, and her mouth—well, you've heard her curse. She's simply not a virtuous woman."

"Maybe she isn't now, but she can be."

"When? She might never change, and if she doesn't, what are we going to do with her?"

"We're just going to have to be patient. I know she's rough on the outside, but inside there's something sweet."

Paige laughed without humor. "Sweet! She certainly looked sweet when she came dragging that awful man in, both of them drunk, and when she wrecked our party with that private detective who tagged along after her."

"He was just trying to look out for her," Kevin said quickly.

"You've got to wake up, Kev. It's just not going to work—and by the way, you shouldn't have given her that motorcycle."

"I thought I ought to do it. I'd never given her anything. None of us has. She hasn't had much, Paige."

"I can see it's no use talking to you. But Brian and I have talked about it, and he, at least, realizes that the situation is impossible."

"Give her a chance," Kevin pleaded. "You can do more for her than anyone else, Paige. You're almost the same age, and you know so many things. You could take her in hand and—"

"You think I haven't tried?" Paige said with exasperation. "I've tried my hardest, but nothing I say seems to soak in. It's just impossible!" She turned and walked toward the door and paused there after opening it. "Wake up, Kev. I know you've got a tender heart, but some things are just impossible. And you've got to understand that she's one of them." She abruptly left the room.

Kevin could not speak, and when she closed the door, he stood looking at it for a long time. Then he went back and stood at the window. His thoughts came slowly, but he knew that Paige was not entirely correct. "It's not impossible. She's rough now, but she can change. It's going to take a lot of love for her to change, but God can do anything." And then at that instant, a still small voice seemed to speak the words that Kevin had been studying: *"Who knoweth whether thou art come to the kingdom for such a time as this?"*

The verse penetrated Kevin Winslow like a sword. He stood still and waited. Silence filled the room, and he heard only the ticking of the clock on the shelf behind him. "Do you mean, Lord, that I'm here to help my sister? Is that what I'm here for?" He got no audible answer, but he knew he had touched upon the truth. He bowed his head and prayed again. "I'll do anything you say, Lord. All I ask is that you guide me."

★ ★ ★

Kevin made a minor adjustment to the motorcycle engine and nodded at Grace, who was seated astride it. She raced the engine and grinned with delight. Reaching out, she grabbed his hair and tugged it. "You're the best mechanic in the whole world, Kev!"

"Cut the engine. I want to do a few more things."

Grace turned it off and dismounted, then watched as Kevin tinkered with the engine. She was standing on his right side and could see the unscarred part of his face and thought again how handsome he was—far better looking than Brian. She had become very fond of Kevin and was grieved over the secluded life that he led. She knew he was a devoted Christian, but somehow the differences in their beliefs did not stand between them. He did not preach at her, but many times his conversation would contain references to the Bible. She watched as his long fingers moved agilely over the engine and thought, *If every Christian were like Kev, I guess maybe I could believe in Jesus.*

Kevin stood up and pulled an oily rag from his pocket. He wiped his hands and said, "This is a fine machine."

"Why didn't you ever get a motorcycle?"

"Just never thought of it."

"As much as you like machinery, you oughta get yourself somethin' really fancy. Have you ever thought about racing cars? The way you can tune up an engine, you could run off and leave the best racers in the dust."

Kevin laughed. "I'd like to try that maybe."

After talking about engines for a time, Grace suddenly frowned. "It's almost time for me to start getting ready. I guess you heard I'm goin' to the opera with Paige and John tonight."

"That'll be great. Your new hairdo looks real pretty."

"That's nice of you to say." Grace had decided to be a good sport and go shopping with Paige to pick out a dress she thought would be appropriate for the opera. That actually went better than either of them had expected, so they also went to the hairdresser and got her hair styled in a new way. To top it off, Paige bought her some new makeup and, when they got home, showed her how to apply it in an understated yet elegant way. It had been a surprisingly good morning.

"What are you going to see?" Kevin asked.

"I dunno. We're going out to a fancy restaurant first. Have you ever seen an opera?"

"Once or twice."

"Did you like it?"

"It's pretty interesting. I don't know enough about it to really understand it, though." He grinned. "You have to believe that there's a world where everybody sings instead of talks. Imagine singing out, 'Please pass the toast!' in great big full tones instead of just saying it."

Grace delighted in Kevin's sense of humor. "Why don't you go with us, Kev? I don't wanna go by myself."

"You won't be by yourself. Paige and John will be there."

"*And* his parents. They can't stand me, but it's mutual. I can't stand them either."

"They're a bit hard to take."

"Hard to take! They're the biggest snobs in the world, and John never had a thought of his own in his life that they didn't put there. I don't see what Paige sees in him."

"He's a nice fellow."

"He's got all the personality of a cauliflower!"

"Oh, come on, give him a break." Kevin saw that she really dreaded the evening. "Look," he said, "you don't want to be like I am, stuck off in nowhere land. You need to get out in the world. You're young and beautiful. You're going to find a young man, and he's going to fall in love with you."

"I've met too many guys already," Grace said bitterly. "I wish I hadn't."

"You can't change the past, but you can do something about today. Start out by going to that opera and get to know John and his family. After all, they'll be part of our family in a way after Paige marries him."

"I can't see that. Mom and Dad are great, but the Asquiths are stuffy. Dad thinks the same thing, but he don't talk about it much."

Despite Grace's uncertainty about the evening, Kevin urged her to go to the opera and enjoy it.

Grace ran her finger along the handlebars of the motorcycle. "Do you remember our discussion soon after I arrived about what I really wanted? You never have told me what *you* really want. You got me a motorcycle. Now it's my turn. What is it you really want?"

Kevin looked at her and appeared embarrassed. "I guess we all want things we can't have. Anyway, you go on to the opera. When you get home, I'll still be awake. You can come tell me all about it."

★ ★ ★

"Say, you look very nice, Grace!" Paige stared at her sister in astonishment. The black velvet dress Grace wore had a low neckline, long sleeves, a tight-fitting bodice, and a long full skirt. To finish off the look, she was wearing black lace gloves and black velvet shoes and carried a burgundy-colored silk wrap and purse. Grace spun around to display the dress and invited her sister into her room.

"Do you really like it, Paige?" Grace asked. Grace really liked the dress and was pleased with the way it looked with her new hairstyle and makeup.

"I love it," Paige said. "And it was fun picking it out with you. We're going to have a good time tonight."

"You do know that I don't know nothin' about opera. . . ."

"John knows all about opera. It's in Italian, but he'll explain it to you as it goes along. Come along now. He and his parents will be here any minute."

The two young women left the room, and twenty minutes later they were in the Asquiths' limousine. John and Paige sat in the front with the chauffeur, which meant that Grace had to sit in the back with the Asquiths. They were pleasant enough, but Grace felt totally ill at ease with them. As they pulled out of the driveway, Helen said, "Your dress is beautiful, Grace."

"Paige picked it out. D'ya really like it?"

"Oh yes. She has exquisite taste in clothing."

"I ain't never had nice things like this before, and I guess I might as well tell you, I ain't never been to an opera."

"It'll be quite an experience for you, Grace," Roger said benevolently. He turned to look at the young woman and could not help thinking of the last time he had seen her, which was when she had shown up at the party intoxicated. "I don't know much about your background, Grace. Would you tell me a little about it?"

Instantly Grace became defensive. She did not know how

much the Asquiths knew about her former rough life, but she suspected that Paige had said as little as possible.

"I grew up mostly in New York with the woman I thought was my mom. She worked a lot, so I pretty much had to take care of myself."

"Your schooling?" Asquith demanded.

"I dropped out of school to go to work when I was fifteen."

"Well, that's unfortunate, but it's not too late to catch up. There are all sorts of things you can do. Isn't that right, Paige?"

"Oh yes," Paige said, turning around and smiling brilliantly. "I'm going to see to it that Grace has every advantage now. And John knows so much! I think between us we can get her ready for college in as little as a year."

"That would be wonderful!" Helen said. "Would you like that, Grace?"

"I dunno. I've never even thought about college. It was all I could do when I was on my own to just make ends meet."

All the way to the restaurant, the Asquiths pried into Grace's life, and she tried to explain carefully. She knew that Paige was on pins and needles waiting for her to expose some awful thing, and she was determined not to.

When they pulled up in front of the restaurant, they all got out, and Roger instructed the driver to wait for them.

The Asquiths led the way, and John smiled and said, "I hope you're hungry. This is the best place in New York to eat."

"Sure is fancy," Grace said, her eyes wide as they entered the opulent foyer.

They were met by the maître d', who greeted Roger promptly. "Ah, Mr. Asquith, it's so good to see you again, sir. I have your favorite table."

"Thank you, James."

When they got to the table, the maître d' pulled a chair out for Grace. She smiled at him and said, "Thanks a lot, buddy."

He raised one eyebrow and then returned the smile. "You're welcome."

When they were all seated, he gave each of them a large menu. Grace opened it and blinked. "Why, I can't read this. It ain't English."

"No, it's in French. Perhaps you'll let me help you with your selection," John said.

"I'll eat anything except snails. I heard the French like to eat snails."

"Yes, they call them *escargot*. You won't have to eat snails. I don't like them myself."

John and Paige helped Grace make her choices; then while they waited for their food, she looked about the restaurant, fascinated by the furnishings and all the people wearing fancy evening clothes. She had only seen such things in the movies. "Are they all going to the opera?" she asked.

"Oh no," Alice said quickly. "Some of them will be going to plays and others to concerts. Do you like plays?"

"I don't know. I like movies," she said. "My favorite actor is Clark Gable. He's the cat's pajamas."

"I think movies are vulgar," Mr. Asquith said stiffly.

This reply stifled Grace, and she remained silent while Paige and John engaged Mrs. Asquith in conversation.

When the meal arrived, Grace watched the others to see which of the three forks by their plate they were using. She followed suit and ate heartily, even though her meal looked much too beautiful to eat. While they ate, the others discussed the opera, the stock market, and people she supposed were famous—some she had heard of, others she had not.

They were just finishing their meal when a disturbance caught their attention. They all turned around, and Grace saw that a fat man with a red face had become displeased with a waiter. The waiter was an inoffensive-looking young man who appeared to be frightened to death.

"That's Craig Matthews, the big railroad magnate," John whispered.

Grace had never heard of Matthews, but she was growing

angry at the way he was cursing out the defenseless waiter. "He's nothin' but a big bully," Grace said loudly.

Paige leaned forward and shushed her. "Don't be so loud. He's one of the most powerful men in New York."

Matthews stood and grabbed the young man by the collar, cursing him roundly, then slapped him. The waiter tried to get away, but Matthews, who was evidently drunk, hit him again.

Grace forgot that she was at a fancy New York restaurant with her sister's future husband and in-laws. She had never been able to stand bullies, and now, without even thinking about it, she shoved her chair back and flew to where Matthews was slapping the helpless waiter. Everyone in the restaurant was watching as Grace plunged into the fray, shouting, "Let him go, ya big ape!"

Matthews turned on her, steaming with rage. "You keep out of this."

"Let him go and I'll keep out of it. Otherwise I'll bust ya wide open!"

Mr. Matthews was not accustomed to being challenged. He loosed his grip on the waiter, who quickly ran away. Then he grabbed Grace by the arm and started cursing at *her*.

"Let me go or you'll be sorry!" she screamed. He began to shake her, and she was vaguely aware that several people were trying to stop him.

Grace's eyes fell on a bottle of wine on the man's table. She picked it up by the neck and brought it down with all of her might on Matthews' head. The bottle shattered, and Matthews went down in a heap.

A pandemonium of confusion broke out. Amid screams and excited chatter, she felt her arm gripped and turned to find a big man in a blue uniform by her side. "You're under arrest, miss."

"You're arresting me? For what? He's the guy you should be arresting!" she wailed, pointing at the huge man on the floor.

"Assault and battery. You may have hurt that gentleman severely."

"He deserved it," Grace said coldly.

"Come along with me."

Grace was pulled unceremoniously away. She looked over her shoulder and saw Paige gaping at the scene, her face as pale as a sheet of paper. She felt sorry for her sister, but suddenly she was not Grace anymore but Ruby Zale. "You let go of me, you creep!" she demanded, trying to jerk her arm away.

The policeman only tightened his grip as he dragged her out to a waiting squad car. "Watch your mouth, sister, or you'll be in worse trouble. You can't hit twenty million dollars over the head like that and get away with it!"

★ ★ ★

Phil was standing beside the sergeant's desk when the jailer brought Grace out. She had not been ill treated but was relieved to see her father. At the same time she knew she had done it again—disgraced the family.

"It's all right, Grace. I paid your fine. We can go home now."

She followed him out to the car silently, and even when he started the engine and drove away, she did not speak. He did not speak either, which made her nervous. "I've disgraced the Winslow name again, Dad, but I have to tell you I'd do it again. That big ape!"

"I guess the fellow deserved it from what I hear. If he weren't a millionaire, he would've been the one arrested."

"What will happen now?"

"Nothing. He could press charges, but I've got a good lawyer lined up. I don't think he'll want the publicity."

"I hate it for your sake and Mom's."

"Don't worry about us," Phil said. "It's Paige I'm worried about."

As soon as they got home and entered the house, they heard Paige's voice. "She's pretty upset," Phil said quietly. "She and John had a big row with his parents and they had to break their engagement."

"I guess that was his folks' idea, huh?"

"I expect so. To tell the truth, I'm not upset about it. I don't think he's the man for Paige. But she doesn't feel that way, of course, so get ready for some hard words."

Hard words were exactly what Grace got. Paige was distraught, weeping, and screaming, "You've ruined my life! Why don't you just go back to the gutter where you came from!"

Grace silently listened to this and worse before Cara finally led Paige off to bed.

When Grace and her father were alone again, she said, "I'm sorry for her, Dad."

"It'll be all right. Why don't you go on to bed too."

When Cara returned to the drawing room, Phil asked, "How is she?"

"Devastated. What are we going to do, Phil?"

"We're not going to do anything. Craig Matthews won't make any trouble about it. If he does, I think I can make some for him."

"You think I ought to go talk to Grace?"

"Leave it until morning. It's been a pretty rough night. Come on. I doubt if either of us will sleep, but we've got to try."

* * *

When Phil sat down to breakfast, neither Grace nor Paige had come down yet.

"Do you think we should go see about them?" Cara asked.

"No, let them sleep as long as they please. It's going to be a rough day."

They finished breakfast, and an hour later Cara interrupted Phil in his study, a troubled look on her face. "What is it, Cara?"

"It's Grace. She's gone."

"Gone? Gone where?"

"She left a note." She handed him a sheet of paper.

Phil took it and read the note:

Dear Mom and Dad,

I'm nothing but trouble for you, so I'm going away. You're both swell people, but this just won't work. Tell Paige I'm sorry for what I did—and tell Kev I love him.

Grace

"We have to go after her," he said.

"Yes, we do. Oh, Phil, this is awful!"

"Don't worry. We'll find her."

★ ★ ★

Finding Grace, however, was not going to be easy. Phil considered calling the police, but after the trouble Grace had already had, this did not seem wise. She had left no clues as to where she might have gone, so he and Cara were not sure even where to begin. "She'll write to us," Phil said, "and when she does, we'll go to her."

This did not satisfy either one of them, but it was all he could think of.

Kevin had no ideas when they told him, and Brian shook his head. "I knew it would come to this. It might be better in the long run."

The next morning Phil came into the kitchen and said to Cara, "More trouble, I'm afraid."

"What is it?"

"It's Kev." He handed her a note, and she read it aloud:

"Dear Mom and Dad,

I'm going to find my sister and bring her back. I think it's what God wants me to do. Don't worry about me. I'll call you as soon as I get a lead on her. In the meantime keep on praying. God's going to do a work in Grace's life."

"Oh, Phil, our world's falling apart!"

Phil took the note and read it again. "Well, this situation has done at least one thing. It's brought Kev out of his cave here. He can't hide if he goes looking for his sister."

"Do you think he'll find her?"

"You know, Kev's pretty close to God. If God told him to do it, then he'll find her." He reached out and pulled Cara close, and the two embraced silently.

Finally she whispered, "Yes, I think you're right. He *will* find her."

PART THREE

April–June 1935

★ ★ ★

CHAPTER SIXTEEN

IN THE SLAMMER

★ ★ ★

Francis Key carefully broke an egg into the hot skillet, waited until the yolk was just right, then flipped the egg over. He salted and peppered it, then scooped it out onto a plate next to the bacon he had already fried. Pulling some toast out of the toaster, he sat down at his work table and contemplated his breakfast with satisfaction. He bowed his head and breathed a quick thanks. No sooner had he taken a mouthful than he heard a knock on the door. Startled, he rose, muttering, "Who could that be this early in the morning?"

He started to open the door, then hesitated, remembering his days as a detective when unsavory characters sometimes showed up unexpectedly. Still, he could not imagine any possibility of this now, so he opened the door and found Kevin Winslow standing there.

"Why, hello, Kevin."

"I'm sorry to bother you so early, Mr. Key, but I had to see you."

"Come on in and sit down. I'm just having breakfast. Let me fry you an egg."

"No, you go ahead and eat."

"At least let me get you some coffee, then." He poured Kevin a cup of coffee. "I'm surprised to see you out and about."

"I came to ask for help, Mr. Key."

"Just call me Francis. What kind of help?"

"It's Grace. She's run away."

"Run away? Why?"

"Well," Kevin said hesitantly, "it was inevitable. She's had a pretty rough time of it since coming to live with us."

"I didn't think it would be easy. Too much of a change for her all at once."

"I tried to help her all I could, but she just hasn't been able to adjust."

"Tell me more. What happened?"

Francis listened as Kevin related various embarrassing incidents. When Kevin told about how she broke a wine bottle over Craig Matthews' head, Francis grinned. "That sounds like the old Ruby Zale. Did Matthews press charges?"

"Dad says he doesn't think he will. Doesn't want the publicity."

"I don't think any publicity could hurt him, but it's just as well." Francis spread jelly on his final morsel of toast and popped it into his mouth. "And let me guess. You want me to help you find her."

"I don't have the vaguest idea how to go about such a thing. Dad says that's your specialty."

"Did you tell him you were coming here?"

"No. I left him a note. I've got to find her on my own."

"I don't think it'll work, Kev. There are just too many things going against her."

"You don't understand, Francis. I think God told me to do this." He expected to see disbelief in Key's expression but saw only interest. "Do you think that happens?"

"Certainly it happens. Tell me about it. Everything." He listened carefully as Kevin explained how God had used the Scripture in the book of Esther and ended by saying, "I think God has put it on my heart to find her."

"Why do you want her to come back, Kevin?"

"I just want her to be happy."

"She wasn't happy when she was there. What makes you think she will be if you find her?"

"I don't think God would have sent me to find her if there wasn't a reason for it."

"I don't think she'll come back. You don't know her, Kev."

"We'll find a way to get her back if you can help me find her first."

"Even if I could, you couldn't help her."

"Why not?"

Key hesitated. "Because you've hidden away from the world so long. You'll have to go public—leave your safe little ivory tower."

"Well, I'm here, aren't I?" he said defensively. "I've thought all this out, Francis. God wants me to find her, and I think He led me here. I've got a little money and an old truck we can use to run around in. I've also brought Grace's motorcycle."

Key studied the man in front of him. *I just don't know how much help he's going to be,* he thought. *The first time he gets out in a real tough spot and somebody laughs at his disfigurement, he'll turn tail and run back home.* He did not voice his thoughts aloud, however, but said, "All right, I'll see what I can do. But I have to tell you that it's not a sure thing." He put his fork down on his empty plate and carried his dishes to the sink. "Did she say where she was going?"

"No. Dad's hoping she'll write, but I don't think she will."

"I don't think so either. So we just have to go out there and find her."

"How will we do that?"

"I imagine we could start with the folks I used to work with at Rader and see if they've heard anything about a new girl on the streets. Listen, why don't you come back tomorrow morning—let me finish this chapter of my book—and then we'll get started."

At that moment Miriam screeched, "Repent! Repent!" and

came sailing down to rest on Key's shoulder.

"What did he say?" Kevin asked, staring wide-eyed at the bird.

"This is Miriam—a she, not a he. She said to repent."

"You taught her that?"

"Sure—but she knows some cussing too that will curl your hair."

Kevin grinned. "I've always wanted curly hair."

* * *

The search for Grace proved to be more difficult than Francis had imagined. The next day he and Kevin went to the detective agency he worked for off and on and enlisted the help of the owner, Matthew Stoner.

"We'll do all we can, Francis," Stoner promised him. "Any thoughts of coming back to work for us?"

"You know I'll be back eventually, Mr. Stoner, but right now I've got to concentrate on my novel. I'm making good progress. But thanks for asking. And thanks for your help."

The two also went to the police station, where Francis had good contacts. Kevin stayed right by his side as they talked with various officers, and Francis watched his behavior carefully. He saw that however painful it was for the young man to be out in public, he was determined to follow through with the search. This pleased Francis, and he thought, *At least one good thing will come out of this. Once this is over, Kevin won't have to go back to being a hermit again.*

Two days went by without a clue, although Francis worked every angle he could think of. As they drove back to Francis's apartment on the second afternoon, Kevin asked him, "How can a woman just disappear? She has to be *somewhere.*"

"There's a thousand places she could be. She could have gone back to California, or even left the country. Do you know how much money she had?"

"No, I just know she left behind all the clothes and jewelry our family bought for her."

"Well, it's pretty hard to trace people who don't want to be found, but I'll keep trying."

* * *

"We've got a lead, Kev."

Kevin jumped to his feet with excitement in his eyes. "What is it?"

"I think I've found her," Francis said with satisfaction. "I had the police check the arrests in all the smaller towns within a hundred-mile radius of New York. There's a one-horse place in Pennsylvania called Eddington. They arrested a young woman there by the name of Grace Winslow. It's probably her."

"What's she charged with?" Kevin asked.

"That's not such good news. She's charged with soliciting."

"You mean prostitution?"

"That's right, but don't make too much of that. When the police pick up a girl who's out on her own, they usually tack that onto the charges."

"I hate to think what the other charges will be!"

"We'll find out soon enough. Come on, let's see if that truck of yours will hold together for a little trip. Say, do you mind if I take Miriam along? She gets awfully upset if I leave her alone too long."

"Not a bit. She can help me memorize some Scripture along the way!"

The old truck did fine as the two men headed to Eddington, about eighty miles south of New York City. When they drove down the main street, Francis said, "This may be touchy."

"Why's that?"

"Some small towns are pretty insular. They don't like outsiders coming in. Usually they're hard-nosed about anybody getting into their business, especially private detectives. You'd better let me do the talking."

"Where do we start?"

"The police station."

They found the police station just off the main street, a small one-story brownstone building with two older-model police cars parked out front. When they went in they were greeted by an overweight policeman with a beefy face. "Help ya?" he grunted.

"You holding a woman named Grace Winslow?"

"That's right. You her lawyer?"

"No, this is her brother. I'm just a friend."

Interest touched the sergeant's eyes. "I guess you want to see her."

"If it's not too much trouble, Sergeant."

"My name's Reed. She's quite a handful. Called me every name you could think of, and I didn't do anything but lock the door on her."

"What's she charged with besides soliciting?"

"That's all of it. Looks like she'll just have to pay a fine. Judge Hardy don't favor tarts in our town."

Kevin started to speak, but Francis drove an elbow into his side while he said, "Thanks, Sergeant Reed."

"Come on. You can talk with her in the interrogation room."

The two men followed the sergeant down a short hall and stepped inside a small bare room with a table and four chairs. When Reed left, Kevin said, "What do you think?"

"I don't think it's going to be too bad. It sounds like it's mostly a matter of money. I hope you've got some."

"I cleaned out my bank account. I didn't know how long this would take."

"We'll probably need it."

They waited until the door opened, and Reed said, "Right in there, honey. I'm not supposed to let you see anybody without written permission, but I guess since it's your brother, it's all right." He shut the door, and Grace stood facing the two. She looked tired, and her face was pale.

Kevin went to her and said, "Are you all right, Grace?"

"Sure. How'd you find me? Oh, I know. The great detective there. You're gettin' to be quite an expert at findin' me, ain'tcha, Francis?"

"You're only charged with soliciting," Francis said. "I think that's how the police make a living around here."

"I didn't do no soliciting. I was hitchhiking and this guy picked me up. He tried to get fresh with me, and when I discouraged him, he pulled out a badge and said he was a deputy. He brought me in here and charged me with hustling."

"It's okay. We'll get you out. You stay here and I'll go see about the fine," Kevin said.

He left and went to find Sergeant Reed. "How do I go about paying the fine?"

"It's fifteen dollars. You can pay me cash, and I'll give you a receipt."

"That's all there is to it?"

Reed grinned. "Yup. It's cash only, you understand."

"That's all right. I've got cash," Kevin said quickly. He pulled out his billfold and counted out three fives while Reed wrote out a receipt. "Can she go now?"

"Sure. I'll get her things together."

Kevin went back to the interrogation room. "We can go now. They're getting your things, Grace."

Sergeant Reed brought in a suitcase and a purse. "Check to be sure everything's there, Grace."

She looked through the purse and snapped it together. "It's all here."

"If I were you, I wouldn't linger," Reed said.

"Don't worry. I wouldn't stay in this stinkin' town if you gave it to me."

Reed grinned. "Been nice havin' you for a visit, sweetheart."

Grace whirled and left the building. When they got outside she said, "I ain't going back there again."

"Okay," Key said agreeably.

"I mean it, Francis."

"So do I."

"That's right," Key said, grinning. "You're bigger than I am, so I don't intend to drag you back kicking and screaming."

"I ain't bigger than you are—but I ain't goin' back!"

"Come on. Let's go get something to eat," Kevin said. "I'll bet you're starved, aren't you, sis?"

"Yeah. They serve slop in that place."

They walked down the street, and Grace suddenly stopped as she spotted the Italian motorcycle strapped onto the bed of the truck. "You brought the bike with you!"

"Sure, you left it behind. It belongs to you. Papers are in your name."

"I didn't want to take anythin' away. I wanted to make a clean break."

"We'll talk about that later."

"Maybe we'd better get our food in the next town. We may not be too welcome here," Francis said.

They all got in the truck and drove for twenty minutes before pulling into a truck stop.

"I always like truck-stop food," Grace said. "You don't pay for a lot of fancy surroundings. Just food."

As they ate their meal Grace's eyes were mostly on Kevin. "I'm glad you came, Kev. I was scared of what might happen. They were even talkin' about sendin' me to the state pen. The cop was the son of the mayor."

"Did you hit him with a blackjack?" Francis inquired.

"No, just my fist, but it bloodied his nose. I wish I had thought of the blackjack."

"You'd probably be in the federal pen if you had," Francis suggested.

They ate quietly for some time, and finally Grace broke the silence. "I can't go back, Kev. I'm sorry. I think a lot of you and of Mom and Dad, but it's just not my place. So thanks for getting me out, but I'll be on my way."

Kevin had thought a great deal about what he would say

if he found Grace, and now he told her, "You know, sis, you've been nagging me for quite a while now to find out what I really want."

Instantly Grace grew still. "Yes," she said, "but you always kept it from me."

"I never told anybody because I never thought it would be possible. But I'm going to tell you now." He hesitated while Grace leaned forward intently, her eyes fixed on her brother. He had become very important to her during her brief stay at the Winslow house, and she was curious about what was on his heart. "Come on, Kev, you can tell me. It can't be that bad."

"It's not bad. It's just so far out of reach. I want to be a pilot."

"A pilot! You want to fly airplanes?"

"That's right, sis. It's all I've ever really wanted. Before my face got all messed up, it was the only dream I had in my mind, and it's still there."

"It shouldn't be too hard to fulfill that dream. You could just get Dad to buy you a plane and take lessons."

"No, it's not that. I want to make a living at it. I don't know. . . . I'd like to be a crop duster, maybe, or a mail pilot. Anything as long as I'm in the sky."

Grace was pleasantly surprised. "I don't think that's crazy at all. Do you think you can do it?"

Kevin leaned forward, his eyes bright. "I *know* I can, sis. I've always been good with machinery, and I'm a great driver, and I've got good balance. And I'm smart enough too. All I need is a chance. Of course, I never thought I'd go out and show this face of mine, but if you'll help me, I know I can do it." He reached out and took her hand and held it for a moment. "Help me, sis. You're the only one who can."

Grace could not remember a time when she had ever been so touched. Her brother was a big, strong man, but he sounded like a child as he pled with her. She studied his eyes and saw the longing in them—not just to fly but to be a man, to do something in the world. "I don't know how I can help you."

"I don't know either. Maybe it's impossible."

"No, it's not impossible," Grace said quickly. "We'll do it somehow."

Francis had listened to all this with keen interest. Somehow his life had gotten tied up with these two people, especially Grace, and he saw the gentleness that showed through despite her rough exterior. Now it was directed toward her brother, but he thought, *If she can be gentle with one man, she could probably be gentle with others.*

The three left the diner, and when they were outside, Grace said, "Francis, you've got to help us do this."

"Me? I can't," he protested. "I'm trying to write a novel."

"You can write a novel anytime, but you owe me this."

"How do you figure that?"

"Because Hack Keller would have killed you back when you first found me if I hadn't been there to help you."

"Do I have to thank you for that for the rest of my life?" Francis was somewhat touchy about this. He had always felt less than a man at having to be rescued by Grace. "I've got Miriam to take care of—anyway, what can I do?"

"You're smart. You can do something."

"I've got to write this novel. Can't you understand that? I want to do that as bad as Kevin wants to be a flyer."

"That's right, sis," Kevin said. "Don't put this on him. He's done plenty just finding you."

"No, he's gotta help." Grace grabbed onto his lapels. "Do you know what day this is?"

"April the twenty-first."

"That's right. Doesn't that mean anything to you?"

"What should it mean?"

"It's my birthday!"

Key suddenly remembered the date from the investigation. "Well—happy birthday."

"All right, then. Are you going to help or not?"

"Not."

Grace turned loose of Francis's garment and grabbed Kevin's arm. "All right. Let's go, Kev."

Francis stood dumbfounded as they walked off toward the truck. He hesitated, arguing with himself, then cried out, "Wait a minute!" He ran forward and caught up with them. They both turned to meet him, and Grace had expectation in her eyes. "All right. I'll do it," he said resignedly.

"Oh, Francis, you're wonderful!" Grace threw her arms around him and hugged him so tightly he gasped.

"Okay, okay. You don't have to crush me."

"Now, what'll we do first? It takes a lot of money, doesn't it, Kev?"

"I have no idea."

They both looked at Francis, and he realized how much they were both depending on him. "All right," he grunted, "I'll think of something."

CHAPTER SEVENTEEN

A Place for Kevin

★ ★ ★

"It's not much of a place, but it'll do for a night," Francis said. He looked around the room and put Grace's suitcase down. "I've stayed in worse."

"Me too," Grace said. "The city jail in Eddington, for one." The three of them had found a seedy-looking motel on the outskirts of town, and Kevin had paid for two rooms. Going over to the bed, Grace sat down on it and shrugged. "It'll be fine. Why don't you guys stow your suitcases, and let's go out and get a bite to eat."

"I've got to bring Miriam in first," Key insisted. He went back to the truck and took out the cage, covered with a piece of bright green cloth. He took it into his room, and when he pulled the cover off, Miriam muttered, "My Francis!"

Grace stood at the door and laughed, her eyes sparkling. "You keep your females in a cage, huh, Francis?"

"Most females need to be kept under lock and key," Francis snapped. He put his finger inside the cage and the parrot at once fastened on to it. "I'll bring you back a piece of nice fresh apple, sweetheart."

"Are you gonna keep your wife locked up—if you ever get one?" Grace teased.

Francis just said, "Let's go find a place to eat," and turned and went back out to the truck, followed by Grace and Kevin. They left the Shady Rest Motel and drove down the highway until they found a diner called Mom's. As they stepped inside, Francis said, "This is a good place to eat."

"How can you tell?" Grace raised an eyebrow skeptically.

"They've got four calendars on the wall," Francis said. "That's how I judge eating establishments. If they only have one calendar—skip it. Two—edible but not much. Three—pretty good. Four—first class."

"You just made that up."

They sat down at a booth with a Formica top scarred with the initials of past customers. "Look at this," Kevin said. "Do you think it's an omen?" He pointed to a poem carved in the surface:

The horror.
Oh, the horror
Of the grilled cheese!
The only thing worse
Are the black-eyed peas.

"Do you suppose that has some kind of hidden meaning?" Francis said.

"No, I think it just means don't eat the grilled cheese or the black-eyed peas," Grace said with a laugh. "Not a real promising sign for your four-calendar establishment, Francis."

A frazzled-looking waitress came up and handed them three food-speckled menus. Grace noticed that her fingernails were bitten off to the quick. She was an attractive young redhead, though a bit too heavy, and she had a ketchup stain on her shirt pocket. She eyed them curiously. "The special is ham and eggs with biscuits and gravy."

"What kind of gravy?" Francis asked innocently.

"What do you mean, what kind?" The waitress looked

puzzled. "Just regular gravy is all." Kevin turned toward her, and she caught a glimpse of his scarred visage. "What happened to your face?" she blurted out.

"A bear bit me," Kevin said without cracking a smile.

"You ought to stay away from bears, then."

"I will from now on. Thanks for the advice. I guess I'll have the special," he said.

"I'll have pancakes, a short stack," Grace ordered. "You got any maple syrup?"

"Sure. You want sausage or bacon with it?"

"Both."

"We don't serve both."

"Oh," she said. "In that case let me have the sausage. Why don't you serve both?"

"I don't know. We just don't. What'll you have?" she said, looking at Francis.

"I'll have the special and a cup of black coffee," he said. "Lots of coffee. Strong and black and hot. That's the way I like my coffee."

The waitress grinned broadly and winked suggestively. "Is that the way you like your women too?"

Grace giggled, and when she saw that Francis was speechless, she said to the waitress, "You shocked him, honey. It's his first day out. You shouldn't make fun of him."

"Oh, gee, I'm sorry!" She reached out and touched Key's head. "I didn't mean to hurt your feelin's."

"I'll live," he said shortly, brushing her hand away.

When the waitress left, Grace said, "I think she's fallen for you, Francis."

"She's just a silly girl."

"She likes you, though." She shook her head. "For a little runt you sure attract women. I wonder why that is."

"Could we talk about something besides me?"

"All right," she agreed. "We'll talk about something else."

When the waitress returned with their food, she lingered next to Francis, pushing her hip against his shoulder. "Anything else you want, honey?"

"No, this'll be fine," Francis said, quickly taking a bite of eggs and ham.

"Okay, suit yourself," she said. "But if there's anything I can do for you—anything at all—you just let me know, toots."

They all found the food surprisingly good, and the conversation died down while they ate. After a bit Grace asked, "So what are we going to do about Kev's dream of learning to fly?"

"I've been thinking about it." Francis took a bite of biscuit and gravy and said, "Kev, your dad would be glad to do this for you, you know. He's got the money."

"I don't want him to do it for me. I want this to be something I do on my own."

"How much money have you got left?"

"Not much after paying the fine," Kevin admitted.

"I know you don't have any money, Grace, or you would have been out of the slammer."

"That's right." She nodded. "How much have you got?"

"Not enough to pay for flying lessons."

"How much do lessons cost?" she asked.

"I have no idea, but I know I don't have enough no matter how much they are."

They finished their meals and continued to drink coffee as the waitress refilled their cups. Each time she returned to the table, she smiled at Francis. Finally she asked, "You stayin' in town long, honey?"

"Not very."

"I get off at six."

"I'll remember that," Francis said gloomily. As soon as she had left, he said, "Let's go back to the motel."

"You afraid she's gonna attack you?" Grace said, grinning with enjoyment over Key's embarrassment. "I've got my blackjack here if you wanna borrow it."

"Come on," Francis said, ignoring her jibes.

When they returned to the motel, Key said, "I saw a phone booth down the road. I've got to go make a long-distance call. Everybody give me all your change."

Kevin turned his pockets inside-out searching for change, and Grace found some coins in her purse. "I'll be back when I get back," he said.

After he had left, Kevin said, "You know, Grace, I'm glad Francis is with us. It makes me feel better somehow."

"He does make you feel that way, doesn't he? I don't know how he does it. I've always gone for big, tall men, not little runts that can get beaten to a pulp. Still, there's somethin' about him."

They sat down on a bench outside the motel to wait for Francis, and Grace lit a cigarette. "Okay, Kev. Tell me more about this dream of yours and why you wanna fly."

Kevin talked for some time about how much he loved aviation as they watched the cars go by. The longing to fly was evident in his voice and eyes. Finally he looked up and said, "Here comes Francis. I hope he's got an idea."

Francis looked unhappy as he approached the two, and Grace said, "You didn't find out anything, did you?"

"Maybe."

"Well, what is it?" she asked impatiently, standing to her feet along with Kevin.

"I found a place you can get lessons," he told Kevin. "But it's pretty far away. There's a flying school in Baton Rouge that was owned by a guy I used to know."

"Did you talk to them?" Kevin asked eagerly.

Francis scratched his head. "It's a catch-as-catch-can outfit. Not fancy, you understand."

"That doesn't matter as long they can teach me to fly."

"You know the owner?" Grace asked.

"I used to be good friends with the original owner, but he died a few years ago. Flying lessons are going to cost more money than I've got."

"I spent most of my money on that motorcycle," Kevin said.

"We may have to sell it," Francis suggested.

"No we won't," Grace said firmly. "I'll get a job."

"Doing what?" Francis demanded.

"Waitressing. I can do that. I've done it before."

"I expect we'll all have to work." Francis sighed.

"So who owns the school now? Do you know him too?" Grace asked.

"It's not a him. It's a her."

"A woman owns a flying school?"

"It was her dad who died, and she inherited it."

"What's her name?"

"Babe Delaney."

Something about the way Francis pronounced the name caught Grace's attention, and she smiled slightly. "Babe, huh? Tell us more about her."

"Well, we were pretty good friends at one time," Francis said guardedly.

When both Kevin and Grace saw that there was more to Babe Delaney than Francis was willing to admit, Kevin said, "I hate to make you go there, Francis. You go on home and work on your novel."

"No, actually, half of my book is set in New Orleans. I was going to go there sometime for background anyway."

"What are we waitin' for? Let's go, then," Grace said.

"Let's get a good night's sleep first," Francis said in his pragmatic way, "and in the morning we'll head out. It's Louisiana or bust!"

CHAPTER EIGHTEEN

BABE

★ ★ ★

Francis became the bookkeeper for the trio and announced that they would no longer spend any money on vain things.

"What do you mean by 'vain things'?" Grace demanded.

"I mean like motel rooms."

"Where we going to sleep, then?" Kevin asked.

"We'll camp out."

"But we don't have any camping gear," he pointed out.

"We'll stop somewhere and get some blankets. It's warm enough we won't need but one apiece, and we can probably use them in Baton Rouge too—in case we have to sleep out in a swamp."

"I'm not sleepin' in any swamp," Grace moaned. "I was there once for a week with a carny, and I went out to one of them swamps. Saw an alligator big enough to swallow me whole! And the mosquitoes weren't much smaller. No campin' in a swamp for me."

"I was just kidding," Francis remarked, "but we do have to conserve whatever money we have left."

"I'll bet you can sweet-talk your old flame, Babe, and she'll give us a discount on flyin' lessons." Grace had figured out that Francis and Babe Delaney had been an item at one time. She was anxious to see the woman, wondering what sort of female Key was attracted to.

Kevin drove the truck, and they headed steadily south, stopping late that afternoon in a small town, where they went into a dry goods store to buy blankets.

"After we get blankets," Francis said, "let's go across the street to that grocery store and get something for supper."

"I'll go with you," Grace said. "I might not like what you pick out."

They went into the grocery store, and Francis had to say no to most of Grace's ideas, which were too expensive. They wound up getting hot dogs and buns and soft drinks. Grace insisted on getting three Baby Ruth candy bars, and Key paid for it all, counting out the money carefully.

They drove another half hour, and Key said, "There's a pretty likely looking spot to camp over there behind those trees."

"There's a creek running along it," Kevin said, pulling the truck off the road and parking behind the trees.

Francis stooped down to take a sip of water from the creek. "It tastes pretty fresh."

"I'll see if I can find some dry wood," Kevin offered.

An hour later it was dark, and Kevin had built a cheerful fire. The sky overhead was spangled with stars, and the moon was a perfect silver circle.

Key cut some small saplings with his pocketknife and sharpened them to a point, handing one each to Kevin and Grace. "Everybody's his own cook tonight."

Soon they were seated around the fire roasting the hot dogs. "I haven't done this since I was twelve years old," Kevin said with a laugh. "We used to go out and roast wieners and marshmallows pretty often—Brian and Paige and I."

"I can't imagine Paige sitting on a log or the grass with a dirty face roasting a hot dog," Grace said.

"She was different when she was younger. So was Brian."

"I guess we all were," Francis said. He suddenly reached

over and grabbed Grace's stick. "You're burning that wiener! Don't stick it right in the fire. Just hold it above the flames until it forms little blisters."

"You're always bossing me around," Grace snapped. "I guess I can roast a hot dog as good as you can."

It turned out, however, that hers was crispy black. Francis shook his head and handed her his. "Here, eat this one. I'll fix myself another one."

"Um-mm. I wonder why things taste better outdoors," Grace said through a mouthful of hot dog.

"I don't know that they do," Francis said. "I'd rather be sitting inside at a cloth-covered table eating a T-bone steak."

Kevin was already putting down his third hot dog. "I think Grace is right," he said. "Things do taste better outdoors. My dad likes to barbecue a lot at our house. I made a barbecue pit out of a huge barrel. I believe we could cook a whole pig on that thing."

They sat talking until the hot dogs were gone, and then Grace said, "Now for dessert." She reached for the sack containing the Baby Ruth bars, but Kevin said, "Not yet." He turned his back and worked busily for a moment.

"What are you doing?" Grace demanded.

Kevin turned around and presented a large cookie to Grace with a candle in the middle of it. "I know I'm a day late, but happy birthday, sis," he said. "Come on, Francis, we'll sing to her." He began singing "Happy Birthday," and Key joined in.

Grace held the cookie with the candle while the two men sang. When the song was finished, Kevin kissed her on the cheek. "Happy birthday, sis." Francis reached over and squeezed her shoulder. "Happy birthday, Grace."

Grace felt something swell in her throat and had to clear it before she said, "This is the best birthday I've ever had."

"Happy birthday, Grace!"

Grace jumped at the raucous screech and turned to the cage that Francis had placed on the ground. "Miriam, you're a scream!" she exclaimed.

"Better make a wish and blow out your candle before it melts all over your cookie," Kevin said with a grin. He watched as she did so and said, "What did you wish for?"

Grace broke off a piece of the cookie and pushed it between the bars for Miriam. The parrot grabbed it and gulped it down. "I wished that Babe would still be in love with ol' Francis here." She grinned mischievously at Key.

He blushed and snorted. "That was a long time ago."

"Aw, that don't matter." She winked at Kevin and said, "I don't know why, but women seem to like you. That secretary of yours had eyes for you."

"Don't be silly!"

"And that redhead in the diner. Remember, Kev, how she fell all over him and ignored us?"

Francis said roughly, "Here, give me my part of that birthday cookie and lay off, would ya?"

Miriam burst into the conversation with "Be ye holy!"

Grace laughed shortly. "Okay, that's enough, Miriam. I don't need none of your preachin'!"

They sat around the fire until finally Kevin stretched and said, "I'm gonna turn in. Hope it doesn't rain tonight."

"I think I'll just sit here by the fire for the night," Grace said.

"You don't have to be afraid," Francis said. "Nothing out here to hurt you."

"I ain't afraid!" Grace acted offended. "I just don't wanna miss nothin'."

Francis grinned. "Not much to miss—unless a skunk wanders into camp."

Grace's eyes grew large. "Do they do that?"

"Happened to me once, but that was a long way from here."

The two sat by the fire while Kevin curled up in his blanket and slept. From time to time, Francis fed the fire with dead branches. Grace looked up at the sky. "All those stars are somethin'. I wish I knew their names."

"You see the Little Dipper there?"

"Little Dipper? Where?"

"Right there. . . . Can you make out the shape of a square dipper? The star at the end of the handle is Polaris. It's fifty times bigger than our sun!"

"Aw, you're puttin' me on, Francis!"

"No I'm not."

"But it ain't bright like the sun."

"That's because it's three hundred light-years from earth."

"Light-years? What's that?"

"Light travels 186,000 miles in one second. A light-year is the distance light travels in a year."

"How do you know all this stuff?"

"I read a lot."

"But what good does it do you to know all that stuff about stars?"

Francis laughed. "What good does it do you to be ignorant about them?"

Grace rolled her eyes.

"I'm going to sleep."

While Francis got comfortable, Grace sat thinking about what would happen when they got to Baton Rouge. Finally she drew her blanket around her and lay back, staring up at the stars. A smile touched her lips, and she thought, *He may know a lot about stars, but he don't know much about women.*

* * *

By the time they pulled into Baton Rouge, all three of the travelers were glad the journey was over. They had slept outside three nights in a row and were feeling pretty grubby by now.

"I'm starvin'," Grace said. "Let's get a real meal where we can sit inside."

"All right," Kevin said. "I'll stop at the next café."

Ten minutes later they pulled up in front of a restaurant called Papa John's Cajun Cooking. When they entered, they were taken by the enticing smells. "I don't know what that is," Grace exclaimed, "but I sure want some of it!"

They sat down at a table, and a lean man wearing blue pants and a white apron came over. He had olive skin, bright white teeth, and dark, liquid eyes. "What can I get for you folks? I hope you're hungry."

Kevin nodded. "I've never had Cajun before. Have you got a menu?"

The man motioned to a chalkboard on the wall with the day's specials. "There—you can't go wrong with any of those dishes."

The three feasted on gumbo, jambalaya, and barbecued shrimp. Francis insisted that they count their money, but this turned out to be discouraging.

"Francis, I wish you hadn't paid off all your debts with the money my dad paid you," Kevin said.

"We can always sell the motorcycle," Francis reminded them.

"No, we're not selling that!" Grace argued. "Not yet anyway." She smiled at Kevin and said, "It's the best gift anyone ever gave me, and I'm not givin' it up. Like I said, I can get a job. We'll make out."

She had a glint in her eye as she put her hand under Francis's chin and turned his face toward her. He blinked with surprise, and she leaned forward and said, "Practice on me, Francis."

"What do you mean 'practice on you'?"

"I mean, give me some sweet talk like you're gonna give Babe so she'll give Kev free tuition."

Francis jerked his chin away and slapped at her hand. "If you say one word in front of her—"

"Oh, I won't. I'll just let nature take its course." She winked at Kevin. "True love will find a way."

"How poetic." Kevin returned the wink.

"I saw that in a movie with Clark Gable and Jean Harlow. If all else fails, Francis, you can always spout poetry. I'm sure you know plenty of it!"

★ ★ ★

The Blue Sky Air Service did not impress the trio as they pulled up in front of what appeared to be an old hangar with a sign that said Office.

"Come on," Grace said as they all got out of the truck and headed toward the building. "Now, remember, Francis—"

"You keep your mouth shut, Grace! I don't want to hear one word out of you."

"My, he's been feeding on raw meat, hasn't he, brother? All right. I won't say a word."

Francis opened the door to let Grace go first, and the two men followed. The low-ceilinged room they found themselves in was no more impressive than the outside of the structure. Two dirty windows admitted a little light, and a ceiling fan turned slowly over the desk. The wall was covered with pictures of planes and aviators, and the air was stale with smoke and gasoline. A table to the right held a coffeepot on top of a portable stove, and two battered filing cabinets stood side by side at the rear, flanking another door that apparently led out to the hangar.

A woman was sitting at the desk, and Grace examined her critically. She looked close to thirty with bright red hair and large green eyes. As she stood up, Grace noted she was tall and had a spectacular figure. She wore a pair of men's trousers and a tight green shirt with several buttons open at the top. From her ears dangled what appeared to be diamond earrings, and a necklace with a single green stone hung down from her neck. Grace had been picturing Babe as rather homely, and she couldn't help feeling dismayed at the impressive-looking woman.

"I can't believe my eyes! Francis, I never thought you'd have the nerve to show up here!" Babe's face looked flushed. "What do you want?"

Key felt the eyes of his two friends on him but ignored them. "I'm glad to see you too, Babe."

The woman stared at him, then burst into laughter. "You've got the nerve of a brass monkey! Now, get outta here!"

"Wait a minute. I haven't told you why I'm here."

"I don't care. I don't need another dose of Francis Key."

"Aw, come on, Babe. At least listen to me before you throw me out." He turned and said, "These are my friends. This is Kevin Winslow and his sister Grace. This is one of my best friends, Barbara Delaney, but everybody calls her Babe."

Francis noted Babe's startled glance when she finally noticed Kevin's scarred face.

"Glad to know you," Babe said, recovering quickly. She studied Grace for a moment, as if making some sort of judgment, but said nothing of her assessment. "When I kicked you out," she said to Francis, "I meant for you to stay out."

Grace laughed. "Francis has been telling us how much you were in love with him, Babe, but I guess the fire has gone out."

"Will you shut your mouth!" Francis said furiously, his face flaming. He turned back to Babe and said, "Look, this is truly business. Kevin here wants to learn how to fly."

Babe's eyes narrowed and she looked at Kevin. "Have you had any experience?"

"Not a bit, but I'd love to learn."

"You think you can crowd him into your full schedule?" Grace grinned sardonically.

Babe did not smile. "I run a business here. If you got the money, I can teach him to fly—if he can be taught."

"Actually, that seems to be the problem, Babe," Francis said boldly. "We're a little short on cash."

"How much have you got?" she demanded.

"The truth is, by the time we rent a place and buy a few groceries, we'll be broke."

Disgust swept across Babe's face. "I'm not running a charity school here."

Grace spoke up. "Come here a minute, will you? I wanna show you somethin'." She walked to the door, and after a calculating look at Grace, Babe followed her out to the truck. "Look at that," Grace said. "A brand-new Italian bike. You know what they're worth?"

"Sure I know what they're worth. You want to trade it in for his tuition?"

"No, I wanna give you the title to hold. I'm gonna get a job and so are those two. We'll make your payments. Don't worry 'bout it. If we don't, you can take the bike and sell it."

Babe chewed her lower lip thoughtfully. "Sounds like a deal to me, but if you don't keep up with your payments, I guarantee I'll sell that bike right out from under your pretty little nose." She lowered her eyes and deliberately took in every inch of Grace. "You his woman?"

"What do you care? You kicked him out, didn't you? Come on, let's get this down on paper."

The two women went back inside, and Babe sat down at the desk. She opened a drawer and pulled out some papers. "Sit down, Winslow. You're now a student at the Blue Sky Air Service. What makes you think you can fly?"

"I just know it, that's all. And I love engines of all kinds. I have an awful lot of experience with car engines. . . . Say, you wouldn't need any help around here, would you?"

"We are a little short staffed at the moment. Our mechanic quit just last week."

"How about if I work for you and you can use my wages to help pay for my lessons?"

"Sounds like a good deal for all of us. Can you start right away?"

"You bet!"

As soon as they had finalized the financial arrangements, she said, "Come on. Let's put you to work."

"Grace and I'll go find a place to stay," Francis said. "I'll pick you up later this afternoon."

As the two got into the truck and drove off, Babe walked Kevin out to a Stinson sitting on the tarmac. Babe asked him about the kinds of engines he had worked on, and he gave her the rundown.

Something about his attitude attracted Babe. He spoke well, and although the left side of his face was a mess, he was handsome enough on the right. "What happened to your face?" she asked.

"Can of gasoline blew up when I was fourteen."

"Can it be fixed?"

"A few doctors have tried."

"Does it bother you?"

"Yes. Now I want you to teach me everything you know about this aircraft."

Babe laughed. "All right. Let's get started."

★ ★ ★

"I can let you have it cheap."

"I just love it," Grace said sarcastically. "It's a palatial mansion."

The man who was showing the small rental house to Grace and Francis gave her a quizzical look. "If you want a palatial mansion, you've come to the wrong end of town."

"It's okay," Francis intervened. "How much?"

"Twenty-three bucks a month. Take it or leave it."

"We'll take it," he said.

"Gotta have a month in advance."

"Sure." Key pulled out his slender roll of bills and handed over the cash.

The owner took it and said, "Don't burn it down. It ain't much, but it brings in a little, and I need it these days."

"Thanks, Mr. Doucett," Francis said as the owner pocketed the money and left. He turned to Grace. "I guess I know what we'll be doing for the next day or so. Cleaning up this place."

"It's filthy." Grace sniffed. "Pigs must have lived in it."

"A little soap and water will make a difference."

"Well, you can start cleanin', but I'm gonna find a job."

"You mean today?"

"I mean right now."

"I need to go buy some cleaning supplies and some groceries. A few pots and pans."

"We'll go together, then. I'll find me a job while you go shopping."

As they got back in the truck, Francis said, "What if Kevin can't fly, like Babe said might happen?"

"He can do it."

"How do you know?"

"I just know."

Francis laughed and got in behind the wheel. "I hope you're right," he said. "What did you and Babe talk about when you took her outside?" he asked as he pulled away from the house.

"She wanted to know if I was your woman."

"What'd she say when you told her you weren't."

"I didn't tell her I wasn't."

Key swiveled his head around. "You didn't?"

"No, she thinks we're an item."

"You shouldn't have told her that!"

Grace laughed. "I didn't tell her that, you ninny, but it ain't none of her business. What I actually said was, if she kicked you out, what does she care? She drew her own conclusions."

Key bent over the wheel and shook his head. "Woman, you have a way of creating trouble everywhere you go."

"Francis, you love it—I can tell. Now let's find the sorry part of town with lots of bars."

"You're not going to work at a bar!"

"You bet your boots I am! Jobs are hard to find, but bars always want a good-lookin' barmaid."

"It's not right, Grace."

"Stop bein' such a preachy old man. You take care of cleanin' the house, and I'll take care of the job. Do you intend to keep that loudmouthed parrot in your room?"

"Of course. She gets lonesome when I'm not around."

"Well, staple her beak when I'm asleep, wouldja?"

* * *

Francis was amazed at how quickly Grace found a job. The place was a combination restaurant and saloon, and it was clear that the liquor flowed freely in the run-down joint. It was called the Green Lantern, although there were no green lanterns in sight. When Kevin saw it the next day, he disliked it as much as Francis did, but there was nothing the two men could do. They needed money fast.

"Grace has got this all figured out, Kev," Francis said with resignation. "First, you and I will clean the house up. After that, I'll do the cooking, and you do the flying."

Francis and Kevin worked hard for two days to get the house more livable while Grace went to work. They were grateful the tiny two-bedroom house wasn't any bigger. The bathroom took all the effort the men could muster to get it presentable. They couldn't use the filthy mattresses that were in the house, so they bought cots for the men and a mattress for Grace's room. The rest of the furniture was worn but useable, and the stove seemed to work fine.

After the house was cleaned up, Kevin went off early each morning and stayed until late afternoon at the air school. Francis did some work around the house but spent most of his time writing. Since Grace worked until late, she also slept late, usually getting up shortly after noon.

"You know," Kevin said to Grace one night when he had waited for her to come in, "this may sound crazy, but this is the best time I've ever had in my life. At least since I was fourteen."

"You're easy to please, Kev." Grace was tired. She had spent the evening fighting off amorous Cajuns and truck drivers, and she was ready for bed. She patted Kevin's cheek and said, "You're gonna learn to fly if it kills us all. Good night, brother."

"Good night, sis."

* * *

Kevin's flight training included a great deal of book study as well as the actual time in the air. One day he was cleaning one of the old biplanes they had used as a crop duster. He longed to try it, but Babe told him, "That's the most dangerous kind of flying there is, Kev. You're a long way from that."

He worked carefully as if it were a new plane and stopped when he heard an unfamiliar female voice. "Hi there. You're new, aren't you?"

Kevin started to stand up and bumped his head on the underside of the wing. It smarted, but he turned around to see a young woman there. She was smiling at him, and he waited to see the disgust on her face when she saw his face. But he saw nothing, and he thought, *She covers her feelings pretty well*. He had given up trying to hide his scars, for there was no point in it. People would see them anyway.

"Are you a student?" he asked.

"Me? No, I'm studying to be a nurse. I'm Babe's sister. My name is Lucy. You must be Kevin Winslow."

"That's me."

"Babe told me all about you." She was not as tall as her sister and was somewhere around twenty, Kevin guessed. She had an abundance of rich brown hair and warm brown eyes, a beautiful complexion, and a trim figure. The woman came closer and smiled up at him. "My, you are a tall fellow. How tall are you?"

"Five feet fourteen inches."

For a moment Lucy looked blank, and then she laughed. "Six-two, I take it."

"That's about right. You say you're a nurse?"

"I'm studying to be."

"Why do you want to do that?"

"Why do you want to be a pilot?"

Kevin grinned. "Fair enough," he said. "Have you ever flown?"

"Not me. I let Babe take care of that. Where are you staying?"

"We rented a house—about five miles from here."

Lucy smiled and nodded. "It's good to have you here, Kevin."

"I'm afraid I'm not a very good student. I think your sister's disappointed."

"Oh, she fusses at everybody, but she's pleased with your progress. She told me."

Kevin's eyes lit up. "She did? Well, she's kept it from me."

"You'll have to come over sometime—you and your friends. You like Cajun cooking?"

"What I've had of it is great."

"Good. I'll look forward to that. See you later."

Kevin watched her go and felt a twinge of regret. Pretty girls were never interested in him, he thought. But he went back to washing the plane and found himself whistling in a way he had not done for years.

★ ★ ★

Francis looked up with surprise to see Babe's Ford Roadster pull up in front of the house. He had been sitting on the porch trying to think his way out of a chapter that wouldn't work, and when she got out, he rose to greet her. "Hello, Babe. Where's Kev?"

"He had some extra work to do. I told him I'd stop by and tell you."

"That's nice of you. Would you like to come in? I just made a pie."

They went inside, and Key brought out the fresh apple pie, still hot from the oven, and two plates. He served up two slices and pushed one of them toward Babe, handing her a fork. He poured coffee into two white mugs. "If you don't like our grub, don't eat here," he announced, grinning. "I saw that once on a restaurant sign in El Paso."

Babe took a sip of the coffee and slowly took a bite of the pie.

"How's Kev doing?" Francis asked.

"Good. He's got what it takes."

"I'm glad to hear that."

"Too bad about his face."

"Yes, it is. He's had a hard time living with it, but he seems to be learning to get along with it now."

"Why hasn't he had it fixed?"

"He's been to several doctors, but so far none of them have been able to do all that much. His dad told me once that it used to be worse."

"He's a nice guy on the inside. All the scars are just on the outside."

The remark caught Key's attention. "You always were pretty sharp, Babe. You're right. Most of the lumps we get on our head don't hurt as bad as the ones we get inside."

When the two finished eating, Key got up and put the dishes in the sink. Babe lit a cigarette and studied him with narrow eyes. Finally she put the cigarette out in an ashtray and said, "I've got to get on home. I'm tired."

"Thanks for coming by." The two walked together to the door, but instead of stepping outside Babe suddenly turned, and Francis found himself standing only inches from her. She put her arms around him and drew him close as he watched her nervously.

"You ever think about when we were together?"

"I try not to."

"We had something, Francis."

"Had something! We fought like cats and dogs half the time."

"But when we weren't fighting, it was sweet." She pulled him closer and kissed him on the lips. She held the pressure against him, and he was aware of the softness of her body against him. But he kept his arms carefully away, and she soon pulled back and laughed.

"You haven't forgotten me. I can tell." She reached out and

ruffled his hair. "Good to have you back, sweetheart."

At that moment they heard a motorcycle pull up front. "There's your girlfriend. Is she special to you?"

"No, not at all. She's not a girlfriend."

"I don't believe that."

They stepped out on the porch, and Grace hopped off the motorcycle. She pulled off her helmet and came forward, and Key said quickly, "Babe came by to tell us that Kev's working late."

"How's he doin', Babe?"

"Fine. He's going to be a good pilot. Well, good night, you two."

Key turned and went inside as Babe drove off, and Grace followed him in. When he turned around, she laughed and cocked her head to one side. "Your lipstick's on crooked."

He quickly wiped his lips with his handkerchief but could think of nothing to say.

Grace laughed at his confusion. "A few coals still there, Francis?"

"No!"

"Why such a big a no? You were in love with her, weren't you?"

"I . . . thought so at the time."

"True love never dies, ya know. There was a song once that said that. I never believed it."

"I think I do."

"Why, you baby! You haven't been around enough to know any better."

"I'm sorry you feel that way, Grace."

"You're a piece of work, Francis. Good night." She turned and went to her room, but after her bath, she lay for a long time thinking of what a strange situation she'd fallen into. She was happy for Kevin, but for some reason she was disturbed about Francis Key. She thought of the lipstick on his face and grunted, "That woman's still got a flame for him. And she'll eat him alive—just like she did before!"

CHAPTER NINETEEN

GRACE GETS A TOUCH

★ ★ ★

The Stearman approached the runway, and the wheels touched down as light as a feather, giving Kevin the thrill of making a good landing. He brought the plane to a halt in front of the hangar, then cut the engine.

"Well, I hate to say it, Winslow, but that was pretty good," Babe said from the back seat.

"Thanks, Babe," Kevin said as they both climbed out of the plane. "That's the first nice thing you've said about my progress."

She arched her eyebrow. "I bragged on a student once, and it got me into trouble. He thought I was trying to make a pass at him."

"Well, I don't think that. You're a good teacher, Babe."

"Here comes Lucy," she said.

Kevin looked across the field and saw Lucy coming toward them, a smile on her face.

When she stopped in front of them, she said, "Did the teacher give you an A?"

"She actually said something complimentary for a

change," he said. "I couldn't believe it. She must want to borrow some money from me."

"I think Kev deserves a reward for all his hard work," Lucy said to her sister. "Can you spare him long enough for me to buy him a hamburger?"

"Sure. You can take my car," she said, pulling out the keys and tossing them to Lucy. "And when you come back, Winslow, sweep the hangar out, will you?"

"Sure thing."

Kevin and Lucy walked to the Roadster. "Why don't you drive?" she said, handing Kevin the keys.

"All right." He quickly went around and opened the door for her.

"Thank you kindly," she said with a sweet smile.

"I always aim to please." Kevin got in the driver's seat and started the engine. "Where do you want to go?"

"Let's go to the Green Lantern. You can tell Grace about your flight today."

"You shouldn't be going to joints like that."

"If Grace can work in one, it won't kill me to go inside. I don't think I'll see or hear anything I haven't seen or heard before."

"All right, if you insist."

As Kevin drove at a fast clip toward the Green Lantern, he asked Lucy a number of questions about her studies.

She answered all his questions, then finally said, "Why do you want to know so much about my coursework?"

"Because I'm interested. It must be pretty hard work learning to be a nurse."

"It is, but I like it."

Kevin fell silent and she asked, "What's the matter? Why so quiet, Kevin?"

"I guess in the hospital you see some people who are hurt pretty bad, huh?"

"Mm hmm."

"The first time I met you, you know what I thought?"

"What?"

"I thought she hides her emotions pretty well. She looks at this scarred face of mine and doesn't even blink."

Lucy did not answer for a moment. "You know what *I* thought?" she finally said. "I thought what a shame it is. It always makes me sad to see somebody who's been hurt. But you know it could have been worse, Kevin."

"How?" he asked, shaking his head in disbelief. "It couldn't have been much worse."

"Suppose you had lost your legs. That would have been worse. Or if you had lost your vision, you couldn't have been a pilot. One of my patients is a young woman who was in a terrible car wreck. It tore both her eyes out."

Kevin gripped the wheel until his knuckles were white. "That's terrible," he whispered. "You're right. I can do plenty of things. I can fly." He turned and smiled at her.

"That's better," she said. "I want you to think like that all the time."

They arrived at the Green Lantern a few minutes later, and when they went inside, they noticed that Grace appeared to have an admirer. "That's Paul Ranier," Lucy said in a low voice. "He's quite a ladies' man."

"How do you know? Has he tried out his ways on you?"

"Well . . . yes, he did once, but my friend was with me. She threatened to shoot him if he bothered me again."

Kevin grinned. "Sounds like Babe!"

As they came closer they heard Grace say, "You just want girls to fall for you, Paul. Why don't you go give one of the others a chance?"

"Oh, come on. I only want *you*, Grace." Ranier was a lean and strong-looking Cajun with olive skin and lustrous dark eyes. He was well dressed and fine looking. According to the local gossip, he was the best zydeco dancer in Louisiana and played a fiddle, which made him popular at all the get-togethers. He was, indeed, a threat to the young women of the town, and more than once he had barely escaped a father's shotgun or a brother's beating.

"Hello, Grace," Lucy interrupted, seeing that Grace was

tired of Ranier's attention. "Come over and wait on us."

"Why, Lucy," Ranier said as he put his hand on her shoulder. "I haven't seen you in a while." She moved away quickly, and Ranier laughed. "You need a man, sweetheart. I could show you a good time. Why don't you and me go out tonight?"

When the Cajun tried to grab Lucy's arm, Kevin intervened, striking the man's hand away.

Ranier's face flushed. "Keep your hands off me!"

Ignoring him, Kevin said, "Come on, Lucy. Let's sit down."

"Don't turn your back on me," Ranier shouted.

"That's enough, Paul!" Grace snapped. "You've had too much to drink."

Ranier ignored her, grabbed Kevin by the arm, and struck him in the chest. Kevin reeled backward, then caught his balance.

Ranier advanced toward him, his fists up, when suddenly something struck him painfully between the neck and the shoulder. It numbed his whole right arm, and he turned around to see Grace standing there, holding a blackjack, her eyes flashing. "Get out of here, Paul, or I'll break your nose. Then the girls won't think you're so pretty."

Ranier lifted his arm and shook his head. "Say, that thing hurts bad. You sure got spirit, woman." He laughed, shaking off the pain and acting lighthearted. "I'll come back later. You and me got things to talk about."

When Kevin rose to forcibly help the man out the door, Grace put her hand up to stop him. "Don't pay any attention to Paul, Kev. He's always in a fight with someone." She led Kevin to a chair. "What can I get you?"

"Bring us two hamburgers and two Royal Crown colas," Lucy said.

"All right. Coming right up." As she turned to go away, she felt her anger at Ranier dissipate as her thoughts turned to her brother. She was so proud of Kevin and how he was showing the courage to be out in public now, and for how well he was doing with his flying lessons. It was also heartwarming to see his friendship with Lucy. *I don't think he's ever had a girl,* she thought, *and she's a good one to start with.*

★ ★ ★

Kevin was changing the oil in the biplane when he heard the roar of a motorcycle. He grinned when he saw Grace's bike heading toward him. He watched as she circled the plane twice, leaning in, then slammed on the brakes until the tires screeched. She came to a stop not a foot away from him, then reached down and shut off the engine. Kicking the stand down, she climbed off and pulled off her helmet. "Hello, brother. What have you been up to today? Any flying?"

"I got in two hours. I'm building it up, sis. Won't be long before I'll be talking about a solo flight."

"What happens after that?" Grace ran her hand through her strawberry blond hair and fluffed it out. Her cheeks were flushed from the windy ride.

"Get enough hours, and then I try for my private pilot's license. I'm just taking it one step at a time. I'll keep going up, up, up until I get to the top. Come on inside. I'll get you something to drink."

The two went into the office and found Babe sitting on her desk talking to Jerome Ruker, one of the other students. He was a balding man in his forties who was evidently well off. He was also one of the worst pilots Babe had ever seen. But he was stuck on her and learning to fly only because it gave him a chance to be with her. She kept him on because she needed the income.

"Hey, Grace. How are you doing?" Jerome said.

"All right, Jerome. How'd the lesson go?"

"He nearly killed us both," Babe said sourly. "Someday he's going to."

"Aw, come on, Babe," Jerome whined. "I'm getting better, and you know it."

Just then Lucy entered through the hangar entrance and

smiled. "Hi, Grace. You on your way to work?"

"No, I got the day off. Just been out riding around."

"How's the famous writer doing today?" Babe asked.

"If you're talking about Francis, he's okay. He's at home writing the great American novel, I expect." Grace laughed at her own humor.

"He and I are going to hear Billy Sanders tonight," Kevin put in. "That evangelist everybody's talking about. Anyone want to come?"

Grace shook her head. "Count me out."

Babe grinned. "That's right, Grace. Stay away from those preachers. They'll mess you up good. Besides, I don't think he'd look very favorably on a barmaid from the Green Lantern."

Grace glared at her. "I never saw a preacher I was afraid of." She lifted her chin. "I changed my mind, Kevin. I'll go with you."

"I want to go too," Lucy said.

"Good! We'll all go," Kevin said.

"Can I borrow the Ford, Babe?" Lucy asked. "Or maybe you'd like to come too."

"You won't catch me going to hear a preacher! I've got better things to do with my time," she grunted before turning back to shuffling papers on her desk.

★ ★ ★

The crowds were already streaming into the huge tent that had been erected just off Airline Avenue. As Grace walked beside Francis, she was sorry that she had agreed to come. She had only wanted to show Babe up. Kevin was walking ahead with Lucy, and the two were speaking excitedly. Grace turned to Francis with a frown. "I shouldn't have come. I don't really want to be here."

"Well, it made Kev happy," Francis replied. As they turned

toward one of the entrances, he asked, "Didn't you go to church much as a child?"

"Not at all—Bertha didn't believe in God." She said no more until the line slowed down and narrowed into a single file as people moved into the tent entrance. "I felt bad about not going to see her in prison. She gave me a hard life, but there were times when she was pretty nice."

Inside, Grace looked around at all the folding chairs that were filling up rapidly. Kevin led the group as close to the front as he could find four empty seats in a row. They moved in, trying to avoid stepping on toes, and Grace was thankful to sit down. A large choir was seated on chairs on the platform, and a lady was playing the piano beside them. Grace noticed that the crowd seemed to be made up of the affluent as well as the poor.

"Did you ever hear this man before, Francis?" she asked.

"No, but everyone I've talked with says he's a great preacher."

Grace felt more uncomfortable as time went on, and finally a man strode across the platform, smiling and holding his hands high. He stood in front of the lectern and said loudly, "Friends, we're going to worship the Lord. Will you please stand while we sing, 'All Hail the Power of Jesus' Name.'"

Grace stood with the others, and soon both the piano and the choir were drowned out by thousands of voices. It seemed that everyone knew the song except for her, and she stood there wishing she were anywhere in the world but in this place. The song was powerful as the tent filled with the sound.

As soon as the last verse was finished, the song leader said, "We've asked the Reverend Henri Duvall, one of your local pastors here in this fine city, to come pray for the service."

A tall, broad-shouldered man came forward, and the room was still as he prayed a short prayer, asking God's blessing on the service and the evangelist. When he sat down the song leader took over again, and for the next thirty minutes the congregation sang heartily. An offering was taken, and then a woman with a beautiful voice stepped to the microphone and sang "What a Friend We Have in Jesus."

As the woman sang the solo, the words made Grace even more uneasy. She could not explain it, but it seemed as though she were somehow the target of the hymn. The words echoed in her mind and brought a sense of great loneliness. Everyone else in the tent seemed happy, but Grace began to feel a longing for something she could not even define.

Finally the last verse came, and the singer's voice was clear and sweet yet powerful. After the last note of the solo died away, a nicely dressed man with white hair approached the microphone. He had a Bible in his hand, which he opened at once, and after stating how glad he was to see them all there, he said, "Sometimes it's necessary to preach to Christians. Much of Paul's writings were directed to the problems that had followed believers into the early church. I am sure that the pastors of the churches of this city do a good job, but tonight I want to speak to those of you who are lonely and perhaps do not even know why. Every city and small town I've traveled to in this country is filled with people who feel alone. Some of them may be in the midst of crowds all day long or may be members of large families, yet there's a longing for something they cannot name. I want to speak to those of you tonight who need a friend. Miss Johnson has just sung the beautiful song 'What a Friend We Have in Jesus,' and I want to offer Jesus to you tonight as your friend."

Grace had come prepared to dislike the preacher and the service. She had had several unfortunate experiences with men who had claimed to be church members, and this had created a resistance in her. But something was happening to her since coming into this place. To her surprise, the service was moving her, and as the preacher began to speak of how Jesus loved sinners, she grew more interested. He read from the Bible many stories of how Jesus sought out sinners and how He was criticized for eating and drinking with them.

Billy Sanders grew more passionate as he spoke of this aspect of Jesus' ministry.

As the sermon went on, Grace wanted to listen but at the same time grew more and more uncomfortable with the message. She was well acquainted with the loneliness that the preacher spoke of and knew that she had been lonely all of her life. A terrible sense of oppression came over her as she realized that nothing was going to change. She was always going to be alone. The Winslow family had tried to make her a part of them, but she was still an outsider. And now she realized that was partly because they were believers and she was not.

The evangelist presented Jesus as a man full of joy. "He was anointed with the oil of joy above His brethren," Sanders said. "Yet the book of Isaiah says He was a man of sorrow and acquainted with grief. We understand this was because He had to come to earth to die, to suffer, for all of our sins. But He was also filled with joy, for He was always at one with His Father. That's the way you can be. Go with joy. Even in the midst of tribulation, even in poverty or sickness, Jesus is always your friend. There is not a friend like the lowly Jesus, the old song goes, and He longs to be your friend.

"In the book of Revelation we read the verse, 'Behold, I stand at the door, and knock: if any man hear my voice, and open the door, I will come in to him, and will sup with him, and he with me.' Doesn't that move you?" Lowering his voice, he said, "All you have to do is open the door, and Jesus Christ, the Son of God, will come into your life. He will come to stay, for before He died, He said he didn't lose one of the people given to Him by the Father. Wouldn't you like to have a friend like that? Someone who would understand you and forgive you for every sin? Maybe you're wondering how many times He will forgive you. The answer is as many times as you ask. There may be some sitting here who say, 'But I've sinned too much. He wouldn't have me. I'm a great sinner.'"

Sanders lifted his Bible and said, "Thank God that you do not have to remain in your sins, for Jesus died to save great sinners! He loves you, dear friend, and this night you can have Him as your friend, both in this life and forever!"

Grace's eyes filled with tears, and she felt weak. Her hands were trembling, and she dropped her head. She could hear the preacher's voice, but there was another voice speaking inside her own heart. And a longing filled Grace Winslow such as she had never known.

Kevin was sitting on her right, and he reached over and put his hand on hers. He said nothing, but the gesture meant a great deal to Grace.

Finally, at the direction of the evangelist, they all stood and sang a song called "Just As I Am," and once again the words seemed directed straight at Grace.

A surprising impulse came over Grace to go down the aisle with the others, but her feet felt frozen to the floor. Many people were gathering in front of the stage, where they were greeted by some men who began to talk with them. Some of them were kneeling with their heads bowed, and one woman wept inconsolably.

"Sis, are you saved?" Kevin asked. "Do you know the Lord Jesus?"

"N-no . . ." Grace said, her voice breaking.

"I wish you did. Jesus loves you."

Kevin said no more, but his words caught at Grace. She whispered, "I-I can't!"

Kev put his arm around her and held her, and she brushed the tears away and blinked her eyes fiercely to keep any more from coming.

Francis too put his hand on her shoulder. Neither man said anything else to her, but she knew that both of them were praying for her.

Finally the benediction was pronounced, and they filed out slowly. Grace walked on ahead, brushing tears from her eyes. Kevin whispered to Lucy, "The Lord was speaking to Grace during the sermon. I want to see her saved more than anything."

Lucy squeezed his arm. "She will be, Kev—she will be!"

★ ★ ★

Babe and Kevin were returning to the airfield after an hour's instruction. Kevin banked the plane to make the turn back toward the field, and Babe shouted, "Okay, friend, land this airplane without tearing the wheels off."

Kevin put the plane down gently, and they finally rolled to a stop. "You did fine," Babe said as they climbed out. "You're ready for a solo. How about tomorrow?"

Kevin punched her shoulder lightly. "I was born for it, Babe!" he said with a grin.

The two made their way to the office, pulling off their leather jackets as they went. "Well, how was the preaching last night, Kev?"

"It was good, Babe. I wish you could have been there."

"That's not for me."

"Yes it is. It's for everybody."

"Did Grace hit the glory road?"

"No, she wasn't saved, but God spoke to her."

"Oh, great!" Babe rolled her eyes. "Now she'll be miserable! That's what religion does to people."

"You're wrong there, Babe. It makes them happy."

Babe turned and studied Kevin. "Are you happy?" They went into the office, and Babe plopped down in her desk chair.

He hesitated, then said, "I've never told anybody this, but I was mad at God for letting my face get messed up, but I'm happy now." He smiled his twisted smile at her, and then pointed to his face. "This has been hard for me to deal with. You know, you've helped me a lot."

"Me? I haven't done anything but teach you to fly."

"That's a lot for me, and I want you to know how much I appreciate it."

"You've paid your way," Babe said, uneasy with the conversation.

"No, Babe, I think it's more than that. I'd like to think we're friends."

Babe Delaney had grown fond of Kevin Winslow. She had a hard streak in her, but there was something in Kevin that appealed to her. She felt pity for him because of his face, and she had learned how hard it had been for him to come out of his cocoon. She also had seen that he had strong feelings for Lucy and was curious to see if anything would come of that.

"Friends it is," she declared. "Now go home and get some rest. Tomorrow's a big day."

CHAPTER TWENTY

A Busy Night at the Green Lantern

★ ★ ★

Cara Winslow rushed into Phil's studio excitedly, her eyes sparkling. "A letter from Kevin!"

Putting his brush down, Phil wiped his hands on a rag and said, "Well, read it."

Cara opened the envelope and took out a sheet of paper.

"Dear folks,

I am sorry I have not written as faithfully as I should, but I have been working long hours. I know that's no excuse, and I will do better in the future.

Things are going pretty well here. The big news is that I have soloed and am now taking advanced training! It was a great day for me, and Lucy and I went out to celebrate. The celebration wasn't much. Just hot dogs and colas, but I wished you two had been there."

"He mentions Lucy a lot. Do you think he's getting serious about her?" Cara asked, looking over the letter.

"I don't know. She seems like a nice young lady from what

he says. Why don't we go down there and visit them?"

"We can't do that. Kevin wants to do this on his own. We'll just have to be patient."

"You're probably right. Go on and read the rest of it."

Cara read the rest of the letter, which was taken up with details of Kevin's flying.

> "Grace is still working at the Green Lantern. She went to the revival meeting with us as I told you in my last letter, and since then she's been rather quiet. I just know God is doing something in her heart. So keep on praying.
>
> Francis is absolutely miserable. He can't get his book to work. He's gotten grumpy, which is unusual for him. Last night I said something about the food not being seasoned quite well enough, and he shouted at me, "If you don't like the way I cook, you can do it yourself!" He calmed down later, but he's usually so easy-going. You might remember him in your prayers too.
>
> I must close now. My training is really tough, but I'm going to make it. God bless both of you, and keep me in your prayers.
>
> Love, Kevin"

"God's doing something in all of their lives, I think," Phil said, taking the letter and scanning it. "How I'd love to rush down there. I want to do something for Grace, but I don't know what."

"We just have to be patient, Phil. You can't rush God."

* * *

At the Green Lantern, Grace wearily pushed Paul Ranier away for at least the tenth time. The lunch crowd had thinned out, leaving just a few regulars in the place. "Paul, you're a real pain in the neck, you know it? Why don't you gimme a break?"

Ranier grinned at her, and his white teeth gleamed against

his olive skin. "We go together, baby. I'm gonna get you to see it someday. How about tonight? Me and you, we'll have us a good time."

"You never give up, do you?" Grace shook her head and walked away. "I'm going home," she said to Luann, the other barmaid.

Luann was chewing gum with her usual vigor. "Why don't you go out with Paul? He's a good-looking guy."

"I've seen enough of his kind to do me for a lifetime," Grace said. "I'll come back at seven and take over, Luann."

Grace changed into her leather motorcycle outfit, and as she made her way out, she received several appreciative whistles from the men who were nursing their beer. She ignored them as she went outside and stepped onto her bike. Starting it up, she felt relief wash over her that her first shift of the day was over. She was sick of working at the Green Lantern but knew she could not quit. Her paycheck was helping to keep Kevin in flying school. She had never for one minute regretted working the long hours and giving all the money to Babe for Kevin's tuition. It was the first unselfish thing she had done in her life, and it felt good. Now as she headed home, she looked forward to a good meal and a nap before facing the night shift. She had agreed to work the breakfast and lunch shift for another waitress on the condition that she could take some time for a break before the evening shift.

When she arrived home, she found Francis sitting at the kitchen table staring at a blank sheet of paper. She looked over his shoulder. "What's the matter, Francis?"

"What's the matter! I can't write. That's what's the matter!"

Taken aback by his sharp answer, she said, "Don't worry. It'll come to you." She looked around and saw that he had not prepared dinner yet. "You want me to cook?"

"I don't care," he snapped.

"Look, I work hard at that bar. It's not too much to ask you to make sandwiches or something."

Miriam was out of her cage, and she fluttered to Key's

shoulder, crying hoarsely, "My Francis! My Francis!"

"He's all yours, you crazy bird!" Grace said and stomped out of the kitchen.

Francis got up and began slapping supper together. He jerked a pan out of the cabinet, opened a can of soup, and poured it in. When Grace came back from washing up, he had a sandwich and soup on the table and was sitting back at the typewriter staring at the blank sheet of paper.

Grace had never seen him like this and knew that the book was really getting to him. She ate the soup and sandwich, then said, "I guess I'll take a nap."

"All right."

She went to her bedroom to lie down and quickly fell asleep. She had been working double shifts lately, and she slept like a rock. It was late in the afternoon when she awoke, and she went to the kitchen to find Kevin coming in.

"Hi, sis," he said, giving her a hug and a kiss on the cheek.

She squeezed him in return. "How did the great flyer do today?"

"Fine, sis. Hey, Francis, why don't you let me take you up? It's against the rules, but I'm sure Babe would look the other way for you."

Key gave him a skeptical look, then griped, "I don't have time for that."

"My, we are touchy today, aren't we?" Kevin said. "What's for supper?"

Francis glared at him. "Bread and water. If you don't like that, fix something yourself."

"Wait a minute," Grace said testily. "That's not what the deal was. You stay home and write and do the meals, and we go to work. You ain't holdin' up your end of the bargain."

"I didn't want to come down to this lousy place to begin with."

"Well, nobody is asking you to stay!" Grace yelled.

A shouting match ensued, and finally Francis said, "I don't care what you do. If you want to be a barmaid, go to it. If you want to kill yourself flying, Kevin, that's fine with me."

He yanked the paper out of his typewriter, wadded it up, and threw it on the floor. He glared at them both and walked out the door, slamming it so hard the windows rattled.

"He's got some nerve!" Grace exclaimed. "What'sa matter with him? Who elected him king?"

"He's worried about that book," Kevin said. "You know how writers are. We'll just have to be patient with him."

"Patient! I don't have to put up with any of his touchy artistic stuff. He can go on back to New York right now for all I care."

* * *

By eleven o'clock that night Grace's feet ached, and she had given up trying to smile at the customers. The restaurant had been packed all evening, and she had had to handle all the tables herself. Between taking orders and dodging hands that reached out for her, she was ready to consign the Green Lantern to the infernal regions.

Wiping off a table, she looked up to see Francis enter. He caught her eye and came over to her. "I need to talk to you," he said.

"I can't talk. I'm working."

She turned around and pushed her cart of dirty dishes into the kitchen. When she emerged again, she found Francis sitting at a table waiting for her. "You got a hearing problem?" she snapped. "I said I can't talk to you now."

She ignored him for a while and continued working, then finally went over and asked, "You want somethin' to eat or drink?"

"No, I just want to talk to you," Francis said calmly, "but I'll wait until you get off."

"How'd you get here?"

"I walked."

She stared at him. She was still angry over the way he had acted, but she said, "Well, what is it?"

"I'm sorry for the way I acted."

She could tell by his expression that he was miserable. She sat down across the table from him. "Well, I wasn't too nice myself," she admitted.

"It's that book, Grace. I've wanted so badly to be a writer . . . more than anything in the world." He looked down, his shoulders slumped. "But I can't do it. I just can't do it!"

Grace's heart melted with pity for Francis. She knew what it was to want something she couldn't have. She reached out and pushed a lock of his hair back. "It's all right, Francis. You'll do it. You're just having a hard time. We all go through those. You'll write that crazy book. I know you will."

He got to his feet and summoned a smile. "You really think so?"

"Sure I do."

"You know, when you say it, I actually believe it," Francis said. "But when I'm alone, I just can't."

Grace got up too and hugged him. "There. You go on back and write something now. When I get home you can read it to me."

"All right, I'll—" Key had no chance to finish for a hand had jerked Grace away. He turned to see Paul Ranier, who was drunk, an angry look twisting his face. "Hey, mister, leave my woman alone!"

"I'm not your woman!" Grace hollered.

"You hush up! I'm gonna make sure he don't come near you no more."

Key had no time to answer or even think as Ranier caught him full in the face with a wicked right cross. He went down at once, and Ranier started for him. Grace grabbed Paul's arm and screamed, "Leave him alone!" He turned around and slapped her full in the face. "You stay out of this. I'm gonna stomp him. You're *my* woman!"

Grace put everything she had into her right fist and caught him in the face, but he hardly noticed and returned her punch with a solid right that knocked her backward. She crashed into a table, and lights flashed in her head as she went down. . . .

* * *

"Yes, this is Kevin."

"Hey, Kevin, this is Gus. I'm the bartender down at the Green Lantern."

"Yeah, Gus?"

"There's trouble down here. You'd better come."

"What is it?"

"You know that Ranier guy who's been bugging your sister? He's roughin' up your sister and that guy that lives with you."

"Have you called the police?" Kevin asked.

"We don't wanna involve the cops. We can deal with it—but you'd better come."

"I'll be right there."

Kevin slammed the phone down, ran out of the house, and jumped into the truck. He got to the Green Lantern in record time, and when he ran inside, he saw Ranier and Grace sitting at the bar, Ranier hanging on to Grace's arm—and he also saw that the side of her face was puffy where he had struck her. Anger surged through Kevin. He was ordinarily the most gentle of men, but the sight of his sister's bruised face caused him to lose it. He rushed over to Ranier and then saw Francis on the floor, his face bloodied. The bartender was trying to calm Ranier.

Kevin had never been in a fight in his life, but he knew just what to do. He threw a punch that caught Ranier in the chin with a terrible force. Ranier was driven back against the bar, then bounced off toward Kevin, who kept swinging and knocked him down again.

"Look out, he's got a gun!" Gus called out.

Kevin had seen the gun Ranier had pulled from his back pocket. He fell forward, grabbed the gun, and twisted it out of Ranier's hand, thankful that the Cajun was drunk and not too coordinated. Kevin stood back at a safe distance and held the gun loosely.

Ranier staggered to his feet. Blood was dripping from his left eyebrow, and he snarled, "You ain't got the nerve to shoot me!"

Kevin lifted the handgun and squeezed the trigger. The bullet hit Ranier's leg, and as he went down, he cried with outraged disbelief, "You shot me!" and lay on the floor holding his thigh.

"You'd better get to a doctor," Kevin said calmly. The rage had left him with the shot of the gun, and he went over and helped Francis to his feet. He said to Grace, "Can you make it to the truck, sis?"

"Sure, but I've got my cycle here."

"If you can drive the truck, I'll take the cycle home."

"All right, Kev."

Kevin looked at the battered faces and shook his head. "I wonder if it's against the law to shoot people in Louisiana."

He handed the gun to the bartender, and said, "Here, Gus. If Paul decides to press charges, you know where to find me."

"Ranier don't want no trouble. He's had enough of the police. So don't you worry none about that."

Kevin and Grace helped Francis out to the car, and when they got him inside, Kevin asked, "Sis, are you sure you can drive?"

"I'm all right, but I'm gonna have a terrible black eye tomorrow." She grabbed his arm. "I'm glad you came, Kev."

"Go ahead," Kevin said. "I'll follow you on the cycle. Take it easy. We don't need a speeding ticket on top of everything else!"

CHAPTER TWENTY-ONE

GRACE ABOUNDING

★ ★ ★

Grace awoke to hear voices coming from the kitchen, and for a time she lay still, unwilling to get out of bed. The violence at the Green Lantern had drained her, and she had fallen into bed and gone to sleep at once but had been troubled by bad dreams. Several times she had awakened during the night frightened. She could not help remembering the sermon she had heard about Jesus, the friend of sinners. More than once she had cried out, "God, I don't know what you want with me. I can't do anything for you."

Glancing at the alarm clock, she saw that it was after eight. Kevin usually left before this, but she heard one of the men scurrying around for at least ten minutes before she heard the front door slam and the house become silent.

Throwing back the covers, she put on a robe and went to the bathroom, where she drew a tub of hot water and soaked for twenty minutes. When she got out and dried off, she went to the mirror and examined her puffy face and the purple bruise under her eye. She went back to her room and dressed, then went out to the kitchen.

Francis was sitting at the table reading a book and holding

a cup of coffee. His face was puffy, and he said in a subdued voice, "Sit down. I'll fix you some bacon and eggs."

She got a large mug out of the cupboard and filled it with coffee, then sat down. Neither of them spoke as Francis fixed breakfast and she drank her coffee. When he put the plate in front of her and refilled her coffee cup, she said, "That was a pretty bad scene last night."

"Terrible. I couldn't believe Kev actually shot that fellow."

"Neither could I. I didn't know he had it in him."

Francis said no more, acting almost as if he were embarrassed, and as she ate slowly, he sat down across from her again. "I'm not too good in situations like that."

"That's okay. There's too much fightin' in the world anyway."

"But a man should be able to fight. I tried to take lessons once in self-defense, but I was never any good at it."

Grace put peach jam on her toast and took a bite of it. Chewing slowly, she shook her head. "I'm not going in to work today."

"Good. You've been working too hard. I think I'll go out and get a job and let you take care of the cooking for a change."

Grace looked at him with surprise. "You don't have to do that. I really don't mind working."

"It doesn't seem right. You work too hard."

Grace finished her breakfast and then went outside for a walk, feeling uncomfortable around Francis. When she got back to the house, she saw that he was gone and thought he had probably left to give her some privacy. She was walking around the house aimlessly when she spotted Kevin's Bible on the coffee table. She picked it up and sat down in the overstuffed chair to read it. She opened up the Old Testament to the book of Leviticus, but that didn't interest her. She flipped the pages to the New Testament, hunting for some of the selections that Reverend Sanders had used in his sermon, and she found one of the stories he had used as an illustration. It concerned the woman caught in adultery whom some of the religious leaders brought to Jesus. They demanded that she be stoned according to Moses' law. Jesus, however, did not answer them. Instead, He sat down and wrote in the dust. One by one the men left Jesus and the woman alone, and Jesus asked her, "Where are those thine accusers?" When the woman said they were gone, He said, "Neither do I condemn thee: go, and sin no more."

Grace read the final words of Jesus again—"Go and sin no more." She closed the Bible and sat thinking. "That's what I need," she said. "To sin no more. God knows I've sinned enough in my life!"

★ ★ ★

That afternoon Kevin came home from the flight school while Grace was enjoying the adventures of Amos and Andy on the radio. Kevin quickly cleaned up and left again, saying that he and Lucy were going out for dinner and a movie. Francis fixed a nice supper—meatloaf, green beans, and mashed potatoes. He asked the blessing, and when Grace lifted her head, she said, "Are you gonna write tonight?"

"I don't know. If anything comes to me, I will."

Neither of them seemed to have much of an appetite. Their faces were still puffy and sore from the fight with Ranier, but neither of them mentioned the incident at the Green Lantern.

"I'll wash the dishes," Grace offered after they had eaten as much as they were going to.

"You don't have to do that."

"You do it all the time. You go in and listen to the radio."

Grace washed the dishes, cleaned up the kitchen, and then sat down in the living room. Miriam flew down and perched on Francis's shoulder, cooing and muttering "My Francis!"

"That bird is downright possessive," Grace remarked. "But you take such good care of her, I guess I don't blame her." The radio was on but Grace's mind was elsewhere. After a time she noticed that the news broadcast seemed to be disturbing Francis.

"What'sa matter? You look worried," she said.

"It's all this trouble over in Europe. That fellow Hitler is a madman!"

"Europe is way across the ocean. It don't have nothin' to do with us," she said, surprised that he would be concerned about something so far away.

"It's not as far as you think, Grace. If there's a war over there, America could wind up involved in it. I think it's likely to happen."

Grace listened while he explained the problems in Europe. She could not understand much about it, for she had never been very interested in politics or foreign affairs. When he stopped to listen to the radio again, she said, "I guess I'll go sit on the porch for a while. It's awfully hot in here."

She went out and sat on the porch swing, and after a time Francis came out and sat beside her. They spoke little, but finally Grace blurted out, "I don't know what's the matter with me, Francis. I'm miserable."

"Why? You're not sick, are you?"

"No, it's that sermon we heard at the tent meeting. I've been worried ever since then."

Her words touched Francis deeply, and he held her eyes with his own. "I think," he said quietly, "that God is speaking to you."

"I don't know what that means. Tell me how you found God."

She listened as he related the story of his conversion. "I just called on Jesus," he concluded, "and He saved me."

"It's not that easy for me. You'd probably never done anything wrong." She dropped her head and stared at her hands. Night was falling now, and murky blackness was gathering about the house and filling the streets. "I've been so bad, Francis," she whispered. "You don't know what I've done—and I couldn't tell you. I wouldn't want you to hear it."

"You don't have to tell me," he said quickly. "God knows everything you've done."

"He must hate me, then."

"Hate you! No, He loves you! Didn't you hear what the evangelist said? Jesus loves sinners. If He didn't, we wouldn't have anywhere to turn for help. He loves you, Grace. Believe that."

The silence seemed to surround them, and Grace felt utterly miserable. Tears welled up in her eyes. "Look at me. I'm squallin' like a kid, and I don't even know why."

"You're lonesome. That's why. We're all lonesome without God."

Francis began to quote Scripture verses—verses of hope and of man's need for God. "You don't have to be unhappy, Grace. That's not God's will. You need to give your heart to Him."

"I can't do it, Francis."

"Yes you can. Look," he said, "the hardest thing for any human being to do is to give up his own will. But that's what God asks of us. You've tried living your own way for quite a few years, and it hasn't worked very well, has it?"

"No, it sure hasn't."

"If you'll just call on God and confess your sins, He's waiting to make you His child. Don't you see?"

"It . . . it all sounds too easy."

"It is easy. If it were hard, we couldn't do it."

He said no more, and Grace held her hands together to stop them from trembling. She wanted to get up and run away, but somehow she knew that this was the moment God had been waiting for. She felt a sense of His presence just as she had during the invitation at the revival. It made her feel frightened and helpless and alone. "Help me!" she finally cried out to Francis.

"It's time for you to come to God, Grace. I'm going to pray, and I want you to pray too. You can pray out loud or silently. Whichever you wish. It doesn't matter. What does matter is that you tell God that you sinned, that you want to leave all that behind, and that you want to give your life to Jesus. Will you do that?"

"I'll . . . I'll try."

Grace heard Francis pray for her; then she knew it was time for her to pray. She did not know how, for she had never learned, but she whispered, "Oh, God, I'm so terrible! I've done such awful things." She thought of the many bad things she had done, and they weighed down on her so heavily she thought she couldn't bear it. "Oh, God, I need to be different! I ask you to make me different. Let me be clean. Forgive my sins in the name of Jesus. . . ."

Grace lost all track of time as she prayed fervently, letting her tears fall freely. When she finally said amen, Francis prayed for God's blessing on her life. He put his arm around her, and she leaned against him, weeping.

When her tears finally stopped, she became aware of a sense of peace in her spirit, and she could only utter thank you over and over again. She finally pulled a handkerchief out and dried her tears. "What do I do now?" she asked.

"You start by telling God you want to please Him."

"I do, Francis. I really do."

"And I think you should call your parents. They'll be so happy to hear this. But wait till Kevin gets in. He's been praying for you ever since he learned you were his sister."

Grace was thankful for Francis's arm around her shoulders. She was still trembling slightly, uncertain about what the future would hold now. After a long time, she said, "Francis, will you help me?"

"Help you with what?"

"With everything," she whispered. "I don't know how to be a Christian."

"Why, sure I'll help you all I can, and so will Kev."

"But I want more than that. I want to go back home to Mom and Dad and learn to be the kind of woman they want me to be."

"They'll be so happy."

"But I don't know how to do that. You'll need to teach

me." She sat up and put her hand on his chest. "Teach me how to talk and which fork to use."

He smiled. "I don't think that will be too hard. I've always wanted to be a professor like Henry Higgins."

"Who's he?"

"Just a character in a play by George Bernard Shaw called *Pygmalion*. He took a young woman off the streets of London and made her into a fine lady."

"That's what I want!" she exclaimed. She looked at him with stars in her eyes. "Do you think you can do that?"

"I think you *are* a fine lady, Grace. And I can certainly teach you which fork to use."

"When can we start?"

"You've already started," he said. He leaned over and kissed her cheek. "I'm happy for you, Grace."

She put her head on his shoulder, and he held her. She felt safe and secure and knew that things were going to be different.

PART FOUR

September–November 1935

★ ★ ★

CHAPTER TWENTY-TWO

A Moonlit Dance

★ ★ ★

The two-seater plane banked as Kevin touched the controls lightly. He enjoyed flying Babe's other planes with the open cockpits, but at times like this it was nice to take this one up and be able to sit side by side with his passenger. "Look down there. There's the football stadium where we went to watch the Tigers play."

Lucy looked down. "Go down closer so I can see where we sat." Even with the enclosed cockpit, the two were practically yelling at each other as they made themselves heard over the engine.

He laughed and kept banking the plane slightly. "I can land on the field if you want me to. Maybe go right between the goalposts."

Lucy turned and smiled brilliantly at him. She was wearing a light blue dress, and her hair glowed in the sun that flooded through the windshield of the light plane. "All right. Let's see you do it."

"I was only kidding. These wings wouldn't fit through there."

"Take me over the river, Kev."

He leveled the plane, added throttle, and gained height. Soon they were over the Mississippi. "I never can get over how crooked the river is," she exclaimed.

"What'd you expect—that it would go straight?"

"No, I've seen it on maps, of course, but when you see the real thing, it's amazing how it twists and turns."

"An old river does things like that. New rivers, like the Colorado, are straight."

"How do they get crooked?"

"They begin to eat away at the sides of the banks, cutting into them until finally you have a curve. Look down there. You see that little lake?"

"The one right beside the river?"

"Yeah, you see, it's curved just like the river. It used to be a part of the river, but over time it became cut off from the river. A lake like that is called an oxbow lake. Funny thing about them," he mused as he kept his hands lightly on the controls, "they don't have life in them like the river does."

"Why's that?"

"Because nothing comes in and nothing goes out. That's the way it is with the Dead Sea, they tell me. It doesn't have any outlets, so it's just a dead lake."

The plane went through a large cloud, and for a moment the earth was blotted from their view. Lucy looked over at Kevin, and even though she knew his face was scarred, she had stopped thinking about it anymore. Now she saw only the man behind the face and knew she was falling in love with him. She could not tell how he felt about her, however, for even though they had been spending a fair amount of time together, he never said anything romantic.

"Why are you looking at me?" he said when he realized she was watching him.

"I was just thinking how much fun I have with you."

"Do you really?" He smiled. "You wouldn't have before I came here."

"Why not?"

"Because I was like the Dead Sea. I was taking everything

in, but I didn't give out anything."

"How do you mean?"

"After my face got scarred, I just quit seeing anybody. I suppose Grace told you that."

"Yes, she did."

"I felt so hideous, and when I saw people looking at me, I couldn't stand their pity. So I just built myself a little world at home and did nothing for years but tend flowers and work on engines. I stayed away from people."

"That's sad, Kev."

"Yes it is, but that's over now. I'm going to be a famous flyer." He smiled at her again. "And I thank the Lord for bringing me out of that prison I was in."

"I'm glad," Lucy said simply. She reached over and put her hand on his arm. "It's good that you're out and into the world, and you are going to be a great flyer. Babe says so."

"You know what I'd really like to do with flying?"

"What? Fly the mails?"

"No, that's a bit too regimented. Same thing over and over. I'd like to try one of those long-distance flights. You know, across the Atlantic—like Lindbergh."

"But that's already been done."

"Sure it has. But I haven't done it yet! And there are plenty of other things I could do. Like break the speed record from coast to coast."

"Take me with you when you try that, Kev."

Kevin laughed. "I'm a long way from that yet. It'll take a lot of money to buy a plane or have one built that could break the record."

He turned the plane and headed toward New Orleans, and soon they were looking down at the Crescent City.

"New Orleans looks a lot better from the air than it does when you're in it," Lucy said. "I never liked the French Quarter. People come from all over the world to see it, but it's really a grubby place."

She knew the city well and pointed out the different sections of it as they flew over.

"We'd better get back, I suppose," he said as the buildings disappeared behind them.

"It's been such fun." She watched several puffy clouds pass by. "What's Francis doing these days? And Grace?"

"Well, today he's out shopping with her. Buying her clothes."

Lucy's eyes grew large with surprise. "Francis is buying clothes for Grace? What does he know about that?"

"It's part of the new Grace. Since she accepted the Lord, she has the idea that she's got to make herself over completely before she can be a part of the family. So she pesters Francis to teach her how to talk and which fork to eat with. I tell her she can just be herself—that the family will accept her just as she is. But she wants to please them."

"What else is he teaching her?"

"He's giving her a complete education. He reads books to her and makes her read them. Makes her keep up with current events—" Kevin laughed—"and he's correcting her grammar! Have you been around her lately?"

"No."

"Every time she says *ain't* he pinches her. Her arm's black and blue, but she's learning." They were descending toward the airfield in Baton Rouge.

"That's a hard way to learn."

"I suppose, but she's really happy, Lucy. When she first came to our place, I could see the unhappiness in her eyes. Since she's been saved, she's a completely different person."

"Yes, she's been to church every Sunday."

Kevin brought the plane in for a smooth landing, and they rolled up to the hangar. He cut the engine, and when they'd climbed out, she smiled up at him. "That was a nice flight, Kev. Thank you for taking me."

He looked down at her as she stood by his side. "I've been wanting to ask you something, Lucy. You don't have to say yes if you don't want to."

"What is it?"

"Would you go with me to New York and meet my family?"

She stood very still. This was the first time he had ever asked her to do something that would involve her in his life. She was surprised and at the same time felt a touch of fear. "I . . . I don't know whether I should."

"I thought you might like it," he said. "But if you don't want to—"

"It's not that I don't want to," Lucy said quickly, "but I'm afraid of them."

Kevin blinked with surprise. "You're afraid of my family? Well, that's silly! You haven't even met them."

"I know, but they're rich, and your father's famous, and Babe and I have had a hard life. I wouldn't know how to act around them."

He squeezed her arm and smiled. "You'll do fine. They'll love you. I guarantee it."

Lucy felt a surge of joy at his confidence in her. "If you're sure about that, Kev, then I'd like to meet them sometime. But only if Babe agrees to the trip."

* * *

Francis felt out of place in the dress department of Bon Marché. He had insisted on bringing Grace to the department store and picking out some clothes for her. Now she was in the dressing room trying on a couple she had picked out, and he stood uncertainly among the racks. From time to time the saleswoman would look at him and smile, and he would smile back.

I don't know what I'm doing here, he thought. *It's ridiculous my trying to be Henry Higgins. I never thought that play made much sense anyway.* He moved around and, from time to time, checked the tag of a dress, occasionally muttering to himself about the prices.

Finally Grace came out, looking self-conscious. "Well, how do you like it?" she asked.

"Turn around and let me see."

Grace spun around and then looked at herself in the mirror. "It's swell, ain't it? I like—Ow!" She grabbed her arm where he had pinched it, temper flaring in her eyes. "That hurt!"

"That was our agreement. When you say *ain't*, I pinch you."

"I didn't mean in public!"

"It's the only way to learn. Education is painful," he said with a grin. As a matter of fact, she was doing very well at improving her speech. She had a quick mind, and the two had worked on grammar every day for an hour. "You want me to kiss your arm and make it well?"

"No! Keep your grubby hands off me!" She examined her reflection in the mirror. "How do you like the dress? I think it's swell."

"It's awful!"

Grace glared at him. "What's wrong with it? You don't like anything I pick out."

"I'll tell you why it's awful. In the first place, pink is not a good color for you. With your hair color and your light skin, you need something darker. In the second place, it's too tight. It makes you look cheap. In the third place, that style was popular several years ago. Now it's outdated. You want me to go on?"

Grace glared at him. "All right, then. You pick out a dress."

"That's what I came for. Now, you just wait a minute."

Grace had often lost her temper during the "lessons" that she endured with Francis. She had asked him to help her with her clothes, with her speech, and with her manners, and he had only agreed after making her promise to do what he said and to take his word for things. As much as she wanted his help, it was hard work changing habits developed over her whole life. She had been willing enough as far as grammar and speech and manners, but the matter of clothes was another thing. She watched as he moved up and down the racks and selected a dress.

"Go put this on."

Grace snatched it and went back into the dressing room. She took off the offensive dress, slipped this one on, and looked at herself in the mirror. A smile came to her face. "Well, I'll be dipped! The runt does know something about clothes."

She went out and Francis smiled. "Now, that dress has class."

The emerald green dress was made of silk gauze with a round neckline edged in black. It had loose three-quarter-length pointed sleeves, an ankle-length skirt, and a matching sash trimmed in black.

"It costs so much," she said. "We don't have the money."

"I've been squirreling some away."

"You can't spend your money on me."

"Yes I can. You go get changed and then we'll pick out some shoes."

"I've got a pair of shoes."

"You've got a pair of motorcycle boots and a pair of sneakers. Don't argue. Go change your clothes."

She changed and then they waited at the counter. The saleslady commented, "Your husband has got good taste, ma'am."

"He's not my husband. He's my owner. I'm his slave."

Francis flushed, but the woman laughed. "He has excellent taste anyway."

As they left the dress department, Francis said, "Let's go find you a nice pair of shoes."

* * *

"I can't learn all this stuff, Francis."

Francis turned the heat down under the gumbo. "Yes you can. Now, tell me again what's happening in Europe."

Francis had insisted that Grace learn about current world affairs. He was shocked at how little she knew and had begun buying newspapers and news magazines for her. He gave her assignments every day and the next day grilled her on what she had learned.

"Well," Grace said, her brow wrinkled, "that man you made me read about, Adolf Hitler, has passed some laws."

"What's the name of them?" He started mashing the potatoes.

"Let me see. I forget. Oh yeah, the Nuremberg Laws."

"And what are the Nuremberg Laws?"

"The paper said they've made Jews second-class citizens."

"And what else?"

"Umm, they've made sex between Jews and non-Jews a capital offense. What does that mean?"

"It means the man's a fanatic. I think he's the most dangerous man in Europe. Did you read the old magazines I found with the stories about him?"

"Yes, but I don't understand most of them."

"Okay, just tell me what you do understand."

"Okay—in 1933 Hitler was the leader of the Nazi party, and he became chancellor of Germany. And he grabbed all the power."

"That's right." He checked on the crawfish. "Let's move on to art. Can you name a famous contemporary sculptor?"

Grace wrinkled her nose. "I remember Barbara Hepworth. But her sculptures just look like odd shapes to me."

"That's called nonrepresentational sculpture."

"It just looks strange to me."

"Well, when somebody talks to you about sculpture, just tell them how great her work is! Now, who's a top movie star?"

"Fred Astaire."

"And what's his latest film?"

"*Top Hat*. I know stuff like that."

Francis had taken her to see the film, and she had been

delighted. "I'm tired of studying. Let me help you with supper."

"All right. You set the table. It's almost ready."

When they sat down to supper, he said, "You ask the blessing."

"I'm not very good at that, but I'll try." They bowed their heads, and she asked a simple blessing. When she looked up, her eyes were sparkling. "I never thought I'd be able to do anything like pray in front of anyone. I still don't do it well."

"Yes you do. You're very simple and direct, and I think that's what God likes." He picked up his fork. "Tell me how you like this crawfish."

She took a bite. "I've finally gotten used to eating it, but I still say they look like bugs—and I'm not gonna suck the heads."

"You'll never be a true Louisianan until you do that."

"I have learned to love gumbo, so maybe I am a true Louisianan after all."

He guided the subject back to her studies. "Did you read *Oliver Twist*?"

"Yes, I read it, but it was awful. Why would anybody wanna write about a poor orphan that gets mistreated by everyone?"

"Dickens wrote to entertain, but he also wrote to educate people and change things. You see, he thought if he'd write about the evils that were in his world, people would read about them and do something about them."

"Did they?"

"A lot of historians say that Dickens changed his world with his books."

"I'd still rather read a nice love story with a happy ending."

"You're an incurable romantic."

The two now made a ritual out of their mealtimes. Grace used to think mealtimes were simply for eating, but Francis had taught her that it was a good time to talk and had managed to teach her to slow down and stop eating in a feeding frenzy.

After they finished the meal and washed the dishes, they turned on the radio in the living room and then went outside and sat on the porch steps. They listened to the song coming through the open windows. "All right," Francis said, "name as many of the constellations as you can."

"Why do I have to do that? They're pretty, and I like them, but who's ever going to care whether I know the names of constellations?"

"You never know what you'll need. That's what education is. You learn a lot of stuff that seems useless, like algebra, but sooner or later you use what you have. Now, what do you see?"

"Okay . . . there's Orion . . . and Ursa Major and Ursa Minor . . . Cassiopeia . . ."

After she named about ten constellations, he said, "That's good. I don't brag on you much, Grace," he said with a smile, "but you're doing well. I'm proud of you."

Grace felt her face glowing. "Thank you, Francis," she murmured. "That's good to hear, but I know I've got a long way to go." She hesitated before going on. "I'm not treating you fairly."

"Why not? What are you talking about?"

"What about your book? You spend so much time teaching me."

"Oh, I work on it while you're at the Green Lantern."

"How's it going?"

"Much better. I've got most of it done in my head now. Sometimes it's hard to get it from your head to paper."

They grew silent and listened as the music came floating out onto the porch.

"Let's dance," Grace said.

"I'm not much of a dancer."

"Well, I'm a great dancer. Come on."

She pulled Francis to his feet, and he put his arm around her waist and took her hand. She sang along as they danced to a popular tune. "Hey, you're not a bad dancer at all." She was very aware that her face was only a few inches from his. "How are you and Babe getting along?" she asked suddenly.

"That's ancient history."

"She still likes you, though. I can tell."

"I like her too."

"Were you going to marry her once?"

"We never talked about it." He seemed hesitant and then finally said, "She was the first woman—and the last—that I ever knew well. She had a lot more experience than I had with relationships. We fought all the time."

She was curious and wanted to ask him more, but a slower song began and she decided to let her question wait for another time.

"Grace," he said suddenly, "I'm afraid I'm going to do something you won't like."

They stopped dancing, but he was still holding her in his arms. "What do you mean? What are you going to do?"

"I'm going to kiss you, so you'd better slap my face now and get it over with."

Grace smiled. "Why don't you just do it and we'll see what I do."

He pulled her closer, and she put her arms around his neck. She had wondered how he felt about her, and now to her pleased surprise, she felt a possessiveness about him. She held his kiss for a time and then pulled away. "Is this where I slap your face?"

"I guess so."

"I don't think I will this time. No harm in a little kiss."

"You know, Grace, there's a sweetness in you. I've always sensed it there, but now I think everyone can see it."

She did not answer, for memories of her sordid past welled up in her mind. She thought of the awful things she had done—the drunken parties and the men—and she felt terrible. "I guess I'll go in now," she said quickly.

"But it's early yet. I thought we could work some more on your lessons."

"Not tonight." She went inside, leaving Francis bewildered. *Maybe it's something I've done.*

Grace went to her room and lay down on the bed fully dressed. She struggled with her memories of life on the road with the carnival. *I wish I had been different. I wish I hadn't done all those things.* She lay there for a long time feeling worse and worse, and finally she told herself heavily, "I can't go back and change the past."

CHAPTER TWENTY-THREE

LUCY'S RELUCTANCE

★ ★ ★

Babe looked up from her desk, which was cluttered with papers. Her green eyes took in Lucy as she entered the office. "What are you all geared up for?"

Lucy flushed. She was wearing a pair of light blue slacks with a tan blouse, and her hair was tied back with a dark blue ribbon. "Kev is going to take me up for a flight."

Babe leaned back in her chair, folded her arms across her chest, and studied Lucy silently. She had always been overly protective of her younger sister, whom she had practically raised after the death of their parents. She had guided Lucy through measles, acne, and all the other perils of childhood and adolescence—including the heartbreaking loss of a boyfriend with flaming red hair at the age of thirteen. She remembered what her last mechanic had said about Lucy: *"That sister of yours is a looker. You better be careful some sneaky fella don't snatch her away when you're not lookin'!"*

Fortunately for Babe, Lucy had never given her the slightest reason for worry. She always seemed to have a built-in desire to do the right thing, and although Babe herself was not religious, she was glad that Lucy walked the straight and narrow—she was even baptized and went to church every Sunday.

"Seems like you've been making quite a few of these flights lately."

Color touched Lucy's cheeks, but she held her head up almost defiantly. "Maybe I have," she said.

"You never liked to fly with me all that much. You're not getting sweet on scarface, are you?"

"Don't you call him that!"

Babe started at Lucy's sharp reply. "What's going on between you two?"

Upset, Lucy ran her hand across her hair. "I think you're awful! Kevin's had enough trouble with people. They stare at him all the time. I'd like to poke their eyes out!"

"Take it easy, little sister!"

"I *won't* take it easy, and don't you ever call him that awful name again! You hear me?"

Babe was shocked at Lucy's rare outburst. "You're right," she admitted. "It's bad enough without people making remarks." She rose from her desk and put her hand on her sister's shoulder. "Are you really serious about this guy, Lucy?"

"I . . . I like him a lot. He's the most gentle man I've ever known, and he's got such a good sense of humor. He keeps it hidden because he's been hurt so much by people. But I have a better time with him than I've ever had with anyone else."

"Does he ever try to get fresh with you?"

"No!"

"Well, that's a good thing. The way you've softened up to him, I believe he could get anything he wants from you."

Lucy colored, then said firmly, "He's never been anything but a gentleman with me, Babe."

Babe felt a sharp pang in her gut, and she drew her lips together into a straight line. "I should've met a few guys like that—or at least *one*."

"You like Kevin, don't you, Babe?" Lucy asked quickly.

"Sure I like him, and he's a good pilot too." She smiled and said, "Don't get to liking him too much, though. I understand he comes from a rich family, doesn't he?"

"Yes, the Winslows are well off."

"Sure, and rich people are all alike. They don't want their baby boys marrying up with women like us."

"Kevin's not that way."

"Maybe he's not, but what about his parents?"

"From what he's told me, they're very sweet."

Their conversation was interrupted as Kevin opened the door. "Interrupting anything?" he asked cheerfully. He was wearing his usual flying outfit: leather jacket, tan slacks, and a pair of well-worn soft brown shoes.

"No," Lucy said almost breathlessly. "Is the plane ready?"

"All juiced up and ready to go."

Lucy went out the door with Kevin, who waved cheerfully at Babe.

She called caustically, "Don't wreck the plane—or my baby sister!"

"I'll be careful with both. Don't worry, Babe."

As the two stepped outside, Kevin asked, "What's the matter with Babe? She forgot to cuss me out. Were you two having a serious discussion?"

Lucy hesitated, then smiled cheerfully. "No, we were just talking. Where are we going to fly today?"

"Well, we've seen about everything around here from the air. You don't mind a repeat performance, do you?"

"Doesn't matter to me. It'll just be good to be up."

The two made their way to the plane that was painted a crimson so brilliant it almost hurt the eyes.

"Wonder why this thing is painted so bright," Lucy commented as Kevin helped her in.

"I don't know," he said. "Maybe the original owner wanted to make sure everyone could spot it if he came down in the middle of the desert." He laughed and then got into the seat beside her. She watched as he worked through his preflight check, then started the engine. He waited until it warmed up, then pushed the throttle forward. The small plane moved under his touch, and he taxied out onto the runway. She noticed that he looked carefully in all directions before taking off. Babe had told her that Kevin was one of the most careful pilots she had ever seen, and the comment had pleased her.

"Here we go." Kevin pressed the throttle forward while keeping his attention riveted to the strip ahead of him. Lucy enjoyed the sensation as the plane lifted off the ground. She watched the earth fall away, and it gave her a thrill, as it always did. Kev climbed steadily to ten thousand feet, then banked the plane. "Let's go look over the Crescent City again today," he suggested loudly enough for her to hear over the engine.

"All right."

As they made their way toward New Orleans, Kevin kept his attention on flying but at the same time asked her a great many questions about nursing school. It was one of the things she liked about him. He was actually interested in what she did. As she told him about one of her supervisors at the hospital who had behaved in an unprofessional way, he nodded sympathetically. "I usually don't talk to anybody else about my work," she told him. "Babe doesn't care what I do."

"Sure she does. She's just busy trying to keep this business from going down the drain."

"I suppose you're right." She looked down and said, "Look, Kev!"

"What is it?"

"That mansion down there. Isn't it beautiful?"

He banked the aircraft and circled the area below, tilting the wings toward her side to give her a better view of the old plantation. "How'd you like to live in that house?" he said with a grin.

"Oh, I don't know. It's one of those ideas that sounds good, but I'm not sure it is. I'd rather just read about it in a book."

"You wouldn't like to live there?"

"No, I don't think so."

"Well, that's okay by me. A person doesn't have to live in a big house to be happy."

He leveled the plane and brought it down low over one of the many swamps in the area, pointing out huge crocodiles sunning themselves on logs. A group of pelicans flew in the distance, and she said, "I've always loved to watch pelicans. They're so homely, aren't they? They stick out in front and nothing at all behind."

"They're pretty smart, though. And good at formation flying. Look at that perfect V they made."

"I guess birds are pretty smart, aren't they," she said.

"I guess so. Especially parrots. Whoever would think of teaching Scripture to a parrot!"

"Francis is a pretty unusual guy, I guess."

"He sure is. That blasted parrot still hates Grace, though. Jealous as can be."

"That's funny that a bird's jealous."

"I guess birds have a right to be jealous just like we do."

"Have you ever been jealous of anyone?" Lucy asked quickly.

"No, I never have. Of course, I never had anyone to be jealous of. My face got ruined just about the time I was getting interested in girls."

He said no more, and the hum of the engine filled her ears. She wanted to ask him some questions, but his attitude was not exactly an invitation.

They spent an hour over New Orleans, and they took turns pointing out the French Quarter, the cathedral, the zoo, and a great many other sights. "We'll have to take in some of those on the ground," he said as he turned toward home.

"That would be fun."

"I expect you've seen most of them."

"I'd like to see them again, though . . . with you."

They flew west, looking down at the cultivated fields as he brought the plane in for a landing. He taxied to the hangar and cut the engine, then turned to her and said, "I'm anxious for you to meet my family, Lucy. Have you given any more thought to going north with me?"

She could not speak for a moment. She had agreed to meet his family but hadn't seriously thought about doing so anytime soon.

He took her silence in a negative way. "Maybe you don't really want to meet them after all."

"Oh yes . . . yes, I'd like to very much, Kev, but . . ."

Kevin couldn't understand why she was reluctant. "What's the matter?"

"I've thought about this a lot, and I'm still not sure they'd like me very much."

"What makes you say such a thing? Why wouldn't they like you?"

"Because I've never been around their kind."

"Well, that's crazy!" he exploded. "They're not stuck up at all. Oh, my sister Paige is a bit, but it doesn't matter about her." He hesitated, then said, "I know my parents would love you, Lucy. I want them to meet you soon."

She smiled, deciding to trust his judgment. "When do you want to go?"

CHAPTER TWENTY-FOUR

A New Kevin

★ ★ ★

"Oh, fuzz! I landed right on Boardwalk!"

Phil leaned forward and rested his chin on his hand. His eyes sparkled as he looked across the table at Cara. "You owe me exactly two thousand dollars."

"But, Phil, I don't have it!"

"That's tough. You lose."

The two were outside on their patio playing Monopoly—the new real estate game that had become an instant hit in America. It was strange that it had struck the fancy of the American people when most Americans were struggling to get enough money together for a loaf of bread and a pound of pinto beans for the evening meal. Monopoly was all about earning thousands of dollars in order to build houses and hotels and buy railroads—big-time finances. Yet for some reason people loved it. Perhaps it was a way for people to dream of a better life.

The Phil Winslow family had been very blessed indeed to have kept their fortunes intact during these trying times. To them Monopoly was just a fun game, an enjoyable diversion for an evening.

Phil grinned and said to Cara, "Two thousand dollars cash, please."

"But I don't have it."

"Then you'll have to sell all your property and give me your money."

Cara pouted at her downfall—a most pleasant sight for Phil, for she had a beautifully shaped mouth, and a pout was just right for kissing. "Couldn't I pay it out over time?" she pleaded.

"There's no mercy in this game, woman. Two thousand dollars or else I'll throw you out on the street."

"You're so mean!"

Phil laughed and leaned across the patio table to kiss her. "All right. You win. You can pay me a hundred dollars each time around the board."

Cara kissed him again. "You're so sweet! Now I know why I married you."

"So you'd have somebody to beat at games, I suppose. But the next time—"

He did not finish his sentence. "Listen," he said. "I hear an airplane, and it sounds like it's close."

Suddenly the roar of the plane filled the sky.

"Look at that!" he yelled. "It must be a stunt pilot."

The two watched as the plane banked steeply and circled the estate. Then Cara gasped. "Look, he's going to land out there on the lawn!"

"Why, the crazy fool, he'll kill himself. There's not enough room."

The two stood on the edge of the patio, not even daring to breathe as the plane got lower. The wheels slammed down on the grass, and the plane shot forward but stopped just short of some hedges.

"It's got to be Kevin!" Phil said. "Come on, Cara."

The two ran toward the plane. By the time they'd reached it, the door was open and Kevin was jumping to the ground, whipping off his cap and greeting them with a broad smile. He embraced his mother, lifting her off the ground, then slapped his dad on the back and hugged him.

"Have you lost your mind, son?" Phil demanded. "You could have killed yourself."

"Nope. No chance of that. I know every square inch of this place. I practiced this landing before I left Baton Rouge. I marked off a spot on our landing field the same size as our lawn. It was a piece of cake."

"What are you doing here? I'm so glad to see you. Why didn't you tell us you were coming?" The words tumbled out of Cara's mouth as she held on to Kevin's arm.

"There's somebody I want you to meet." Kevin pulled away and helped a young woman out of the plane. He brought her forward and said, "I'd like you to meet Lucy Delaney. Lucy, these are my parents, Cara and Phil Winslow."

"I'm so glad to meet you, my dear." Cara hugged the girl while Phil stood behind her.

"You must be very brave," Phil said, "letting this crazy aviator put you through a stunt like that." He was very impressed with the young woman. She looked clean and fresh, and there was an honesty in her sparkling brown eyes.

"Oh, I knew he could do it! He's told me all about this place," Lucy said breathlessly. "And he did practice over and over."

"Well, I still say he should have been more careful," Cara said. "You could have hurt this young lady."

"Not a chance of that, Mom," Kevin said. "I'm very careful with young ladies—especially this one." He smiled his crooked smile at Lucy and she blushed.

"We already had our breakfast, but I'm sure I could get Betty to cook up some more," Cara said.

"You think you could talk her into some of her pancakes?" Kevin said. "I've missed them."

"I believe she'd cook anything for you," his father said. "She always spoiled you rotten, and I got the leftovers."

"Poor Dad!" Kevin laughed. "You get no respect, do you?"

The party moved back toward the house, and Cara said, "Come along, Lucy. You'll want to wash up after such a long trip. You must have been flying for days."

"Only about two and a half days," she said, "but it was fun. I've never had such a good time in my life! We made plenty of stops for gas and to eat, and we camped out both nights."

Cara led the young woman into the house, leaving the men to wrangle some breakfast out of Betty. She led the girl into the guestroom and told her, "There's a bathroom right over there. You can take your time and even lie down if you want to."

"Oh no, Mrs. Winslow! I'm starved, and I do want to see the place. Kevin's told me everything about it."

"Did he tell you that he made it the most beautifully landscaped place on Long Island? Or in all of America, I think. He's a genius with growing things."

"He's told me all about it, but I want to see it for myself."

"I believe he told me you were a nurse."

"I'm studying to be one. I'll be finished in another six months."

"Always nice to have a medical expert close at hand. Come downstairs as soon as you wash up now, and we'll have breakfast."

Phil and Kevin were back out on the patio, where Phil was firing questions at his son. "Do you like flying, Kev?"

"I like it better than anything I've ever done, Dad."

"Do you think you'll make a career out of it?"

"Yes. That's what I'm going to do."

Finally Kevin lifted his hand and said, "Dad, we'll be here for several days. If you'll have us, that is. So you don't have to ask me everything right now."

Phil smiled, and for the first time since the accident, he knew that Kevin was going to be all right. It had been the tragedy of his life that his younger son had had so much potential and talent thwarted because of his disfigurement. Now he saw a freedom and excitement in Kevin's face and in his manner that gave him great pleasure. "Let's go find out what's taking Betty so long with that breakfast."

Betty was fussing about the kitchen, fixing an extra-special breakfast for Kevin and had a huge stack of pancakes ready to serve. When Kevin and Lucy were seated in the small dining room, she brought a syrup pitcher and set it down beside him. "Here's some of that sorghum you like so much, Mr. Kevin. Nobody else will eat it but you. You always liked it—ever since you was a boy."

Kevin reached out and hugged Betty's generous waist. "No pancakes in the world like yours, Betty. We should go into business. We'll call it . . . Aunt Betty's Pancake House. We'll get rich."

"I ain't startin' no business!" Betty said indignantly. "And besides, you gonna fly them crazy airplanes. You ain't gonna be no pancake salesman."

Kevin and Lucy ate the pancakes with delight while Cara and Phil drank coffee and listened as Kevin told them about his flight training.

"So you're all through now? You have your license?" Cara asked.

"I have my private pilot's license, but there are others. You have to have a different rating to fly multi-engine planes and another to fly commercially. I'm going to get those too," he said confidently.

"Tell them what you really want to do, Kev," Lucy said.

"It might be a little soon."

"No it isn't," Lucy said, her eyes bright. "Tell them."

"Well, this is a long time off, but what I really want to do is try for a record flight."

"You mean like across the Atlantic?" his father asked.

"Something like that. Lindbergh's already done that alone, but there are still a great many flights that have never been made. I'm not experienced enough yet, but I will be someday. And then, of course, I'll have to get somebody to trust me with an airplane. They can be pretty expensive."

"When you're ready, son," Phil said quietly, "your mother and I will furnish the plane."

Lucy gasped. "Oh, that's wonderful, Mr. Winslow! Kev will make you proud of him."

Phil smiled. "We're already proud of him, Lucy."

"Yes we are," Cara agreed. "Now tell us all about Grace. When's she coming home?"

"I don't know exactly," he said. "Francis is encouraging her to come, and she really wants to, but she keeps putting it off."

"Why?" Cara asked in a puzzled tone.

"She's afraid."

"Afraid she won't fit in?" Phil asked. "That's nonsense."

"Actually it isn't, Dad. She's really very sensitive." He poured some more sorghum onto his pancake. "It took me a while to figure that out, though, because her manners are so rough. But she's working on that. Francis is teaching her all sorts of things."

"Like what?" Cara asked.

Lucy broke in with a smile. "Like how to dress."

"I don't believe it!" Cara exclaimed.

"It's true, Mom. He took her to a department store and helped her pick out clothes and shoes. He's even taught her how to use makeup properly and which perfumes to wear!"

"And he's working on her grammar," Lucy said with a laugh. "They have an agreement that every time she says *ain't* he pinches her arm. I couldn't believe she agreed to that arrangement."

"But it's working," Kevin added. "She gets the word half out, then flinches and looks over at Francis and changes it to *isn't*. Hard way to learn English, but it works."

"I wish she'd come back now," Phil said.

"Just give her some time, Dad. She's had a lot to learn and a lot of hurts to overcome, but she's making progress! Now that she's a Christian, she goes to church every Sunday and reads her Bible. There's a huge difference in her. You'll see it at once, I'm sure."

The Winslows had heard about Grace's conversion in Kevin's letters but wanted to hear the story all over again. As the four sat talking comfortably, Lucy felt relief wash through her. She had been very nervous about meeting Kevin's parents—afraid they wouldn't accept her—but now she knew it was going to be all right. *They're just as sweet as he is,* she thought.

★ ★ ★

The table in the smaller dining room was covered with a white cloth and was laid with gleaming china, silverware, and crystal. Betty had worked hard on the dinner, and now she glanced around with satisfaction, muttering to herself. "It's good to see Mr. Kevin home again, and that young woman he brought—she's quality folks. She don't pay no attention to his scar. I likes that!"

Brian and Joan were there along with their three children, and Paige sat beside Lucy, who was feeling shy and apprehensive. Kevin had warned her that Paige could be difficult, and she feared they might not get along. But Paige had greeted her warmly and said kind things about what Kevin had said about Lucy in his letters.

This had won Lucy over at once, and she wondered how Paige could have been so unfeeling toward Grace. She looked down the table at Brian, noticing the resemblance between him and his father. He was indeed handsome, full of life and energy. His wife, sitting next to him, was a pretty woman with fair hair and a quiet expression.

"If I can get this thundering herd to be quiet," Phil said over the noise, "we'll say the blessing."

Joan reached over and rapped the knuckles of the four-year-old, Scott, who was talking loudly to Kevin, demanding a ride in the plane.

"Ouch! That hurt, Mom!"

"Then you hush and behave yourself."

"That's right. Be good like your dad." Brian winked at him.

"Be better than that," Cara said.

Brian smiled at his mother, then bowed his head as Phil asked the blessing. They started passing the food around the table, and everyone was full of questions for Kevin.

As her brother spoke, Paige could not believe how much he had changed. Her shy, retiring brother who had hidden himself away for all these years was now as outgoing as anyone she had ever met. He didn't seem in the least bothered by his scarred face anymore, and she was truly astounded by the transformation. Her eyes met Brian's more than once, and he nodded and smiled in understanding.

When little Scott saw that his mother wasn't looking, he yanked on Kevin's arm and said, "Uncle Kev, you've gotta take me for a ride in your airplane."

"Only if your mother and dad say so."

"Can I, Dad? Can I, Mom?"

"I suppose so . . . but I'm afraid of those things," Joan said.

"Don't do anything you don't want to do. You can wait until I'm a full-fledged professional before trusting your kids with me," Kevin said. "But I'll tell you what—maybe I can just taxi them around. We could just ride on the ground. Then next time I come, I'll be fully licensed and we can all go up. How's that?"

This satisfied both Brian and Joan, and the boy was ready to go right then.

Betty's special meal was magnificent, and the family made sure to compliment her over every dish she served. Kevin was extremely pleased to see how well received Lucy was. He knew she had been afraid to come, and he was proud of Paige and of Brian as they both made every effort to include her in the conversation.

At the end of the meal, Paige took Lucy off to show her some more of the estate, and Kevin pulled Brian aside to talk privately. "How's Paige taking things, Brian?"

"You mean her broken engagement?"

"Yes."

"You know, after she got over the initial shock of it, she

was really relieved. I hate to say it, but she was becoming as much of a snob as the Asquiths—and even she realizes that, looking back on it."

"Does she still talk about John?"

"Not at all. For a while, she didn't go out with anybody, but here lately she's been out twice with a young fellow she met playing tennis. Nice guy as far as I can tell. Works for a big life insurance company. Their up-and-coming star, I understand."

"Do you think they might be serious?"

"Oh no, nothing like that. They've only just met. But I'm really glad to see her get out into the world again. Did you know that John got engaged to someone else already?"

"No, I didn't know that."

"A real society girl—someone his parents picked out."

★ ★ ★

The next day Kevin had a chance to speak with Paige, and he asked her directly about her feelings about John Asquith.

She made a face. "I can't believe I was about to marry him. He'll never change, Kev. He'll be doing what his mama and daddy tell him to do when he's fifty years old. I want my husband to have a mind of his own." She dropped her head for a moment and said, "I guess I never thought I'd hear myself saying this, but Grace really did me a favor. I could have killed her for a while, but looking back on it, her short stay here was the best thing that could have happened to me."

★ ★ ★

The visit was in its third day when Cara had a chance to spend some time alone with Lucy. They were walking around the estate, and Cara was pointing out the different things that Kevin had done.

Lucy was awed by the estate, and she said frankly, "This is all so great, Mrs. Winslow. My sister and I have had a hard life. I've never even been near anything like this before."

"It's just a house."

Lucy laughed as she looked at the mansion. "Just a house with twenty bedrooms!"

"Oh, it's not quite that many." Cara smiled. "Phil didn't want to buy it because it was so big, but he loved the studio so much, that settled it. Besides, it's big enough we can always have our children and grandchildren come back to visit."

As the two walked along, Cara skillfully induced the young woman to talk about herself. She found out that Lucy had never had a serious attachment to any man. She also got the impression that she had very special feelings for Kevin but was too shy to say so.

"I've always been very direct," Cara said, "so I hope I don't offend you by what I'm about to ask. But I would really like to know how serious you are about Kevin."

Lucy caught her breath and looked frightened. Turning pale, she found it difficult to meet Cara's eyes. "Why . . . I like him a lot," she whispered.

"Is it more than that?"

She swallowed and shook her head. "I . . . I don't think I'd ever learn to fit in here."

"There's no need to think that way. You already fit in."

Lucy did not know how to say what was on her heart.

Finally Cara asked, "Do you love him, Lucy? I ask because I've always wanted Kevin to have a wife. His accident cut him off from the world. He's never had a girlfriend. He's never had a romance in his life. But he obviously cares for you deeply."

"You really think so?"

"I know he does just by the way he watches you and the way his voice gets tender when he speaks of you."

Lucy struggled to speak for a moment, then looked up and said eagerly, "Yes, I love him."

"I'm glad, but I must warn you about something."

"What is it?" she asked, frightened.

"Kevin has come a long way these last few months, but he's very sensitive by nature. Far more so than my other children. I believe he loves you, but he may never ask you to marry him."

"Because of his scars?"

"Yes, that's it. He might be very afraid that you'd reject him."

Lucy looked at Cara with a new determination and said, "Then I'll ask him."

Cara reached out and pulled the young woman into a quick embrace. "I think you'll have to, Lucy," she whispered.

* * *

Lucy thought all day about what Cara had said. She knew she loved Kevin as she would never love another man, and she also understood that Cara was right. Kevin *was* sensitive. He might think that no woman could love him with his scarred face. She had already sensed this in him and knew that several times he had almost told her how he felt but then had lost his courage. She had not understood at that time what it meant, but now she did, and she determined that she would make the first move. It was a difficult choice, for she was usually quite shy, but she also had a steely thread of courage running through her.

She found her moment that night after supper. The family had been listening to Fibber McGee and Molly on the radio. When the show was over, she said, "Let's go see what the fish pond looks like at night, Kev."

Kevin had looked at her with surprise but agreed at once. "It's very pretty," he said. "I used to go there all the time."

After they walked out of the room, Phil said, "They're going to look at the fish in the dark?"

"Never you mind," Cara whispered.

The moon was high overhead, casting silver shadows on

the ground. As they reached the fish pond, the water glowed, and a jumping fish broke the moon's reflection into wavy patterns. "I helped build this pond. As a matter of fact, I designed it. The fish come all the way from China. They're called koi—a fancy name for carp."

"They're so huge."

"Yes they are. Some of them weigh up to fifteen pounds. But they're not very good to eat."

"Ooh, who'd want to eat one of those beautiful things anyway?"

"Deer are beautiful," Kevin said with a grin, "but I've eaten a few of those."

Lucy had no good reply for that observation, and the two watched the fish and listened as the waterfall gurgled pleasantly. It had been a warm day, but now that it was dark, the fall air felt cool. As they stood silently beside the pond, she desperately wondered if she could go through with her plan. Finally she turned to him and touched his arm. He smiled at her, which gave her courage. Without a tremor in her voice, she spoke up. "Kevin, I love you. Will you marry me?"

He straightened up as though he had been struck by a bullet. His lips parted, and he swallowed hard. He must have recovered quickly though, as he immediately took her into his arms and kissed her. She clung to him, and her eyes filled with tears. She did not know whether he was simply kissing her out of pity or out of deep feeling for her.

When he lifted his head, he said, "I'll always be sorry for one thing."

"What's that, Kev?"

"That you beat me to the punch. I was going to ask you to marry me, and you did it before I could get up my nerve."

"I was afraid you'd never ask me," she said simply.

"Let me ask you, then. Will you marry me, Lucy Delaney?"

Lucy's breath caught as her heart leaped with joy. "Yes . . . oh yes, I will, Kevin Winslow."

They kissed again, and this time Lucy knew she had found her man.

CHAPTER TWENTY-FIVE

OLD FLAME

★ ★ ★

Babe Delaney stepped into the Green Lantern and saw that there was only a handful of customers. Two old men sat at the bar, one of them with a long white beard like Santa Claus, the other balding and with a round, red face. They were arguing in muted tones and did not even look up when she came in. A couple sat at the back drinking silently with morose expressions on their faces, and another couple was dancing but appeared half asleep. The jukebox was playing "Cheek to Cheek," and the music seemed to cut through the smoke-filled air.

Babe took a seat at a table close to the bar. She picked up a saltshaker and tapped it nervously on the table until Grace approached.

"Hi, Babe. Can I bring you something to eat?"

"No, just a beer, I think."

Babe waited until Grace returned with a stein of beer and put it before her. "You're not busy tonight."

"No, I think everybody's at the LSU football game."

"Can you sit down a minute? I need to talk to you."

Grace checked her customers and then sat down. She kept

her back erect, and there was a cautious light in her eyes as she studied the woman across from her.

"I got a call from Lucy today," Babe said after taking a sip of the beer. "She tells me that Kev has asked her to marry him, and she's going to do it."

"I know. Kevin called me. I think it's great. Your sister's a nice girl."

"Yes she is. I'm proud of her. Never had to worry a minute about Lucy. She's a straight arrow all the way." She took another sip of beer. "Not like me."

"Not like me either," Grace said.

The remark caught at Babe, and she cocked her head. "You think she'll make it okay with his family? Your family, I mean. You know, they're so rich and all that."

"From what Kev tells me, she's already made it. They've welcomed her with open arms. I don't think you understand how much that family has worried about Kevin." She thought for a moment, then added, "It's like they've all been praying for him to come out and do something, and all he would ever do was grow flowers and work on engines. Now he's a changed man, and I'm pretty proud of him."

"Yeah, well, I guess I am too. He's one of the best students I've ever had. He's going somewhere in the world of flying. You just watch."

The two women sat there, and the jukebox started playing "Stars Fell on Alabama."

"I hate that song. It's so sappy," Babe said.

"What's on your mind, Babe? I know you didn't come here to drink beer and talk about jukebox songs."

Babe laughed. "You're pretty sharp, Grace. You've come up the hard way just like me. All right. I do have something on my mind." She sipped at the beer and then put it down firmly. "I've come to tell you that I'm going after Francis."

"I thought you were already doing that."

"Not really. When he first came back, I didn't give him much of a thought. But there's something about that guy. I don't know what it is. Back when we were together, we had something, and it was good."

"Why are you telling me this, Babe?"

"Because I think you're in love with him." Babe was watching Grace carefully and saw something change in her expression. Babe's hard life had formed her life philosophy: Keep what's yours and don't let anyone get to you. Only where her sister Lucy was concerned was there any softness in her—except for what she had felt in the past for Francis Key. He had been different, and she had never been able to explain how the two of them had come together. All she knew was that there was something special about him that made him different from other men. Ever since they had broken up, she'd had faint stirrings of regret. Since that day she had felt an emptiness she could not define. When he unexpectedly walked back into her life, she was honest enough to realize that she was responding to him in the old way. She had met old flames before, and it had never been like this. "I know something's going on between you two, but I can't figure out exactly what it is."

"Neither can I," Grace admitted.

Babe was shocked at this statement. "Come on," she said. "You've been around the block. You know what life's like. Francis is like a baby as far as women are concerned, but you're no baby."

"That's right. I'm not."

Babe had expected antagonism, but there was a mildness in Grace Winslow that had not been there when they had first met. "I expected you to come after me with your claws out."

"No, I won't do that. Listen, don't think about me. If Francis loves you, I want him to be happy."

The words displeased Babe. She got up abruptly, searched in her purse, and threw some money on the table. "I'd like it better if you'd fight me for him."

Grace smiled and shook her head but did not answer. She watched as Babe abruptly left the restaurant. Finally she heard the bartender, who had walked up beside her. "Anything wrong, Grace?"

"I don't know, Gus."

Her answer puzzled him, and when she got up and went back to work, he scratched his head and muttered, "I gave up trying to understand women a long time ago."

⋆ ⋆ ⋆

Francis typed a line, then straightened his back and reread it. He glanced over at the clock and saw that it was after nine. He studied the line again, staring at the typewriter as if it were a crystal ball; then he heard the sound of a car pulling up. He'd had no company since Kevin had gone to New York, and now hearing a knock, he went to the door and opened it. "Why, Babe," he said with surprise. "Come on in."

"Are you working?" she asked.

"I guess so." Babe saw that he was troubled and said, "You're not worried about Kev and Lucy, are you? I'm not."

"No, of course not. I think it's a good thing. Has Lucy called you?"

"Yes, she's happier than I've ever known her to be."

"They'll have a good marriage. Kev's a good man, and she's a fine woman." When she didn't respond, he asked, "Can I fix you some coffee?"

"All right."

He poured two mugs of coffee and handed one to her. "You want to go sit on the porch? It's a little cooler out there."

"Sure—that would be fine."

They went out and sat down on the porch swing, and for a while they talked about Kevin and Lucy. The conversation gradually turned to some of the things they had done together in earlier days. Babe suddenly blurted out, "I missed you after you left, Francis."

"You were the one who ran me off."

"I know that. I didn't think I'd miss you." The swing moved slowly back and forth, and she could see a smile come to his lips. "Did you miss me at all?" she asked timidly.

"Sure I did. You were the only woman I'd ever loved, Babe. When we separated it was as if I'd lost a leg. A man can get by, I suppose, when he loses a leg, but he has to hobble around. He's not the same anymore. It was pretty bad for me."

Babe's features became soft and she took his hand. "I didn't know you felt that way," she whispered.

"Well, I did."

Babe released his hand and put her hands on his shoulders. "We could have it again," she said. She put her arms around his neck and kissed him firmly. He didn't resist her kiss, which pleased her, for she knew how to make a man want her. His nearness was sharpening all the old memories, bringing back the past like a powerful flash. When their lips parted, she whispered again, "We could go back to the way things were. You can't hide your feelings for me. You never could, could you?"

"I guess not." Francis sat perfectly still and did not move for a long time. Finally he cleared his throat and said, "I have this theory that you should never move backward."

She felt a stab of disappointment at this comment. "Why not, Francis? We're still the same people."

"I don't think so. You might be, but I've changed."

Frustrated, she said quietly, "No you haven't—not really. It's this religious thing, isn't it?"

"That's right. I wasn't a Christian then, and I pretty much did what I wanted to do. But now, well . . . there are things I can't do no matter how much I want to."

"You want me, Francis. Don't deny it. You wouldn't have kissed me like that if you didn't."

"I can't deny it. You're a beautiful woman, and you know how to stir a man. But I can't go back to being what I was. I've moved on."

Sighing, she knew that their relationship was indeed over. She had begun to build faint hopes of rekindling the love they'd once had, but now she understood that he had spoken the truth. "I guess I knew it, but I'd hoped we could get together again."

"You'll find a man who really loves you someday, Babe."

"No, I don't think I ever will." She got to her feet, and he rose with her. "You're really serious about this Christianity thing, aren't you?"

"Yes, I am."

"But even if I were to change, it wouldn't matter, would it?" When he hesitated, she smiled slightly, but there was bitterness in it. "You've got someone else on your mind." She did not say any more but saw that her words had hit him. "I wish you the best, Francis, I really do."

"You too, Babe."

He stood and watched as she went back to the car. She started it up and drove away, and as she disappeared into the night, Francis knew that a chapter had finally closed in his life. His love affair with Babe Delaney had been the most turbulent drama in his life, and he had struggled with fantasies that one day it might happen again. But now as the sound of her car faded, so also faded any such thoughts. And with that realization came great relief that his inner struggle was over.

★ ★ ★

When Grace got home from work, Francis was sitting in the easy chair in the living room. He usually had a book in his hands, but this time he was simply staring at the wall. The radio was playing softly, and she came and stood over him. "What are you doing up this time of night?"

"Couldn't sleep."

"It's after midnight."

"I know it. I went to bed but just lay there staring at the ceiling, so I got up. Are you hungry?"

"No, not really." Then after a moment's consideration, she said, "I'll just have some milk." She opened the icebox and pulled out the milk bottle. She poured herself a glass of milk, and as she set the bottle down, she noticed a cup in the sink with lipstick on the rim. At once she understood that Babe had been there, but she said nothing about it.

Francis had followed her into the kitchen and saw her expression change when she looked into the sink. "Babe was here," he said quietly.

Neither said a word, and the music on the radio was the only sound in the room. Finally Grace said, "She's in love with you, Francis."

"No, not really."

"You're blind. She's cared for you a long time."

"We never got along, Grace. We fought like cats and dogs, and she threw me out."

"Why was she here if she doesn't still care for you?"

Francis sighed. "Maybe she does, but with Babe love is always . . . physical." He dropped his head for a moment. When he lifted his gaze to meet hers, Grace saw the pain in his eyes. "There's got to be more to it than that, hasn't there?"

Grace was touched that he would ask her this question, knowing what a struggle she'd had in life over issues of love.

"Yeah, I think it does, but I'm no expert," she said bitterly. She wanted to say more, but considering her history, she did not consider herself worthy of offering any advice on the subject.

Francis had expected her to say more, and he was disappointed when she started toward her bedroom. "I mailed the book off today," he called out.

"You finished it? Oh, Francis, that's wonderful!" Grace spun around and came back to him at once, her eyes bright. "I'm so proud of you."

"Well, don't be. That might be the last we ever see of it."

"What are you talking about?"

"It may never get published. I thought it was good when I started, but now I don't know. I've lost any sense of objectivity. It may be the best book or the worst book ever written—I just don't know."

"What if it don't get published? Will you write another one?"

"I don't know, Grace." His voice was weary. "I've thrown myself into this for so long, I haven't even considered what

I'd do if I failed. But now I've got to think about it."

Grace felt compassion for this man who was so strong in so many ways, yet almost fragile in others. She wanted to put her arms around him and comfort him, but she refrained. "Can I read it?"

"If you like. I've only got the carbon copy, and that's a bit hard to read." Going over to the table where he kept his books, he picked up a thick manuscript tied together with a blue ribbon. "It may be the only blue ribbon it ever wins," he said wryly and handed it to her.

"I hate to see you like this."

"Maybe I'm just a sensitive artist who needs to suffer," he said with a faint smile.

She did not smile back, however, for she hurt for him. "I'll read it. I'll start it tonight. I wish I knew more about literature."

"I hope you like it."

She did smile then. "Oh, I know I will."

She took the manuscript to her bedroom and put it on the nightstand beside her bed. She showered quickly and put on a gown. Getting into bed, she picked up the first few pages and began to read. She read slowly and carefully, for this book meant a great deal to her. She had come to love Francis, and she felt that these pages represented his life. She desperately wanted it to succeed. She stopped reading, thinking about how Babe must feel, having missed out in her relationship with Francis. *Babe missed her chance at love . . . but maybe I will too.* Frightened by that thought, Grace put it from her mind and began to read again.

★ ★ ★

Three days later Kevin returned from New York. He swept into the house, put his arms around her, and swung her around the room. "Well, sister, everything went great!"

"Did they really like Lucy?"

"They loved her! Even Paige and Brian. I was proud of all of them."

"I'm so glad!" Grace exclaimed. "She was so afraid to go."

"I know, but they made her feel completely at ease. Now it's your turn. When are you going home?"

"Francis says we should go next week."

"Good. It's time for you to be there."

Grace was thrilled for Kevin and Lucy, and the next time she saw Lucy, it was evident that the young woman was as happy as Grace had ever seen her. She listened as Lucy excitedly spoke of the family, and she finished by saying, "They're so anxious for you to come home, Grace. They love you so much."

Grace smiled but said nothing. In all truth she was so caught up with reading Francis's book that other matters had faded into insignificance. She took every spare moment to read, reading after work into the early hours of the morning until her eyes burned. The book, she had discovered, had a power she could not fathom. She had read romances before, but none of them had ever stirred her quite like this. The very words in these pages seemed to leap out at her and enter her mind and heart.

The story concerned a woman who wasted her life, having made a wrong turn while she was very young. The story keenly reminded Grace of her own life. Although there were no specific details that matched, she suspected that Francis had at least partially modeled his heroine after her.

By the time she finished the book early one morning, Grace was weeping. The main character in the book had found only one way to make her life bearable, and that was through Jesus, the Savior. She had given her life to Christ, but she'd still had problems afterward, and this is what intrigued Grace. The heroine had been troubled even after becoming a Christian with thoughts of past sins—exactly as Grace herself was experiencing!

At the end of the book, the character had finally learned that God forgives completely and never brings up our past errors once we have confessed them and forsaken them. In the last scene, the young woman was able to tell her sweetheart that she had learned God's forgiveness is complete. He doesn't forgive one day, then come back the next day tormenting us with our past sin.

Grace had suffered terrible remorse over her past. Now she slipped out of bed, knelt down, and began to pray. "Oh, God, I can't go back and undo the things I did when I was lost. You know I've repented of them, and I know I've cried out and called on you to forgive me. Now I pray, O Lord, that you take away this guilt once and for all. Let me trust in you and in the Lord Jesus Christ that these sins are under the blood. . . ."

She finally crawled back into bed, feeling totally exhausted. She slept deeply and the next morning felt a curious lightness of spirit. After she dressed she tied the ribbon around the manuscript and took it into the kitchen, where she found Francis fixing breakfast. He greeted her, and she smiled at him. "I finished the book, and it's been such a help to me, Francis. Have you got time to listen?"

"Sure."

The two sat down, and breakfast was forgotten. Key listened intently and saw the happiness that was in this woman he had come to care for so much. "I've been struggling with what I did as a lost person and have been tormented by it," Grace confessed. "And when I read in your book and saw how Angela found forgiveness and relief from guilt, it made the Bible make sense for me. All the Scriptures you've been reading to me and I've been finding on my own are all true."

Francis reached out and took her hand. "That's what I wanted my book to do, Grace. To make people see the truth of the grace of God."

Holding on to his hand, Grace felt great joy. "It's a lovely book, Francis. It's going to help so many people. I just know it!"

CHAPTER TWENTY-SIX

A Close Call

★ ★ ★

Grace awoke and glanced at the clock—a few minutes after ten. She did not have to work that night, and she was determined to spend the day getting away from the thoughts that had troubled her lately. She put on her leather motorcycle outfit and examined her image in the mirror. It brought back memories of a time she would rather forget, but ever since she had prayed for God to take away her guilt feelings, she had experienced a lightness of spirit that had brought her great joy. The outfit was comfortable, and she looked at her reflection again and said firmly, "That woman is dead forever. Now it's just an outfit to wear when riding a beautiful Italian motorcycle."

She went into the kitchen and found Francis typing rapidly. "Hello," she said cheerfully. When he turned to look at her, she saw his eyes widen with surprise. "I'm going for a ride, and I want you to go with me."

"You mean on that motorcycle? I hate that thing!"

She playfully grabbed his hair. "You're going with me, so don't argue. Or do I have to get my blackjack?"

"Ow, you're pulling my hair out!" He freed himself and

stood up. "I'll fix you breakfast, but no motorcycle ride for me."

She pinched his arm, which drew a yelp from him. "You've pinched my arm black and blue over my grammar, so I'm gonna pinch you every time you say no to me. Now, fix me a good breakfast. I'll eat it, and then we're going to New Orleans."

Francis laughed. "You must be feeling better."

"I am. I feel great!"

"I wish I did. I keep worrying about that manuscript."

"Just forget about your book. I want some pancakes and sausage and a big pot of coffee. We'll take some in the Thermos."

"What about your lessons? How am I going to make you into a refined lady when I'm on the back of a dumb motorcycle?"

"You can teach me as we go."

Her good humor was infectious, and Francis laughed. "I don't think I want to teach you anymore, Grace. I don't want you to be smarter than I am."

"No danger of that," she said, squeezing his arm firmly. "Now, fix those flapjacks!"

Francis did her bidding, and as soon as she had finished eating, she said, "Throw the dirty dishes in the sink and get your helmet."

"I don't have one."

"Yes you do. I got one for you yesterday." She pulled a leather helmet and goggles out of the closet. "Here, put it on."

Francis fumbled at the helmet and snapped the strap under his chin. "I feel like an idiot wearing this thing."

Grace pulled the goggles down over his eyes. "Now you're ready for anything. Let's go."

They left the house, and after she had kicked the machine into life, Francis got on behind her. He reached around her waist and held her tightly. "Don't hold on so tight!" she protested.

"I will too," he shouted over the roar of the engine. "If I

fall off, I'm taking you with me."

"I know what you're doing. You've been looking for an excuse to hug me, and now you've got it."

He squeezed her harder and said, "If you're determined to go, then let's get going."

"All right. Hang on, Mr. Key."

Francis actually enjoyed the ride to New Orleans, especially since he got to hold on to Grace. Feeling the wind in his face and conscious of every bump in the road under them, he found himself enjoying it greatly but would never admit it to her.

As they entered the city, she hollered back, "Let's go to the French Quarter and get us some good hot Cajun food."

Francis agreed, and they found an excellent restaurant and devoured some of the best Cajun cuisine they'd had so far in Louisiana. After eating, they wandered slowly around the French Quarter watching the street entertainers. One man played an accordion so enthusiastically and sang so fervently, albeit off-key, that Francis put a dime in the cup at his feet. "God bless you, brother," Francis said.

"Why, God bless me! That's right enough, sir. Thank you very much."

They wandered into the cathedral and sat down for a while, soaking in the peace they found in the cool silence. When they finally emerged, Grace said, "What was that, Francis?"

"What was what?"

"What was that I felt inside the cathedral?"

"That was the presence of God."

"Let's go back. I want to feel it again."

He laughed. "You can feel it just as well at home."

Grace stared at him. "I don't believe that. Otherwise, why build cathedrals? Why not just stay home?"

"I think it's just a special quiet place after all the noise of our lives. Sometimes I find God's presence when I'm sitting out on a creek even more than I do in a church. Finding God, I think, is just a matter of waiting for Him no matter where you are. You can even be close to God driving a motorcycle."

She loved it when he spoke like this, helping her understand the mysteries of God. He took her hand as they continued down the street. She was startled, but his grip remained firm, and she liked it. It gave her a sense of belonging she had never felt before.

Late in the afternoon, Grace said, "I guess we should be heading home."

"You don't have to work tonight, do you?"

"No, I don't."

"Good. Then we can have a grammar lesson when we get back."

"No, I'd rather do something exciting."

"Like what?"

"Anything but work on grammar! You've done a lot for me, Francis, but I'm always gonna make mistakes in grammar."

"We all do. You've learned so much, Grace, you'll do fine anywhere you go now."

She beamed at his praise. "Come on," she said. "On the way home we'll think of something fun to do when we get back to Baton Rouge. Maybe we'll go down on the river and watch the big boats."

"That sounds good."

They got on the cycle and left New Orleans, Grace operating the machine with care, for the local police officers were not known for their generosity with speeders. Once they had left the city limits, she felt free to speed up until they were flying along at a fast clip. Francis was holding on tight, thinking what a nice day it had been. Suddenly, however, he was thrown forward roughly against Grace. He grabbed at her wildly. "What is it?" She did not answer, for she was intent on avoiding the danger ahead. He peeked around her to see that a big semi was blocking the rather narrow highway. He quickly spotted a car that had been knocked off onto the shoulder on the left-hand side. The stationary truck loomed ahead of them, and he thought, *She'll never miss it!*

Grace slowed the cycle as much as she could and leaned sharply to the right, pulling Francis with her. They missed the back corner of the truck by a fraction of an inch. In fact, Francis thought he had grazed it with his left forearm.

The bike spun out and deposited the riders on the thick grass by the side of the highway. Francis's first thought was *I'm glad we're not on the concrete.* He lay on the grass for a minute while he determined he wasn't hurt.

Grace rolled over and squatted in front of him. "Francis, are you all right? Are you hurt?"

"I'm all right," he said as he sat up. "Just roughed up a bit."

"I was so afraid!" Grace cried, hugging him.

"I don't see how you managed to miss that truck."

"I don't either. It must have been the Lord."

"I think so. Come on. Let's see if anybody's hurt. That wreck must have happened just before we got here."

The family in the car had been shaken up, and the wife had sustained a severe cut on her arm.

"Do what you can for her, Francis, while I find a place to call for an ambulance and the cops."

"Hurry as quick as you can," he said.

As Grace climbed back on the bike and left the scene, she was aware that her heart was beating fast, and her hands were unsteady. She had had close calls before but none quite this close. She knew they had been only inches away from death or serious injury. She raced to find a phone, saying over and over, "Thank you, God . . . thank you, God . . . thank you, God."

★ ★ ★

"I don't think I'll ever forget this night," Francis said in a subdued voice when they finally arrived home.

Grace was thinking of how close death had been. The family in the car and the truck driver could have all been killed, but they had miraculously survived with only minor injuries. Grace and Francis had waited with the others until the ambulance and police had arrived. They had given their part of the report and then come directly home.

"I really thought we were going to hit that truck," Francis said quietly.

"We could have easily been killed," she said. "What were you thinking about when you saw that truck?"

He looked at her, startled. "Thinking about? You mean just before I thought we were going to die?"

"Yes."

"I thought of how many things I'd never get to do."

"Like what?" she pressed.

"Mostly of how I'd never have a family." The accident had sobered him, and his face still had a pallor to it. "I've always wanted a family more than anything—a wife and kids and a house somewhere."

"I didn't know that, Francis."

"Well, it's true, and for that split second I thought I'd never have it, and it made me very sad. What did you think about?"

"I thought about you," she said simply.

Her answer caught him off guard. He put his hands on her forearms. "Not about yourself?"

"No. I guess I got used to facing danger in that stupid carnival act I was in, but I did think about you. You're so talented and have so much to give, and I felt terribly sad that I had ruined it all for you."

He tightened his grasp on her arms, and she grew very still, her eyes steadily on his.

"The other thing I thought of," he said, "was how much I love you and how very thrilled I would be if you would agree to marry me."

Grace could barely breathe. "Do you really love me?"

"You must know that, but I don't know how you feel about me."

She had difficulty speaking. "I . . . I love you too, Francis, but . . ."

"But what?" he said. "What's wrong?"

"You know what kind of life I used to lead. I wasn't a virtuous girl."

"But you are now. God has made you into a virtuous woman."

He slipped his arms around her as she whispered, "I wish I hadn't done all those awful things. I know God's forgiven me, but I still wish I'd lived differently."

"It doesn't matter now. All those things are forgotten." He kissed her, and she began to weep as she clung to him. "Don't cry for yesterday, Grace. Today is the day the Lord has made."

The two stood there embracing, and finally he kissed her again. "You didn't answer my question. If I'm a success and get my book published, will you marry me?"

"You *are* a success," she said firmly. "And yes, I'll marry you! I love you, Francis. I don't know when I started loving you, but I know you're the kindest man I've ever known."

Francis smiled. "I'm not very big," he said with a grin.

"You're big enough for me to marry!" She put her cheek next to his. *He may not be a very big man on the outside, but that doesn't matter,* she thought. *He's big on the inside, and that's all that counts.*

CHAPTER TWENTY-SEVEN

BABE'S ADMONITION

★ ★ ★

Francis pulled the truck up in front of the airfield office and turned the engine off. Grace was watching him with a peculiar expression in her eyes. "Why are you looking at me like that?" he demanded.

"Is this going to be hard for you, Francis?"

"Is what going to be hard for me?"

"You know what I'm talking about. Will it be hard for you to say good-bye to Babe?"

"Of course not," he said quickly. He reached over and twirled a strand of her strawberry blond hair around his forefinger. "Are you going to be jealous, Grace?"

"No, I don't think so. As a matter of fact, I feel sad about Babe."

"Sad? Why is that?"

"She's missing out on so much. She's got it in her to be a very good woman, but she's not willing to trust God."

He released the strand of hair and shrugged his shoulders. "I'm sad for her too, but it's not too late. She's young. She can change. Come on, let's go in."

"Are you sure you want me to come?"

"Yes, I'm sure."

The two got out of the truck, and Grace stopped long enough to check the ties that held down the motorcycle and their luggage. "This is all we've got," she said with a laugh. "A few suitcases, a typewriter, a couple blankets, and a motorcycle. Not much in the way of worldly goods, is it?"

"No, not much," he agreed. "But it means we can travel light. Come on."

The two went inside and found Babe sitting at her desk. She did not get up but studied them with a strange expression. "I thought you two would be long gone."

"We're on our way," Francis said. "We just came to say good-bye."

"Good-bye," Babe said in a tense voice.

"I'll miss you, Babe," he said. "I don't know where we'll wind up, but I hope we'll get to see you again sometime."

Babe rolled her eyes. "You are something, Francis Key. You reject a woman and bruise her feelings until she's like a piece of raw hamburger, then come by smiling with your cheerful little innocent face. I oughta kick your rear out of here like I did the last time!"

He dropped his head. "Well, I wish you luck," he said lamely.

She got out of her chair and came quickly around her desk. Francis's eyes flew open with alarm, and he took a step backward. "Now, wait a minute," he said nervously. "You don't have to—"

Francis never finished his sentence, for Babe threw her arms around him and kissed him full on the lips. She held it for a long moment before pulling away, her hands on her hips. "Well, Grace, there's one kiss you won't get."

"I guess not." She stepped forward and embraced Babe. She whispered, "I'll be praying that you'll find just the right man to make you happy." Stepping back, she smiled and took Francis by the arm in a protective gesture.

"Don't worry. I'm not gonna hit the little pipsqueak. Just get him outta here, will ya?"

"All right, Babe. I'll send you an invitation to the wedding," Grace said and smiled.

"Just take care of the little shrimp. And you"—she fixed her gaze on Francis—"you be good to her."

"I will. So long for now." Francis turned and walked out, allowing Grace to go before him. When they got to the truck, neither of them said anything, but as he started the engine and looked at Grace, he was concerned to see a tear rolling down her cheek. "What's wrong?" he asked.

"I feel so sorry for her."

Francis reached over and squeezed the back of her neck. "So do I," he said softly. Then he gunned the truck, and as they left the airfield, neither of them spoke for a time. After a while he put his arm around her shoulder and pulled her close. "You heard what she said. I'm supposed to be good to you."

She smiled brilliantly at him. "All right, Francis, you can start right now."

★ ★ ★

They drove hard all day, and when it started growing dark, they looked for a place to camp. An hour later they were sitting beside a campfire, roasting hot dogs. "You're still burning yours," Francis said. "Let me do it for you."

"I can roast my own!" Grace protested.

"No, I'm the man; you're the woman. It's time you started practicing up on your obedience."

"What are you talking about?" She glared at him.

"That's what you've got to promise when we get married. To love, honor, and obey me."

"I never did like that part of the wedding ceremony," she muttered. "But I have to admit, you are a better cook than I am."

Francis tossed the blackened wiener over his head and lanced another one onto the roasting stick he had cut. He held it carefully over the flame, and when it was done, he smeared mustard on a bun, inserted the wiener, and topped it off with bubbling hot chili he had heated in a can near the blaze. Grace bit into the hot dog and cried out, "Aaahh—that's hot!"

"Hot dogs are supposed to be hot, silly! You'd complain if I gave you a cold one."

She made a face at him and bit into her dog. After having their fill, they drank coffee they had brought in a Thermos.

"This is nice," Grace said. "I hope we'll always do things like this."

"It looks like we will whether we want to or not. Can't afford to go first class."

Grace noticed that his mood had changed. "What's the matter, Francis?"

He rearranged the fire with his hot dog stick. "We don't even have a roof to put over our heads. After we get married, we'll have to honeymoon in the woods."

"No we won't. Your book will be published by then." She moved closer to him and put her hand on his knee. "Tell me, how do you get paid for writing a book?"

"First you have to get it accepted by a publisher."

"I mean after that."

"The theory is that you sign a contract, and they give you what's called an advance."

"An advance? What's that?"

"It's money paid out against the royalties. For instance, they might give me a check for three hundred dollars. Then after the book has been out a while, they count up all the copies that have sold and see how much money they've made."

"Do you get half of it?"

"Half! No! No writer gets half. Ten percent's more like it."

"Ten percent! That's highway robbery! Those thieves will be keeping ninety percent of your money."

Francis laughed. "Actually, they don't even get half of it." He put his hand over hers and squeezed it. "Half of the price of the book will go to the bookstore."

"That still leaves fifty percent."

"But the publisher has to spend a lot of money to pay their editors, hire an artist to design a fancy cover, print it, and distribute it, so depending on how many copies it sells, they might not make any money from it. They're taking a chance with every book, especially if the author is not well known. The big writers, Hemingway and Faulkner, probably get fifteen or maybe even twenty percent. But I'd be thankful for ten."

"Let's see. If a book costs a dollar, you'd get ten cents. Is that right?"

"Just about."

"Then all you'll have to do is sell . . . umm . . . ten million books and you'll be a millionaire."

He laughed. "You know how many books sell ten million copies?"

"No. How many?"

"Not many!"

Grace was happy because she had taken his mind off of his fears. *I can't let him worry about things like this*, she thought.

"I know what you're doing," he said. "You're trying to take my mind off my problem. Don't worry about me. It does me good to be miserable once in a while."

She grabbed a handful of his hair, jerked his head over, and kissed him firmly on the lips. "You don't have to worry. I'm a rich heiress, anyway. Remember, I'm a Winslow."

"We can't live off your folks!"

"I know it, Francis. I was just teasing. But I can go to work."

"I know," he said, deviltry sparkling in his eyes. "We can do an act."

"An act? What kind of an act?"

"We can do the Ring of Death. We'll get another cycle, and you and I can go around to carnivals."

She lunged at him and knocked him backward off the log he was sitting on. He hit the ground with a grunt, and she threw herself onto his chest, pinning him down. "Don't you even mention that awful thing! The Ring of Death indeed!"

With her weight pressing against him, Francis reached up and put his arms around her. "Let's just stay out here. I've had more fun tonight than I've had in the last six months."

She kissed him soundly and then stood up. "Remember, we have to behave ourselves on this trip. We're not married yet."

He got to his feet and dusted himself off. "That's a tall order, Grace. Maybe we should have gone to a motel and gotten separate rooms."

"I doubt that would have helped," Grace said with a laugh. "No, I think we'll just have to sit up all night and keep the fire going."

"And what else?" he asked.

"You can tell me about the next book you're going to write."

"I'm not even sure what it'll be yet."

"Then you can tell me some more about how to be a lady."

They did sit up that night until the wee hours of the morning. They leaned against the log and held hands, and from time to time he put his arm around her. Grace felt safe and secure, knowing that Francis wanted to keep their relationship honorable before God as much as she did.

Finally Francis said, "I'm getting awfully sleepy. If I'm gonna drive tomorrow, I need some rest. Guess we'd better bed down."

"All right. Which side of the fire do you want?"

"Either one. I'll try to wake up once or twice and keep the fire going."

They each laid a blanket out on either side of the fire, and then she turned to him almost shyly. "Good night, Francis. I love you."

"Good night, sweetheart. I love you too." He put his arms around her, and for a moment she was afraid he would not hold up his end of the bargain. She did not want him to change from what he was. He gave her a soft, quick kiss. "I'll see you in the morning," he said gruffly.

"Good night, Francis."

★ ★ ★

The sun was high in the sky when Francis pulled the truck up in front of the Winslow home. "Here we are," he said. "There come your folks. They must have been sitting there waiting for us."

Grace almost fell out of the truck in her eagerness. Her mother swept her into an embrace and held her tightly, and her dad then took his turn. Phil shook hands with Francis and asked, "Did you have a good trip?"

"Very good."

"I'll help you carry the suitcases in."

Before they got to the door, Paige came out of the house and went straight to Grace. "I'm so glad to see you, Grace."

Grace hesitated for just a moment, then stepped forward and embraced Paige. Francis felt a glow of satisfaction. *Well, she never did that before. I think everything's going to be all right.*

"It's good to be back, Paige," Grace said shyly.

"In front of Mom and Dad, I want to tell you how sorry I am that I treated you so abominably," Paige said.

"If we start apologizing, I'll have the most to do," Grace said quickly.

"Let's start all over again, all right?" Paige said. "Come inside and tell me everything you've been doing."

They went inside, and Cara and Phil were very glad to see that Paige was bending over backward to be pleasant. Cara had talked with her earlier and knew there had been a change of heart in her daughter, and now she whispered to Phil, "It's going to be all right, dear. They're going to be good friends."

They sat down to a quick lunch and had no more gotten started when Brian pulled up with his whole family. Grace immediately went to Brian and smiled at him. "Brian, I was awful the last time I was here, but I promise you I won't take any of your children's money from the inheritance."

Brian flushed and was so startled he could hardly talk. Then he laughed aloud and said, "Well, it's all in the family.

It's good to see you, Grace. You look wonderful."

The day went very pleasantly, and late that afternoon Francis managed to find Phil alone in his den. "Come on in, Francis. Have a seat."

Francis sat down, and his face had a determined expression. "I don't know if this will come as a huge shock to you or not, Mr. Winslow, but I have to tell you that I'm in love with your daughter and have asked her to marry me."

Phil got up at once and put his hand out. "No, it doesn't come as a surprise, but it comes as very good news." Francis stood up and took Phil's hand. "It looks like we're going to lose a daughter almost as soon as we found her, but I can't think of any other man I'd rather have for a son-in-law."

Francis shook his head. "It's kind of tough on me. I finished the novel I was working on, but it hasn't been accepted yet."

"It will be, I'm sure."

"I'm going back to work for the detective agency."

"Are you sure you want to do that?"

"I don't mind it. It's interesting work. I can write at night. Grace and I have talked it over. I don't want to marry until I'm able to take care of her."

"I can understand that. Well, sit down and tell me about the book. I don't know anything about the publishing business."

As Francis told about the characters in his book, Phil Winslow reflected on the day he had first met the younger man. He had liked Francis from the start, for he saw in him a depth and a steadiness that he admired, and now he was pleased to have him as a son-in-law. As the conversation turned to wedding plans, he said, "Why don't you stay here instead of finding a place of your own?"

"Oh, I couldn't do that!"

"Of course you could. This is a big house. It'd be good to have you."

"That's very kind of you, sir."

"Why don't you just call me Phil? I'd feel more comfortable. Come on up to the studio. I want to show you some new things I'm working on."

CHAPTER TWENTY-EIGHT

A New Grace

★ ★ ★

"I'm going to throw a party."

Cara looked up, shock in her eyes. "You? A party? You hate parties."

Phil was in bed watching Cara brush her hair. She turned to stare at him, and he laughed at her expression. "You must think I'm an awful person," he said. "I don't see why you're so surprised. I'm very good at parties."

Cara sniffed. "You're terrible at parties! I'm always afraid to drag you to them. I know you're going to look bored."

"I won't look bored at this one." Phil turned onto his side and propped his head up on his elbow. "You know, you're just as beautiful now as you were on our wedding night."

Cara, after all her years with Phil, could still blush. She dropped her eyes for a moment, then laughed. "I was the world's greenest bride. I'd been cooped up in a sick room for years."

"You were the most beautiful thing I'd ever seen."

"I didn't know the first thing about . . . about being with a man."

"But you had a good teacher," he said impishly.

"Oh, you, I'll throw this hairbrush at you! What kind of a party?"

"An engagement party for Kevin and Lucy."

"Oh, darling, that's a wonderful idea!" Cara put the brush down, then came over to the bed and turned out the light. She got in bed beside him. "How long have you been thinking about this?"

"Ever since they decided to get married."

Cara put her arms around him and kissed him. "You are getting to be a sly thing. But it's a great idea. Say, why don't we have a party for both of the couples?"

"No, I think we need to wait and have another party for Francis and Grace later. Francis doesn't want to announce their engagement publicly until he feels that he can support Grace financially."

"Oh, of course you're right. When do you want to have this party for Kevin?" she asked.

"How about tomorrow night?"

"Tomorrow night! Why, that's impossible! You can't—" She laughed and poked him in the chest. "You're teasing me. When will it really be?"

"I'll let you decide when it should be, but I want it to be fancy. Invite all the big shots we know. I'm so proud of Kevin I could simply bust. He's going to do great things, Cara. You wait and see."

"Yes, he is, and Lucy's so sweet. They're going to make a perfect couple."

"Another thing," he said, stroking her back, "it'll be a good time to introduce our new daughter."

"Do you think that's wise?"

"Yes, I do. Have you noticed the change in her? She's like a new person."

"Of course I have. I spend more time with her than you do. I think you ought to pay Francis a bonus. He's really done wonders for her speech, and she's even showing good taste in clothes."

He continued to stroke her back and then pulled her close.

"I like being married," he said. "I hope Kevin and Grace like it as well."

"You're crushing me!" she protested.

"It's the caveman in me. I have to keep you under submission. You're an unruly wife." When she opened her mouth to protest, he closed it with a kiss and then laughed softly. "There, now be still or I'll drag out my club."

They lay there for a while discussing details about the party. She reached up and held her hand against his cheek. "I love you, Phil," she said quietly.

"And I love you too, sweetheart. I hope our kids are as happy as we are when they've been married a hundred years."

★ ★ ★

Phil Winslow rarely threw himself into social life, but he had determined that the party to introduce his new daughter and daughter-in-law-to-be to New York society would be absolutely top drawer. His family was amazed at how he put himself into it. He hired a top caterer and a special decorator. He insisted on picking out the musicians and even conferred with them about the music that would be played. The house was turned upside down for a few days. But when the night of the party came, Brian stood looking at the house with admiration. "Dad, I didn't think you had it in you. You're getting to be as bad as old man Asquith."

"That's right," Phil said with a grin, looking very distinguished in his white tie and tails. "Just an old social climber, that's me. No riffraff around here."

"The way Kev's come out of himself is a miracle. Are you really going to buy him an airplane, Dad?"

"Yes, I certainly will. He'll make us proud of him, Brian."

"Well, I'm proud of *you,*" he said. He smiled at his father and hit him lightly on the shoulder. "You've done a great job on this party. It must have cost a fortune."

"I wanted a celebration Lucy and Kevin would never forget."

"I don't think they'll forget this. Who all is coming?"

"All the big shots that bore me to death."

"Oh, come on, Dad, they're not that bad."

"No, we're having all of our friends in and all of yours too. Do you think this monkey suit looks all right?"

"You look great, Dad." An impish light danced in Brian's eyes. "If you drop dead, we won't have to do a thing to you."

"Why, you young whippersnapper! I ought to pop a knot in you!"

"You look great, Dad, and Mom's dress is beautiful."

"It should be. It cost enough, but she's worth it." The doorbell rang, and they heard the help greeting their first guests at the door. "I guess I'd better go welcome them," Phil said.

"Have you seen Grace yet?"

"No, I haven't. She had some kind of a disagreement with Francis about her dress, I understand."

"Really?" Brian looked interested. "What was the fight about?"

"Francis thought he ought to help her pick it out. You know he's given her a crash course in how to dress and things like that. She politely told him to paddle his own canoe." Phil laughed, his teeth white against his tanned skin. "I think he'd gotten used to the idea of making all of Grace's decisions for her."

"He's done a good job of it. You know, I've spent some time with Grace. Everything about her is better. Especially her attitude. She's got a gentleness about her now that was lacking before."

"I think giving her heart to the Lord has done some of that."

"You're right, Dad. Have you seen the dress?"

"No, it's a big secret. Look, the Asquiths are coming in."

"I'm surprised you invited them. And John too? After the way they treated Grace, I'm surprised they'd have the nerve."

"Your mother put some pressure on them. Come along. Let's go greet them."

Phil shook hands with Mr. Asquith and John and said, "I'm so pleased you could come tonight."

"I'm glad to be here, sir," John said. "Where's the prospective bridegroom and his bride?"

"They're right over there, John. I'll introduce you momentarily."

The Asquiths looked ill at ease, especially Roger. He could not help remembering the last time he had been at a party with this man's daughter and what a disaster it had been. "I congratulate you," he said. "I understand your son is going into flying as a profession."

"He's been learning since the spring. I have it on the best authority that he's a great pilot."

Mrs. Asquith was looking around nervously. She was obviously looking for Grace, and Phil smiled inwardly. "Mrs. Asquith, I know you're a busy woman. It was so nice of you to come to Kevin's engagement party."

"I'm anxious to meet the young woman."

"You'll like her, I'm sure."

Phil Winslow had an impish streak in him that surfaced from time to time. He knew that the Asquiths had come partly out of curiosity to meet Kevin's fiancée, but he knew they had also heard that Grace had come back. "Come along," Phil said. "I'll introduce you to Lucy." They had started across the room when a movement on the stairway caught Phil's eye. He looked up and smiled. "Just a minute. Here comes someone you'll want to greet."

The trio followed Phil's gaze and watched as Grace came down the stairs. Phil had never been so proud as he was as he watched his daughter descend the stairway gracefully, her head up, a smile on her face. And the dress! It was the most beautiful thing he had ever seen. The deep blue sequined evening dress by Chanel had a rather low neckline in front and a plunging V down to her waist in the back. It was sleeveless, and the fluid lines of the dress ran smoothly along the curves of her body. The back of the skirt had a series of pleats that started at the waist, gathered together by a small sequined bow, and a short train trailed behind her as she walked.

Grace greeted the Asquiths with a calm graciousness that delighted Phil. She smiled and said, "How are you, John. I'm glad to see you again."

John stepped forward and took her hand. "You're looking beautiful, Grace."

"Why, thank you, John." She greeted his parents. "Mr. Asquith. Mrs. Asquith. It's so good to see you."

The Asquiths, Phil saw, were absolutely astonished. This was a woman they had never seen before! There was a quiet dignity about her, and her voice was low-pitched instead of shrill. There was no gum chewing, and as she welcomed them to the party, they stared at her as if she were a strange specimen.

Francis had drawn near off to one side and witnessed Grace's entrance. He came forward to stand by her side and greeted the Asquiths pleasantly. Everyone in the room had turned to watch the group. Most of the guests knew of the difficulties the Asquiths had experienced with Grace and were curious about the ongoing drama.

The most interested person there was Paige Winslow. She had been standing beside Kevin and Lucy, and when Grace had started down the stairs, she had nudged Lucy. "Look, there comes my sister."

Kevin had whistled low at the sight. "Wow, is she ever something!"

"She's so beautiful and regal—she looks like a princess!" Lucy whispered.

Paige waited until Grace had spoken with the Asquiths; then she joined the group, touching John's arm as she did.

His eyes opened wide when he found her standing next to him.

She smiled at him. "How are you, John?"

"F-fine," he stammered. "You're looking beautiful tonight, Paige."

"Thank you, John. Good to see you here, Mr. Asquith, Mrs. Asquith. I'm so pleased you could come."

Once again the couple was taken aback. They had been the instrument of separating their son from this young woman, and now she was acting so graciously. And they were very aware that their son couldn't take his eyes off her. When the others moved on to greet other guests, Roger said, "Now, John, don't go getting any ideas."

John stiffened. "Ideas?" he said, his face sober. "What do you mean?"

"I mean about that woman. Remember that you're already engaged."

"Father, you and Mother are responsible for separating me from the finest girl in New York. I plan to break off my engagement to Margaret. She was *your* choice for me, and I have no feelings for her whatsoever! I'm going to talk to Paige and beg her pardon for being such a milksop. And furthermore, I'm not taking any more of your suggestions about whom I shall marry." He walked quickly away, leaving his parents gasping like two fish.

He walked straight over to Paige and asked if he could have a word with her.

"Why, certainly, John. What is it?"

He led her into a private corner. "I was a fool to let my parents tell me to break our engagement, Paige. I've just told them that from now on I will see whom I please, and I'll choose my own friends."

"Did you really? That's wonderful!" She smiled broadly.

"I know you can never forgive me, but I think for the rest of my life I will be kicking myself for being such a fool."

Paige was touched. "I understand you're engaged, John. What about that?"

"I plan to break that off immediately," he said. "She was my parents' choice for me. She's not a woman I could ever love."

"You'll find a woman who loves you, John. I'm very glad

you've told your parents that you're your own man now. I like you better for it."

He smiled shyly and said, "Maybe we can have a dance?"

"Of course. You're the best dancer I've ever known."

* * *

Kevin invited Grace to dance and told her how delighted he was with the party and how happy he was for her.

"It's your night, Kevin," Grace said. "I'm proud of you and Lucy. Everyone loves her."

"Yes, I believe that's true. But I'm proud of you too. You've come so far."

"Thank you, Kev."

"It's good to have a new sister."

"And it's good to have a brother."

Kevin surrendered Grace to a young man who cut in, then went to talk to Francis, who was standing by the refreshment table. Kevin took a glass of punch and said, "She's beautiful, isn't she, Francis?"

"She sure is. You're a lucky man."

"Oh, I didn't mean Lucy—although of course she's beautiful too! I meant Grace. You're a lucky man too. We owe all of this to you, Francis. You're the one who found her, and you're the one who brought out the woman God created her to be."

Grace approached Francis with arms outstretched. "Dance with me, Francis."

He put his punch down, and they joined the others on the floor. She was wearing heels and was slightly taller than Francis. It did not bother either of them, however, and he said, "I'm so proud of you tonight, Grace. You're beautiful."

"Do you really think so, Francis?"

"Yes. Don't ever let me pick a dress out again. You did a marvelous job picking that one out by yourself!"

Grace's face grew serious, and she said, "I'd like to ask for a favor."

"Anything you want."

"Wait until I ask," she warned. "You may not like it."

"Try me."

"I want Dad to announce our engagement tonight." She saw the uncertainty in his expression. He could be stubborn when it came to changing plans. "Please, Francis, it would mean a lot to me."

"I'd do anything for you, Grace, but I just don't think it would be wise."

"Why not? You've got a job. You love me, and I love you."

"It's not much of a job. Wait until I'm successful as a writer. Then we can announce our engagement."

Grace remained silent for a time, and finally she said, "I thought Christians were supposed to have faith."

"Why . . . yes, they are."

"Don't you have any faith in yourself? Don't you believe God's going to bless what you're doing with your writing?"

"Well, sure, but it may take a while."

"Francis Key, I've wasted too many years. I'm not going to waste another." She pulled out of his arms and left him standing there as she walked straight to the bandstand. He watched with astonishment as she tugged on the band leader's sleeve and whispered to him. The man held up his hand and the music trailed off. Everyone else in the room turned to see why the music had stopped, and they all saw Grace standing by the band with a determined look on her face.

"I think I know that look," Phil whispered to Cara. "That daughter of ours has something on her mind."

"She looks like you, Phil," she whispered back. "She's got that determined look you get sometimes."

When it was quiet, Grace said, "I want to tell you all how very proud I am to be a member of the Winslow family."

Kevin began applauding, and it spread across the room. Francis joined in, smiling, for it had been a courageous thing for her to do. *She knows everybody in this room is aware of the things she did when she first came here, and she's facing them down. What a woman!*

"I never had a family, and now I have one. I have a father and a mother, a sister and two brothers. I have a niece and two nephews, and I have something I never dreamed about. I have a Savior, Jesus Christ. He has forgiven me all my sins, and I thank Him for it."

"By George," Phil said, whistling low. "What a testimony! She's got boldness."

"Yes she has," Cara said, her eyes filled with tears. "I'm so proud of her."

Grace looked straight across the room at Francis. She smiled at him and said, "I also have an announcement to make. My father should be making this announcement, but I have a problem."

Francis suddenly felt very conspicuous, for he sensed what was coming. He looked about nervously but knew there was no escape.

"I am very much in love with Mr. Francis Key, that short gentleman right over there."

Francis wanted to sink into the floor when every eye rested on him. At that moment he would have liked to throttle the beautiful woman who was speaking!

"He loves me very much, but he won't marry me until he's successful. But I will tell you this. In my eyes he's a success right now. I think he's wonderful, and I'd like to ask all of you to talk to him tonight and persuade him to marry me as soon as possible. Thank you."

The room exploded in laughter and applause, and Francis was immediately surrounded by Grace's siblings. Paige grabbed his elbow and said, "You've got to marry her. You've just got to."

Kevin said, "Look, you either marry my sister or I'll break your neck. You hear me?"

Brian grabbed Francis's free arm and held it tightly. "Who do you think you are, refusing to marry my sister?"

And then Cara and Phil were there. Phil looked down at Francis, who appeared miserable and confused, but he smiled and said, "Son, I've got a shotgun, and I know how to use it."

Cara, however, put her arms around Francis and said seriously, "You've got to marry her, son. She loves you so much."

Grace stood to one side smiling, and finally she came forward and stood directly before Francis. "It's now or never, Francis. It's the Ring of Death for you. Will you have me or not?"

And then Francis Key knew he had no choice. He laughed and reached for her. "You crazy woman! I'll have to marry you to keep you under control."

He kissed her, and applause filled the room. She whispered in his ear, "I'll be good from now on."

Francis held her tightly. "I'll believe that when I see it." Then he realized everyone was waiting, and he nodded to Phil. "I think, sir, it's time for you to make an announcement concerning your daughter's engagement."

"Good! I won't have to use that shotgun after all." Phil lifted his voice and said, "I wish to announce the engagement of our daughter Grace to Mr. Francis Key. The wedding will take place as soon as possible."

CHAPTER TWENTY-NINE

"MY FRANCIS"

★ ★ ★

The wedding of Kevin Winslow and Lucy Delaney was one week away. The two of them were as happy as human beings could be. Francis, who was working again at the Rader Detective Agency, had started on another book, but he spent every available moment of his time with Grace.

The two of them were walking out beside the fish pond, and she exclaimed, "Those are the ugliest ducks I've ever seen!"

"Those are mergansers," he said.

"So? They're still ugly."

"I'm sure they're not to another merganser," he said. "Besides, their eggs are very good to eat, and I think they mate for life like swans and Canadian geese."

"Do they really?"

"So I've read."

"I think you make up most of that stuff you tell me. How would I know if they mate for life or not? How would anybody know?" She grabbed his arm and laughed. "I can just see a scientist following a pair of mergansers around for ten years, following them everywhere they go just to see if they cheat on each other."

"They look faithful to me," Francis said with a smile.

She smiled back. "You know, I have more fun with you than I do with anyone. Let's always have fun, Francis."

"That's my plan. After we—" He broke off when he heard his name being called. "Looks like your mother wants me."

The two started back toward the house, and Cara was standing on the patio. She said excitedly, "Francis, your agent, Mr. McCartney, is on the phone."

He blinked with surprise but didn't move.

Grace nudged him. "Come on, let's go find out why he's calling."

"I don't want to."

Grace and Cara gave him questioning looks, and he laughed shortly. "I'm afraid it'll be bad news."

"It won't be. The Bible says a righteous man has no fear of evil tidings," Cara said. "Now, you go right in there and talk to him."

Francis made his way inside, and Cara turned to her daughter. "I do hope it's good news, Grace!"

"So do I, Mom. He's been so nervous waiting for this call."

The two women waited on the patio until Francis finally came bursting out. There was no need to ask if the news was good, for joy flowed out of him. "It's sold!" he shouted. "Random House bought it!" He ran forward and embraced the two women, and they all three tried to talk at the same time. Finally Cara broke away. "I've got to get Phil and Paige."

As soon as she left, Grace kissed Francis. "I'm so proud of you!"

"I'm a little dazed. It's really happened."

"And that means you can support a wife!"

Francis laughed and put his arms around her. "So I can. Say, why don't we get married on the motorcycle?"

"Mom and Dad would hate that. No, I want a big wedding." She rested in his arms, and then a shadow passed over her face. "Francis, I don't know the first thing about being a wife."

He kissed her and then put his lips close to her ear. "Don't worry. I'll give you instructions. The first lesson is—give your husband everything he wants."

She laughed and they clung to each other. Suddenly a flash of green appeared, and Miriam flew right at them, separating them in their surprise. "She's gotten out of her cage!" Francis said.

The parrot fluttered around the pair, screaming, "My Francis! My Francis!"

But Grace came back to the arms of her man and laughed. "No, Miriam—this is *my* Francis!"

HEIRS OF ACADIA
More Bestselling
LARGE PRINT FICTION
FROM YOUR
FAVORITE AUTHORS!
Large Print EDITION
T. DAVIS BUNN & ISABELLA BUNN
The Innocent Libertine
JANETTE OKE SAYS,
Large Print EDITION
T. DAVIS BUNN & ISABELLA BUNN
The Solitary Envoy
JANETTE OKE SAYS,
"THE FASCINATING STORY OF A NEW NATION BEING FORMED AND NEW RELATIONSHIPS FORGED."
THE ACADIAN SAGA CONTINUED FROM
THE BESTSELLING OKE/BUNN SERIES
History comes to life in this captivating
new story of an American woman reared
in the shadow of the Court of St. James.
BETHANYHOUSE